I Can Read Comics introduces children to the world of graphic novel storytelling and encourages visual literacy in emerging readers. Comics inspire reader engagement unlike any other format. They ask readers to infer and answer questions, like:

1. What do I read first? Image or text?
2. Why is this word balloon shaped this way, and that word balloon shaped that way?
3. Why is a character making that facial expression? Are they happy, angry, excited, sad?

From the comics your child reads with you to the first comic they read on their own, there are **I Can Read Comics** for every stage of reading:

LEVEL 1 — Simple stories for shared reading.

LEVEL 2 — Engaging stories for children reading on their own.

LEVEL 3 — Complex stories for independent readers.

The magic of graphic novel storytelling lies between the gutters. Unlock the magic with…

I Can Read Comics!

Visit **ICanRead.com** for information on enriching your child's reading experience.

I Can Read *Comics* Cartooning Basics

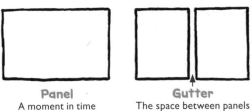

Panel
A moment in time

Gutter
The space between panels

Tier
One row of panels

Word Balloons When someone talks, thinks, whispers, or screams, their words go in here:

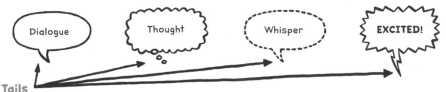

Dialogue   Thought   Whisper   EXCITED!

Tails
Point to whoever is talking / thinking / whispering / screaming / etc.

A quick how-to-read comics guide:

In a **panel**, read the text on the **left** first.

Then, read the text on the right.

Remember to...

Read the text along with the image, paying close attention to the character's acting, the action, and/or the scene. Every little detail matters!

No dialogue? No problem!

If there is no dialogue within a panel, take the time to read the image. Visual cues are just as important as text, so don't forget about them!

On a page, **start here**, in the **top left** corner!

After that, read the panel immediately to the **right**.

When you're done up there, come down here and read **this** panel **next**!

ME NEXT! ME NEXT!

You're almost there...

YOU MADE IT! You just read a comic page!

YAY!

To Comics Club —B.L.

Clarion Books is an imprint of HarperCollins Publishers.
HarperAlley is an imprint of HarperCollins Publishers.
I Can Read® and I Can Read Book® are trademarks of HarperCollins Publishers.

Cool Buds: To the Rescue!
Copyright © 2025 by Barbara Lehman
All rights reserved. Manufactured in Malaysia.
No part of this book may be used or reproduced in any manner whatsoever without written permission
except in the case of brief quotations embodied in critical articles and reviews. For information address
HarperCollins Children's Books, a division of HarperCollins Publishers, 195 Broadway, New York, NY 10007.
www.icanread.com

Library of Congress Control Number: 2024932956
ISBN 978-0-06-338906-9 (trade bdg.) — ISBN 978-0-06-338905-2 (pbk.)

Book design by Rick Farley
24 25 26 27 28 COS 10 9 8 7 6 5 4 3 2 1   First Edition

LEVEL 3

I Can Read! Comics

COOL BUDS

To the Rescue!

by Barbara Lehman

CLARION BOOKS
Imprints of HarperCollinsPublishers

HARPER alley

BLUE
Arctic Fox

PUFF
Atlantic Puffin

TIP
Arctic Hare

SEALY
Harbor Seal

To the Rescue!

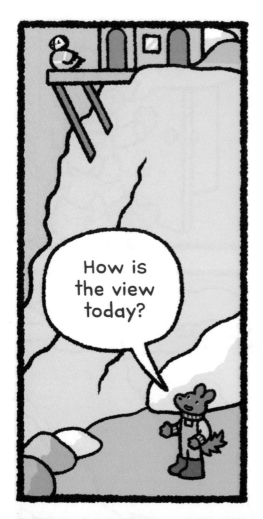

Oh no!

BLUE!

What is it, Puff?

20

26

27

30

Arctic Extras!

Blue Arctic Fox

Foxes are often red or white. Blue is a rare kind that has grayish-blue fur. The blue Arctic fox is most commonly found living along rocky coasts. Arctic foxes are known for storing food—the more the better!

Arctic foxes have thick, bushy tails that they can use as a toasty blanket to snuggle in when they need to keep themselves warm.

The Russian grabbed him by the wrist and put the knife to Tim's neck. "If you try anything funny, you won't see tomorrow."

Tim took out his keys and opened the rear lobby door. He knew the monks were asleep downstairs, five floors below, so it was unlikely they would hear them. The monastery was dark as he slowly made his way across the lobby. Tim felt relieved when he heard the familiar panting that often filled the halls and realized his plan might just work. As he silently opened the locked cabinet to the collection box, he shouted, "Bernardus, attack!"

A mountain of fur and muscle that dwarfed the Russian appeared out of the darkness. Sergio screamed in pain, and the monk's giant St. Bernard guard dog growled like a rabid wolf. Russian expletives echoed off the walls like gunshots. Tim turned on the light and was witness to a struggle between the evil Russian and the immense guard dog of the monks. The dog's teeth were sunk deep into the Russian's tattooed forearm, spewing blood everywhere. Sergio went for another stiletto knife near his pants leg, but Bernardus attacked his leg, forcing him to drop the knife. In an impressive feat of strength, the dog lifted the large killer off his feet and slammed him against the marble stairway with a huge thud. Unfortunately, the Russian landed next to his knife on the floor and agilely whirled around to face his opponent, knife in hand.

Timothy was not a violent person, but he could not bear to think of their poor dog being stabbed by this killer. He grabbed one of the heavy sterling silver candlesticks off a cabinet. Channeling his muscle memory from years of playing doubles tennis at Stanford, he swung a perfect cross court forearm shot, connecting the candlestick with the Russian's right temple and knocking him out cold.

Timothy jumped into the air. "Game, set, match!" he shouted.

The sweet Saint Bernard happily sat on the unconscious Russian, and Tim quickly gave him two well deserved dog biscuits. Then, Tim, even though he struggled at first, securely tied up the Russian in case he woke up.

Tim again thought of poor Brother Adolphus. He grabbed a flashlight and went out to examine him. Shining the light over his body, Tim confirmed he was indeed dead. He brought the monk inside and cleaned his wound. He said some prayers and knew this saintly man was certainly on his way to Heaven. With some difficulty, he dragged the Russian back outside and checked his bonds. Then, he walked back inside and attempted to straighten up their mess. He washed some of the blood off Bernardus but realized he would probably need a bath after all his efforts. Though he wanted to call the police, he didn't. He knew the monks and authorities would find the murderer in the morning, and he still had to complete the task he and his father had promised Brother Adolphus. He took the diamonds he had from his pocket and locked them in the collection box for the monks. He was well aware his father would have wanted him to keep the diamonds, but his father was ten thousand miles away.

Tim kissed Brother Adolphus on the head, patted Bernardus, and then headed out into the night.

2 LUCKY BALDWIN'S

Clint maneuvered his Harley into the small parking lot behind his favorite Pasadena bar, Lucky Baldwin's. He took a deep breath after his long drive from the valley in LA. He smiled as he slid the transmission into neutral and revved the engine. That loud, throaty Harley roar was almost palpable and reverberated against the surrounding buildings and trees. He could envision his friends on the patio behind the bar groaning at the signal of his arrival. He laughed to himself about the sexual references one could make about motorcycle riding, comparing his stimulating drive and climax with the Harley roar. He knew he best keep such thoughts to himself though as his friends would give him no end of grief.

He was happy that the drive tonight had only taken an hour. With LA traffic, it could take two to three times as long and could seem even longer thinking of a cool draft beer and a sandwich at Lucky's. Lucky's was an English pub that specialized in Trappist Belgian beers—the bar was a gift to Pasadena. He wondered what the original Elias "Lucky" Baldwin would have thought of several iconic pubs being named after him. As long as they made money, Clint figured he likely would not have cared. After twenty years, Lucky's was becoming a real part of the community, sandwiched between the historic

Green Hotel and the last vestige of Route 66 that ran through town.

Clint stretched his legs and headed to the patio behind Lucky's where he knew he would find his friends. His long legs were a bit stiff from the ride, so he walked in long strides, hoping to stretch them out. He took off his leather jacket as he started to feel the heat and music radiating from the bar. His jacket was one of his prized possessions with beautiful stitching of a cartoon clown wearing a judge's wig and robes across the back. The jacket proclaimed "President," but this was his own private joke since it didn't say what he was president of, not to mention he was the only member.

Despite his thirty-eight years, Clint felt in fairly good shape, aside from a slight limp from an old knee injury. Even with his long hours working as a city attorney, he still managed to exercise, and other than an occasional beer with his friends from their beer club, he tried to take care of his body. His friend David had started the club, the Drunk Monks, only to get a discount at a number of bars, but it had since morphed into a social event for the four friends.

The music and throng of the crowd at Lucky's hit Clint as he came into the back patio. As usual, the Belgian beer fest brought out a large boisterous crowd. There weren't many places one could find fifty Belgian beers with over twenty of them on tap. The motley collection of his beer buddies had set up shop in a corner with reasonable access to the passing staff. His three friends,

David, Bartley, and Smithers, lifted their glasses of beer to Clint when he joined them.

Bartley had cornered one of the barmaids and was holding forth about his favorite brew. He was shaking his finger and bald head in unison, and his ample belly shook with the rest of him. "Why even bother selling all this other swill when you know St. Bernardus is a much better product and even comes close to the top beer in the world, Westvleteren."

The pretty young woman finally broke free from Bartley's diatribe. "I have other customers to serve, and I'm sure you could find plenty of people who would disagree with you and some who might even agree. St. Bernardus is a great beer, but it's not a true Trappist beer. It's actually a spin-off of Westvleteren and made in greater quantity. You can discuss this with your friends, but I have work to do and thirsty customers to help." She twirled her tray and was gone in a flash.

Clint chuckled at the barmaid's quick tongue as he pulled out his latest beer fest glass. He had thirty more at home, including a real beer boot from previous fests, but he really liked the artwork on this one. He liked this year's bell-shaped glass both for its design and its supposed ability retain the foam of the beers. He found it fascinating that each of the Belgian beers had its own glass, usually designed by an artist to reflect some character of that beer. His three friends let out a communal belch as he sat down.

"David, I think your belch was a bit flat tonight," Clint said.

David laughed. "My belch was a whisper compared to the roar of your bike tonight. I think you may have awakened Lucky himself, and he has been dead for over one hundred years. Even worse, your entrance almost made Bartley spill his beer."

Clint was David's closest friend, though perhaps his polar opposite. Clint had a rough childhood growing up in Detroit and had the scars and tattoos to prove it. He looked hard and tough, but was really a gentle giant type. David Collins, on the other hand, was short and energetic, almost hyperactive, and definitely brilliant. His features and intellect reflected his Jewish heritage. He often led the discussions among his bar friends as well as his business associates. David had used Clint as a compatriot in a number of his schemes, or "negotiations" as he preferred to call them.

Clint masked his laugh with a swig of beer. He knew his friends would give him a hard time about his bike.

"I'm sure the Scientology group across the alley has already notified the police about how you parked in 'their' alley and disturbed their sanctity. We should be seeing one of Pasadena's finest any minute now," David joked.

Right on schedule, Officer Michael Faraday arrived and headed directly toward the group. As usual, he gave them a friendly greeting, but quickly got serious, playing his official role. "Clint, I'm sure you know why I'm here. I do wish you would park your bike around the corner and avoid this encounter every time you come here."

Clint laughed and, on cue, took out his official honorary Pasadena Police consultant license. "Michael, please give the police commissioner our greetings. Let him know David and I are happy his daughter was able to get her money back from the fraudulent realtor we advised him about. Did you know he told me I can park wherever I want to in your fair city?"

The officer rolled his eyes. "I will let your friends across the alley know I've advised you to please try to be quieter in the future," he said and left them to their beers and thoughts.

David launched into his usual discussion on Lucky Baldwin's and its namesake. "As you know, Lucky Baldwin was an entrepreneur back in the 1800s. He reportedly even sold brandy to Brigham Young's brother when he headed west. He had many investments, including shares of silver mines in Virginia City, hotels in San Francisco, large tracts of land in Southern California, and the Santa Anita racetrack. He loved horses and became good friends with Wyatt Earp who even got married on his yacht off the coast of California. We should feel honored to be able to drink in an establishment named after him."

David paused and raised his glass to his friend Clint. He then added, "You are already two beers behind us. You have some catching up to do. Actually, better go easy since you are riding your bike back to the valley tonight. I'm lucky. I just have to get back to Santa Monica."

"C'mon, David. I've already been talked to by one officer tonight," Clint responded.

"I know we don't have to worry about you. Despite your muscles and tattoos, you do behave yourself. My brother nicknamed you Mother Teresa in leather, and I can't disagree." David then signaled to one of the wandering bartenders and put in his order for his next beer. He had been at this long enough that, despite the fifty beers available, the bartender knew exactly what David wanted. In fact, he knew what their whole group wanted.

Clint sighed. "I think I've heard about enough of this Mother Teresa reference. You better be careful or this Mother Teresa will ride over your foot with my bike in the parking lot."

Smithers, the thin, morose friend across the table, made no effort to hide his rising anxiety. "Will you two quit blathering? I want to talk to you about something serious. I don't know if you have heard, but Brother Adolphus of the Lavro Monastery died. Supposedly, he fell off a ladder while checking one of the batches of beer and broke his neck. Who knows if that's true, but no other information is available. That only leaves five monks to run the Lavro Brewery, and the youngest one is seventy-nine! There are only four approved Trappist breweries in Belgium and twelve worldwide. If Lavro falls, that will really impact the number of superior beers we have to enjoy."

Clint took a long gulp of his beer. It wasn't just the taste of the beer he enjoyed, but it was the experience as well—the beautiful amber liquid with just the right amount of head, the smell of the hops, the sound of the bubbles, the fruity taste from the Belgian yeast, and of course, the slight buzz from the 10 percent alcohol. It took him a while to digest both the beer and Smithers's words.

"I've heard the tragic news of Brother Adolphus and think a moment of silence, as best we can do in this establishment, is in order," Clint said solemnly.

The four friends stood and had a long drink to honor the fallen monk.

As usual, David took the floor. "I understand your concern about Lavro, but most of the other monasteries sublet the production of their beers to other manufacturers and simply supervise the end product. I'm sure Lavro could do the same. Perhaps we could offer our services to produce their brew. Clint, how are your Dutch and French? Could you manage if we went to Belgium to help them out?"

Clint laughed. "I can speak a little French. *Voulez-vous coucher avec moi?* Or, in other words, do you want to sleep with me? But I don't know Dutch."

"Yeah, that line might not work on the monks, but it could come in handy sometime on the trip," David said with a laugh. "Maybe you'd be better utilized figuring out what really happened to Brother Adolphus. I still don't buy he fell off a ladder, and I know you've been itching to try out some Sherlock Holmes tactics you've been reading about."

"I have been getting interested in detective work. Some of my legal cases are not as straightforward as one would think, so I have found it helps to look at things from a different angle. Who knows? If I get tired of practicing the law, maybe I'll get into detective work."

Smithers, always the most negative of the group, persisted, "I am serious about this. Aren't any of you worried about the quality of the Belgian beers deteriorating, especially as all the monks get older?"

Clint held up his glass. "I can only say that the quality and availability of Belgian beers in the US has been improving. Five years ago, we had to make our own Belgian style beers in some of the DIY brewing establishments, but now we can go to places like Lucky Baldwin's and delight in twenty or more Belgian style beers on tap. I think your worries are unfounded. Actually, I think your *real* concern sprouts from your recent divorces. I can't imagine two high-profile divorces in less than five years."

Smithers groaned. "True. My lack of marital bliss is one of the reasons I'm here with you deviants. Thanks for reminding me my two alimony payments are due this week."

Clint stretched. "With all due respect to Brother Adolphus, I think it is time for a monk joke. In a Belgian monastery, a young monk had just joined the order and was meeting with the head monk. 'Do you have any questions, Brother Stanus, before you begin your work today?' asked the senior monk. 'I've noticed that when the monks here are copying old documents, they use previously copied documents rather than the original documents. Over hundreds of years of doing that, I wonder if mistakes have been copied and then carried forward over the years. Maybe it would be worth reviewing some of the original documents to see if they are consistent with our current texts,' the young monk replied. 'That is a noble idea, and I will check on some of the old texts myself today. Go work with the others, and I will let you know what I find out.' The senior monk disappeared into the bowels of the monastery and was gone most of the day. Brother Stanus became concerned and went looking for him. As he descended deeper into the caves below the monastery, he could hear a loud banging and cries from below. He could make out some of the yelling. 'We forgot the R! We forgot the R! We forgot the R!' He heard the senior monk yell. Eventually, the young monk found his superior distraught and bloodied from hitting his head against the wall. The senior monk held the original text from hundreds of years ago in his arms, turned to Brother Stanus, and said, 'The word should have been *celebrate!*'"

The rest of the beer club laughed in appreciation and raised their glasses to Clint.

David, always the entrepreneur of the group, smiled a devious smile. "Okay, okay, but I mean it. Perhaps there is a financial opportunity at the Lavro Brewery, and maybe they would consider a business arrangement to produce their beer since their monks are getting quite old."

Bartley had been unusually quiet, possibly because he was on his fourth beer. His wife would not let him drive after these club meetings, so he was free to indulge a bit more than the rest. "You forget how reclusive and mistrustful these monks can be," Bartley chimed in. "They have had hundreds of years of isolation. Some sects don't even talk. Remember how upset the Westvleteren monks were when they found out the distributers in the US were reselling and overcharging for their beers? The monks cut off selling to the US. Well, that is, except when they had to redo the roof of the monastery, and then, they temporarily lifted the ban. I don't see the monks at Lavro jumping into a financial bed with you, David, just because you are so damned charming."

David got up to address his friends, but Clint interrupted, "Gentlemen, we are in deep trouble. The last time David got up like this to address a hostile board of directors of thirty high powered, angry assailants, they all left crying and agreed to do whatever he wanted them to do. We might as well agree with him now and avoid further mental anguish."

David laughed. "Actually, it was only twenty-five board members, and three of them did not agree with me even at the end. Fortunately, they were outvoted. Let me remind you, we are happily seated here at Lucky Baldwin's by the grace of God or whatever brought us here. It is appropriate that we remember the namesake of this establishment and just what it means to be 'lucky.' Some people feel that luck is a capricious force in the universe, and others feel we can influence these forces ourselves. I like to think of Carl Jung's description of luck as synchronicity—a meaningful coincidence. I feel we can influence luck by taking advantage of certain situations. Certainly, Lucky Baldwin was able to take advantage of many situations in his life and was, therefore, called 'lucky.' He wasn't always lucky though, as his hotel in San Francisco burned to the ground without insurance, but overall, he wound up owning a large chunk of Southern California. I'd say that's pretty lucky.

"I think we should seriously look at the opportunity the Belgian beer market presents, and I propose that Clint and I go to Belgium and check things out. At worst, they'll turn down our offer, but we'll get to sample some of the best beers in the world."

Clint choked on his beer and almost spilled it—a Class A violation in Lucky's. "We have not been drinking Delirium Tremens that I know of. Are you out of your mind? Last I checked, I had an ex-wife, a family, and was working for the city of LA as an investigative attorney. I can't just drop all of that and go off gallivanting to Belgium just for some scheme of yours. Your little plans always wind up being far more involved than you let on. I vaguely recall being trapped in Toronto, Canada during your last scheme and having to pretend I worked for some museum of antiquities. Luckily, I didn't get arrested, but that's the only 'luck' I remember."

"You might also remember that we each pocketed a fair amount of change from that little gambit and got your niece into McGill University, on scholarship to boot," said David. "I don't think we'll have to do anything patently illegal in Belgium, and I'm sure I can work out something with the city and your family to get you out of here for a few weeks. It won't be a big deal. All you'll have to do is pose as a potential novice for the monastery to get us through the door."

All three of his friends started choking on their beers, and Bartley actually fell onto the floor laughing hysterically. Even Smithers cracked a smile for the first time in weeks.

Clint jumped to his feet. "A monk? You want me to pose as a fucking monk? I'm sure that would go over very well with my family and my friends in my biker club. You are truly nuts!"

David put his hands up. "Settle down, settle down! Smithers, please help Bartley up off the floor. Lord knows what is down there. Clint, I just want to arrange an appointment to meet one of the monks at Lavro, and I don't think I can get in to see one without some ploy. If you played my brother who was considering becoming a monk, they would be more willing to see me."

Clint shook his head. "You don't look anything like me, and now we're brothers? So, I'm Jewish now as well? At least I'm already circumcised, so we don't have to go that route."

Bartley was now laughing so hard he was sobbing. "A Jewish monk with tattoos. Now that would be a first! It sounds like an episode from *Seinfeld*," Bartley said as he hung onto Smithers, laughing.

David let out a chuckle. "Well, okay. So, you can't be a Jewish monk, even if you are circumcised, but you could be my cousin raised by a very religious Christian family. You have been to church on occasion, Clint. We went to some sort of church function with your family last year, so a monk wouldn't be too much of a stretch."

Clint continued shaking his head. "It is a huge stretch from going to church on occasion to pretending to be a monk or even a novice. You had a Bar Mitzvah, so what does that make you? A rabbi?"

"Let's just give this some thought," David said. He finished his beer and began tapping his temple with his pointer finger.

"Oh, no!" said Clint to Bartley and Smithers. "I hate it when he does that. It usually means he's concocting a plan, and I know I won't like it. A monk for God's sake! I would have to be celibate—well, at least I'd be a Belgian monk, so I'd get to drink beer. Not that I'm actually considering this ridiculous escapade."

Smithers joined in, "Actually, the monks are limited on how often and how much they can drink. In fact, I think they're only allowed to drink weaker beers. Sorry, man."

Clint winced. "This keeps getting better and better. Do I have to cut off an appendage or become blind to make my appearance more appealing too?"

"No," said David, deep in thought. "We'll keep you just as you are. Your rough upbringing from the streets of Detroit may actually be a benefit. Anyway, we all have lots of thinking to do. Brother Clint, perhaps you best get an early start back to the valley. I'm going to call it an early evening myself. This, by far, has been one of the strangest meetings of our beer club, but maybe the most propitious."

Clint half-heartedly raised his glass. "L'chaim! Here's to those who wish us well and those who don't can go to hell."

3 THE LADIES

Molly put her car keys in her mouth as she reached behind her to close the front door. She enjoyed the definite slamming noise and finality of the feeling from her effort—joy and sorrow combined in a rush of release. She had managed the almost impossible by showering, dressing, and packing up her most important things this morning in only forty-five minutes. More impressive was how she had managed to coordinate her stunning bright yellow outfit with matching Jimmy Choo shoes to her adorable little yellow Mustang convertible.

Ralph, what an asshole, she thought.

Ralph, her boss, was a private detective—more like a private dick. They had worked and lived together for the last two years. Ralph, however, made the mistake of accidentally taking pictures of himself with their recent client's slutty girlfriend. He was supposed to be staking out her house, but the pictures showed him doing far more than that. When Molly found the pictures, she knew it was definitely time to move on.

As she walked down the cobblestone walkway, she tried to look reasonably stylish, which was not so easy to do while carrying most of her possessions and in four-inch heels. She could see Ralph peeking out behind the drapes. She would have to send her brother Tony over later that afternoon to get the rest of her things. He would be thrilled as Tony never did care much for Ralph and let her know that often.

She made it to her car with dignity and put her things in the trunk, making sure not to disturb her five-inch, red Prada heels she kept with her in case of an emergency. She got in the car and did a quick check of her hair and makeup in the rearview mirror. *Not too bad for pushing thirty,* she thought. Her blond curls and *Vogue* features could still turn more than a few heads. Still, here it was, not even 8:30 a.m., and she had already lost her job and her boyfriend. Aside from collecting her possessions, she didn't know what to do next, but she knew who would—Giselle. Giselle was a good friend who always knew just what to do.

Giselle answered the phone on the third ring. She always answered the phone on the third ring, whether she was sitting at her desk, on the treadmill at the gym, in the shower, or having sex with the Thompson twins. In fact, when she answered the phone, it sounded like she was participating in the last option, but it turned out she was only on the treadmill.

"Darling, I told you that sleeping with your boss was a bad idea," Giselle responded after hearing of the morning fiasco.

"But you occasionally sleep with your boss when you need a favor from him," Molly teased.

"Yes," Giselle answered, "but I also sleep with his boss just in case something like this might come up. In any case, this is an emergency, and the only solution is to go immediately to Spa Heaven. You need the works, and since I am your friend, I might as well get that myself."

"Don't you have to work today? You mentioned something about a corporate power play and some meeting this morning. I wouldn't want to get you into any trouble."

Giselle laughed. "Me in trouble? Please. They know the place would fall apart without me, and after my last corporate takeover, I am essentially untouchable. The only trouble you could get me into would involve more young studs than you could imagine and lots of Jell-O, preferably red. I'll see you at Spa Heaven in fifteen minutes. Bring that pretty little yellow toy convertible of yours. We may need to troll Rodeo Drive afterward to pick up some escorts."

"Your wish is my command, and thanks," said Molly.

Within half an hour, Molly was at the spa and changed into her white cotton robe, ready to start with a massage from Enrico, a handsome Italian masseur with hands of steel and the touch of a feather. Giselle burst through the spa doors in her typical hurricane fashion. She wore a tight leopard print dress that showed off her ample breasts. Her hair was done to perfection in a short, dark manicured style, and of course, she wore her famous five-inch heels, partly to compensate for her five-two frame.

"Darling, I thought you would be naked by now and having Enrico's famous hands turning your muscles into jelly." Giselle gave Enrico a kiss on the cheek and of course a pinch on his bottom. "I'm going to start with a pedicure, and then who knows, I might have to let Enrico at my body."

Molly got on the table, and Enrico began to work on her tight muscles. "I'm sorry," he said, "but I do have another client after Molly, and she is out in the waiting room. I'm sure I can fit you in after that."

Giselle eyed Enrico and said, "Young man, no one fits me in to anything. If anything, I fit them in when I'm good and ready!"

Just then, they heard someone crying out in the waiting room. Molly threw on her robe, and they all went out to see what was going on. A pretty young woman sat sobbing in her chair. She was startled to see them all. From her Coach purse and designer accessories, one could tell she was quite used to a degree of opulence.

Though Giselle didn't typically play the motherly role, she put her arms around the young woman. "Sweetie, what can we do to help you? In my experience, when most women cry, it has something to do with a man. We can always find you another if that's all you need."

"Oh no," the young woman began as she managed to stop crying. "It's my brother Timothy. He seems to have disappeared, and I can't get ahold of him. He has been gone for over a week, and my family won't listen to my concerns. This is not like him to not call me."

"Have you contacted his friends or the police?" asked Molly.

"His friends haven't heard anything, and my father doesn't want to contact the police. He is quite wealthy and is afraid of the publicity."

Giselle gave the young woman a closer look. "I think I know you from the fashion news. Who are you, and what can we do to help?"

"I'm Marguerite Marcum, and my father is the business tycoon Cornwell Marcum," the young woman responded.

"Holy cow!" Giselle exclaimed. "Your father owns more real estate than Donald Trump and Bill Gates combined. Last I heard, he was worth some $2.7 billion."

Molly's eyebrows went up. "I can see why he doesn't want to get the police involved. Why do you think your brother may have disappeared? When did you last talk?"

"I spoke to him last week. He was in Europe and looking into something he called 'exciting.' Then, all of a sudden, nothing," said Marguerite.

"Sounds to me like your family should hire a detective on their own and see what is going on," Molly ventured.

"My father won't do that since he is angry with my brother about something. I don't know what. And I don't know who I could hire or what I should do," said Marguerite. She started to cry again.

"Molly, you've worked for a detective agency for the last two years, and you did more of the work than that stupid boss of yours. I don't think he could find his own dick in his pants to pee, even on a good day," said Giselle.

When she saw the girl's wide eyes, she added, "Sorry, Marguerite, I can be a bit direct at times."

"Wow," Marguerite perked up. "Molly, you may be just the person I need. Would you be willing to help me find my brother?"

"Hold on!" Molly replied. "I simply worked in a detective's office. My experience is limited, and I'm not even licensed."

Giselle gave Molly a stern look. "Molly, with your detective work experience and my brains, we can solve anything. We can hire someone if we need added help. You need a job, and I need to get out of my office for a while."

Marguerite jumped up and hugged her new friends. "You have to help me! I'll pay you whatever you want! When can you start?"

"I guess we could start right away," said Molly. "What country was your brother in when you last heard from him? We will need funds for travel and incidentals. Giselle, do you have your passport? Okay, this could be good. We could really do this!" Molly said, thinking out loud. "I'm certain, Marguerite, if anyone can find your brother, Giselle and I can."

"That's more like it," said Giselle. "We will need at least fifty thousand dollars to start, and we'll keep tabs on our expenses. My secretary will set up the flights. We need some pictures of your brother and a detailed description about his past habits, education, and interests—anything that might help us find him."

"My brother last called from a hotel in Brussels, and I can get you the name of the hotel and his contacts there. I can text you some pictures of him. He is twenty-six, two years younger than me, and is five-ten with sandy blond hair. He was very into tennis in college and still has a thin, well-muscled build. He graduated from Stanford with a degree in political science, which my father always felt was useless. He has never had a formal job, but he has done some odds and ends for my father, even though he lacks my father's killer instinct in business. The two have not always gotten along, but my father grudgingly still supports him. He has traveled often to Europe and is quite comfortable in finding his way around there. He is sweet, and the two of us are very close. I don't know what I would do if something happened to him." Marguerite paused before she added, "I'll get you the funds this afternoon and arrange an account for you at a bank in Brussels. I am so thankful. I can't express how grateful I am you both are willing to do this."

"Well, we haven't found your brother yet. Unfortunately, he may not want to be found, or you may not like what we find. But we will do our best and keep you informed," Molly explained. She hoped she wouldn't have to be the bearer of bad news. "I think the sooner we leave, the better. Does your brother have an iPhone? Maybe we can pick up on his location from his phone. That is, if he still has it with him and the battery is still charged."

Marguerite was ecstatic. "I know you can find him! Here is his phone number, and yes, he does have an iPhone. As I said, my brother and I are very close. We even have power of attorney for one another. I just pray he's okay."

"We will certainly do what we can to find him and help him," said Molly.

Giselle ended their meeting. "I'm off to pack and buy shoes for the trip and let my office know I will be gone for a while. Molly, finish your massage, and, Enrico, do your best to whip her into shape. Unfortunately, I will have to put off a rendezvous with your talents, but I'm sure we can arrange something when I return. I'll have my secretary send over our flight schedule. Molly, good thing that cheating bastard screwed you over or you'd be stuck at that job."

4 THE AIRPORT AND BEYOND

David and Clint rode in the backseat of the Uber to the airport and said nothing. There could not have been greater contrast in their moods, dress, or physiques. David wore his three-piece Brooks Brothers suit and Ferragamo tie. His Burberry leather shoes were polished to a high gloss, and his mustache was neatly trimmed. He was quite focused, thinking of his coming negotiations with the monks. He was already working on a battle plan. He knew that the monks were a different kind of opponent than he usually dealt with. He did feel, though, that everything in life was a negotiation, and at least Clint would get him through the door. He knew Clint was not happy with his role in this process, but he never was. Still, Clint had always played his part well in their past "negotiations."

Clint, on the other hand, was fuming in the backseat of their Uber. He had played a number of roles with David in the past, but this one took the cake. He was dressed in a simple monk's habit with a cotton top, pants, a rope for a belt, and sandals. He felt ridiculous, knowing this garb did not fit his tall, muscular frame and handsome appearance. He wondered how long he would have to play this role and hoped none of his friends would see him dressed like this. The only silver lining in any of this was his chance to build his detective skills. He had told David he would only agree to the getup if he could bring along his detective paraphernalia.

He had studied up a bit and knew that monks tried to live a simple life with few possessions and limited interaction with the outside world. They ate simply and did Yoga-type exercises and meditation. Of course, they were celibate, though that was not an immediate problem because he had no current female companions. He could stand to shed a few pounds around his waist, so maybe the monastic life wouldn't be so bad, at least for a few days. However, beyond a few days, he might need to escape and call this whole thing off. He knew the intrigue of "the deal" always pushed David to further involve them in bizarre schemes. For this one, they had to fill out a ton of paperwork and call in a few favors to get an interview with the head monk. Clint was surprised he even had to submit blood work and a saliva test as part of the screening process to try out as a novitiate at the monastery.

Dressed in monk clothing, Clint wondered about Brother Adolphus. He couldn't help but feel suspicious about his death. It seemed odd that he would fall with no one around to catch him since the monks supervise the brewing process and their English workers were much more hands-on in the day-to-day operations. He hoped to poke around the monastery for more answers, assuming he could get in as a novice monk.

They arrived at the airport in silence, each in their own thoughts. Their driver got their bags out of the trunk, two Louis Vuitton bags for David and a small cardboard satchel for Clint. They wheeled their bags to the international flight departure for Air France. David knew he better not press his luck and had booked them both in first class. They were flying LA to Charles de Gaulle in Paris and then on to Brussels. Flying first class certainly made checking in a breeze, though Clint did get some odd looks from the airport staff and other passengers.

As they stood at the counter, they couldn't help but notice a porter hauling a cart with at least six large Fendi suitcases. A loud diminutive buxom woman and a beautiful statuesque blond younger woman accompanied him. They all headed right for the first class station at Air France where David and Clint were standing.

"If you're done checking in, can you two get out of the way so someone else can get a little service?" the busty woman shouted.

"Sorry about my friend and her brusqueness. She can be a bit impatient at times," said the beautiful blond.

Clint was entranced by the blond and felt like a total idiot in his monk outfit. "No problem, miss. We were just finishing checking in for our flight to Brussels. The counter is all yours," Clint said.

Looking at David, the older woman said, "What's with your friend flying first class and wearing pajamas?"

Somewhat offended, Clint responded, "Ma'am, I am studying to be a monk, and this is my habit, the clothes I wear. We try to limit our possessions."

"My mother is called ma'am, and even she would object to the term. You can call me Giselle. This is Molly, my associate. I guess I haven't seen too many monks floating around Los Angeles, but you may be on to something. I might have to try a monk outfit on myself. Maybe I'll have to wrestle you for yours at some point," Giselle said with a wink.

"Oh no, miss," said Clint. "We monks are supposed to avoid any female contact. I am only allowed in this airport with women since I am traveling to study in a monastery in Belgium."

"Doesn't sound like too much fun to me, but to each his own," said Giselle.

David coughed. "Allow me to introduce us. I am David Collins, and this is my brother Clint. We are traveling to Belgium where he will decide if he is to become a monk." Giselle eyed David up and down. "And you must be his Brooks Brothers brother. Do you call him brother, Brother Clint?"

David smiled. "Oh, brother. I can see you are a force to be reckoned with."

Giselle eyed him. "Don't end your sentences with a preposition, Brother David. Something tells me you are a lawyer and should know that."

David eyed her back. "As a matter of fact, I am a lawyer, but only to help in my business negotiations. I wasn't aware we had started our negotiations as of yet. I will be more careful in the future."

David and Giselle stood facing each other like how a male and female pit bull might, unsure whether they were going to fight or hump each other in front of the ticket counter.

Suddenly, Molly let out a shout. The lock on her suitcase was broken, and some of her beautiful and intimate things were falling out onto the floor as the ticket clerk lifted the luggage onto the baggage conveyor. Clint, always the gentleman, grabbed the suitcase and started cramming designer panties and bras back into it. It was quite a scene—a monk holding up sheer lingerie, turning red as a beet while doing so.

"Now that's not something you see every day," said Giselle. "Molly may have ended your brother's religious calling without even trying."

Molly thanked Clint, and it was a toss-up as to who was the most embarrassed. The ticket clerk said they would need another suitcase or at least something to hold the bag together, so Clint graciously offered the rope he was using as a belt and secured the suitcase. Molly was most appreciative and made Clint feel like a hero.

Giselle laughed. "Brother Clint, don't stop at the belt! I'm dying to know if monks wear underwear. You're lucky that tunic goes down to your knees."

Clint excused himself, and he and David headed off to the plane while Giselle and Molly finished checking in for their flight.

David and Clint arrived in plenty of time for their flight and settled into their first-class seats. For once, Clint was happy to be in his monk's clothes as he was quite comfortable for the long flight. It was, as Giselle had suggested, like he was wearing his pajamas. David loosened his tie, took off his shoes, and was already downing a glass of champagne before they had even lifted off.

Not surprisingly, Giselle and Molly arrived close to takeoff and, with much fanfare, settled in across the aisle from David and Clint. Giselle complained about the type and quality of the champagne and demanded more pillows and blankets than the crew could find. By the time they took off, the crew was rolling their eyes and wished Giselle would fly another airline in the future.

David nudged Clint and said, "We'll stay in Brussels tonight and then drive to the abbey tomorrow afternoon. Don't let anyone know what our real plans are, especially Molly. I saw how you were looking at her, and I need to know you can keep your mouth shut about what we're really doing. I don't trust her friend Giselle at all, and I doubt they're just sightseeing in Brussels. Who knows what their real plans are."

Clint gave David a dirty look. "You sound more like my father than my brother."

"Fine, you can talk with Molly for a while, but remember, for the moment, you are a monk in training. When we are back in the states, you can track her down if you like."

"Let me remind you to keep your hands off both Giselle and Molly, and I will continue to play this stupid monk role for now. If the monks at the monastery don't want to negotiate with you, all bets are off, and I return to my normal self with a new wardrobe courtesy of you," Clint stated.

Giselle and Molly were also whispering across the aisle.

"Wow," said Molly. "I just feel like tearing that monk's clothes of his back and joining the mile high club—although, I guess we haven't even left the ground."

"Slow down, girl," said Giselle. "Imagine me saying that! I know there is something almost irresistible about a handsome man with a religious calling that you can't seduce. It's like having this amazing piece of fudge that you can't eat. No fudge for you today, girl! I don't know what is going on with those two, but I bet it is much more than they are telling us. Keep your panties on until we figure out what they really are doing. We are here on a case and have to keep that in mind. After that, be my guest and have at the monk. I do have to confess there have been at least one or two priests over the years that I have led astray."

Molly sighed. "I can almost taste that fudge, but I will behave and so will you! No fudge for me means no fudge for you either."

Giselle frowned. "Well, I may have to play hide the salami with the attorney just to figure out what they are up to, but I do promise I won't get distracted by the event. Can't say the same for him."

Without much fanfare, the plane taxied to the runway and eventually took off. Since they were leaving LAX, they had to wait at least twenty minutes for the ten planes in front of them. Once they were in the air and the seat belt sign went off, Clint got up to go to the bathroom.

David leaned over to Giselle across the aisle. "Would you care to join me over here for a glass of champagne and to discuss the real reasons you and I are flying to Europe?"

"Said the spider to the fly," Giselle said coyly. "Although, I'm not sure in this case who is the spider and who is the fly, but I never pass on champagne. We will just have to keep an eye on our younger protégés since your brother's monastic intent could be sorely tested with Molly."

Giselle got up and moved over to Clint's seat, and she and David ordered another glass of champagne. They sipped it and sized one another up.

"We can skip the small talk. I already Googled you on the way to the plane," said Giselle.

David raised a brow in disbelief.

"Don't believe me? You were born in Chicago from a stalwart Jewish family. Your father, Lou Collins, was an attorney and real estate developer after WWII and did quite well. You were brought up in Milwaukee and got a business degree from the University of Wisconsin—Madison has a nice campus and is quite the party school. I visited a friend there while in college. You moved to LA twenty years ago and, starting with a small business firm, rose like a meteor to your own firm, focusing on mergers and acquisitions. Along the way, you picked up a law degree from UCLA, but looks like you are your only client. I read two of your papers on mergers in the LA area. They weren't bad but were a little dry. You could have punched them up a bit. Nothing in your bio about women in your life, certainly nothing about marriage or significant others. But I saw you check out Molly's derriere when she was picking up her underthings, so I assume you are not gay. I suspect you have made a conscious decision not to have a long-term romantic relationship at this point, but I could be wrong. Google only goes so far, so I would need more time to check you out more."

"I'm not sure whether I should be impressed or alarmed," David said with a grin.

"Oh, I'm not finished yet. I researched your travel companion too, and I have a feeling Clint isn't following a true calling to be a monk. Though, he does seem to be a genuinely nice guy, which is a truly rare commodity in LA. Clint Daniels does not have as extensive of a bio as you do, but I was still able to find some information. He was born in Detroit into a simple working class family, and his father worked for the auto industry. He went to a local college in Detroit and then later graduated from Michigan State in East Lansing. He went on to attend law school in California and has been practicing general law with some family law for the last fifteen years in LA. He was married and divorced and has a fifteen-year-old daughter." Giselle paused, looking David right in the eye. "So, what the hell are you doing traveling to Brussels? I assume you are not working on a deal with the European Union or NATO, and I doubt you have thoughts of a major charitable contribution to one of the abbeys."

David gave an appreciative laugh. "That is a fairly reasonable summary of my life to date. Do you know what I had for breakfast? If so, then I'll really be worried."

"You should be worried anyway. I would guess coffee, an egg white omelet, whole wheat toast, and grapefruit juice," she ventured.

"No toast, but pretty damned close. You are right that I am going to Brussels for a negotiation of sorts, but I can't reveal what I am working on now. It is far too early in the process to leak any information. Clint is not really my brother as I am sure you already know. He is a close friend and may or may not choose to pursue a monastic path."

"I think it's clear who the spider is," Giselle said triumphantly.

"Not so fast. You're not the only one who knows how to use Google," said David. "You are a California girl, born and bred in LA. Your father, Carl Larson, was an attorney as well, but there's not too much about him online. He was a bit of an entertainment promoter, but not into the big time. Your mother was a ballerina of some note. You were named after the renowned French ballet, but were never the dancer your mother was. You had other talents. Plus, you are only five-two, and most ballerinas are around five-five. But that's not a disadvantage in my book since I am only five-seven. You were schooled at Stanford, also in business and also an impressive campus, though a bit formal. You wrote for the school newspaper and got into a bit of trouble for being a bit too forthright. You chose to work for a large merger and acquisition firm and are one of their chief VPs. At this point, you pick and choose what projects you want to pursue. You also have not been married and, from what I have found online and have recently experienced, I think you too have a healthy heterosexual appetite. I have no idea what you had for breakfast. So, what the hell are you and Molly doing in Brussels? I am certain you are not going to Belgium for sightseeing or to try their chocolates."

Giselle laughed. "You are right that Molly and I are not on vacation, though Belgian chocolates are addictive. We are actually working on a real live mystery and have a client who we are trying to help. Molly is the real detective, and I am here more in a supervisory capacity. I can't tell you more specifics on what or who we are trying to unravel. I guess we both have some secrets to keep for a while. Perhaps we can meet in Brussels in a few days and see how each of us is doing."

David nodded. "There is great restaurant, Comme Chez Soi, where we can meet in a few days. Clint may be ensconced at the monastery by then, but we can try to meet and catch up. He has actually been studying detective work and might be able to help you at some point. Even though he is an attorney for the city of LA, he enjoys detective investigations."

Giselle thought for a moment. "Maybe that could come in handy. I'll have to think about that and discuss it with Molly." They exchanged cell phone numbers and sat back to drink their champagne.

Clint returned from the bathroom and without reluctance sat next to Molly. "If you don't mind, I'll sit here for bit while David and Giselle talk," he said.

Molly smiled. "No problem, make yourself comfortable. I have to be honest though, I am still confused as to why you would want to become a monk."

Clint was conflicted. He didn't want to lie to Molly, but he couldn't break his promise to David—at least not yet. "It's hard to explain," said Clint. "At this point, I just want to see if this is the right path for me. I will have the opportunity to change my mind if this doesn't seem like it is working. I meet with the head monk tomorrow afternoon and will see what he says. What are you doing in Brussels? Your friend Giselle certainly seems like an aggressive sort. She is pretty funny though."

Molly smiled. "Yes, Giselle is something else, but her heart is in the right place. We aren't supposed to tell anyone the specifics of why we are here, but it is for a new job. I am starting to do some detective work. It is very exciting."

"Wow," said Clint. "I work as an attorney, but lately have been studying detective work, partly for my clients and also as another employment option. I really enjoy the intellectual challenge."

Molly was quite excited. "If you have time before you start at the monastery, maybe you can help us with our case. I'll talk with Giselle."

Giselle leaned over. "I need to retake my cocoon so I can watch a movie and get some sleep before dinner.

These overseas flights are murder with the sleep deprivation, but at least these reclining chairs in first class make it somewhat tolerable."

Giselle and Clint changed seats. David looked over at Clint. "I hope you kept your mouth shut."

Clint winced. "Sure, Dad."

Molly told Giselle about her talk with Clint and his interest in detective work. The two agreed that Clint's skills may come in handy, especially when they go to investigate the hotel room Marguerite's brother was last seen. Giselle had booked the room in Brussels he had been staying in so they could see if any information was left there. Of course, she and Molly would be staying at a much nicer hotel in Brussels.

Giselle leaned across the aisle and asked, "Clint, before you officially enter the monastery, could you spare a few hours in a hotel room with the two of us?"

Clint's cheeks flushed.

"To do some detective work of course. We could use your help investigating the disappearance of our client Timothy Marcum," Molly clarified.

Clint was relieved and started feeling like this trip may actually pan out to be fun, but he noticed David's apprehension. Even still, he agreed to help them and suggested he sleep at the Sabina, the hotel where Marguerite's brother had stayed, that evening since he soon would be at the monastery.

"I know that name from somewhere, Clint. I'm not sure we want to be involved in this," David said quietly.

"Don't be so paranoid. We'll still have time to execute your plan. I just want to have a little fun," Clint stated.

David was not thrilled with the distraction, but eventually he got on board as well.

Molly and Giselle decided, once they landed in Brussels, they would freshen up at their hotel and then meet Clint back up at seven that night at the Sabina. David begged off, planning to study his proposal and a few Belgian beers as well.

5 TIMOTHY IN PARIS

Timothy stretched his legs as his flight approached Charles de Gaulle Airport in Paris. Normally, he would have been excited to arrive in this amazing city, even the mere mention of its name would make his mouth water, but dealing with his recent trauma and cohort's death at the monastery put a damper on that. Still the excitement of finding the next clue for his father intrigued him. He just wished his father would let him know more about his task and why he needed so many diamonds. He tried to piece together the bits of information he had: the flash drive from the monk that showed him part of a chemical formula and process, a name of a contact he would meet at the Louvre, and a possible description of where to find the next bit of information in the museum. He had no idea how he was going to find the next clue among the millions of artistic treasures. Searching for a needle in a haystack paled in comparison to his next mission, but his father, as a billionaire, had untold resources. He had assured Tim that the staff at the Louvre would be most cooperative. In addition, his father sent him a "special" watch his AI team had been working on. When paired with his iPhone, it could search the internet and provide an amazing amount of information. All Tim had to do was lift the watch to his mouth and say a command.

Aside from the safety of his father's resources, Tim couldn't help but worry about the real possibility of encountering more Russian thugs. Tim wondered whether the police arrested the Russian at the monastery for the murder of Brother Adolphus. Tim fought back a tear or two thinking of the sweet monk. He would have to keep his wits about him to avoid more encounters.

"***Mesdames et Messieurs***," a voice chirped loudly over the plane's speaker. The flight attendant went on to inform the passengers that they would be landing soon. Tim brought himself back to the moment and tightened his seat belt. At least he would have time to catch a wonderful lunch with buttery croissants at a French restaurant before heading off to the Louvre for his next adventure to meet Monsieur Gerard Malbec.

6 THE ABBEY

Brother Antiochus sat at his desk eating his modest breakfast of oatmeal, a few grapes, and tea and uncharacteristically was in bit of turmoil. He had been up since five that morning as usual and had done his morning prayers and exercises. Little had changed in this routine or his breakfast for the last twenty of his eighty-two years. As senior monk, he certainly had issues come up over the years, but nothing as serious as this. He was a very pious man and felt even this conundrum would be ultimately handled by the Almighty. He just needed to help move things along in a propitious way. The abbey had existed for hundreds of years and hopefully, God willing, would continue for hundreds of years more. He smiled thinking of the formation of the monastery almost nine hundred years ago. Various orders of monks occupied the site until the French revolution when it was burned to the ground. In the 1930s, the monastery was rebuilt, and the current monastic order established. The brewery was reestablished in 1931 and follows Trappist protocol in using its proceeds to support the monastery and charity.

Brother Antiochus shook his head thinking how he actually had to lie to the police and press about Brother Adolphus passing away from a fall. He did, however, tell his good friend Detective Karven what had really happened, that Brother Adolphus had actually been killed protecting the young novice Timothy outside the abbey. He and the detective were still trying to figure out what to do.

Poor Brother Adolphus. May he rest in peace, he thought. The senior monk could not help crying when he thought of the surveillance tapes from outside the abbey that he had reviewed time and again with Detective Karven. *Why did the Russian criminal try to stab Timothy? Was he trying to steal the money?* Brother Adolphus had acted bravely and had given his life protecting the young novice. The senior monk wished he knew where Timothy was so he could find answers to his questions. Knowing the Russian thug had escaped and the police were still searching for him made Brother Antiochus feel even more anxious. He couldn't help but feel responsible knowing he had contributed to Brother Adolphus's death in some way. He knew he should not have agreed to the proposal from Timothy's father, but the abbey sorely needed the money from the diamonds for repairs and maintenance. However, in hindsight, nothing was worth Brother Adolphus's life. He felt guilty for putting the saintly monk in harm's way, but he knew the monk faced death with grace and peace.

To add to the puzzle, he looked at the packet on his desk sent from someone in the US who had set up a meeting at the abbey tomorrow. Normally, he would not have agreed to this, but he had no idea if this was somehow linked to Brother Adolphus's death and Timothy's disappearance. The monk pulled out the papers from the folder and again looked at the picture of David Collins. He was certain that, if this was some sort of business proposal, it would be totally out of the question. He then looked again at the enclosed picture of the potential novice, Clint, and was surprised to get the same overwhelming sensation he had had when looking at this yesterday: this young man was being sent to help him resolve their current problems. How that was possible, he did not know, but who was he to question? He again reviewed Clint's information and smiled at his lab studies, including his DNA profile. He would greet him warmly and go from there.

Brother Antiochus looked up and was greeted by their massive Saint Bernard as he came bounding into his room. What a devoted protector he was for the monks at the abbey. Their Russian intruder had certainly found that out. The monk cradled the dog's massive head in his arms and happily scratched him behind his ears, just where Bernardus liked. Contrary to rumors of his pet's advanced age, Antiochus was all too aware that Bernardus, who happily licked his hands, was nearing his allotted time on earth. Fortunately, the Almighty saw fit to allow Bernardus, and their eleven previous Saint Bernards, to live out double what most Saint Bernards lived to, resulting in nearly twenty years with their loyal guard dog, which was about twice the average life span of a typical Saint Bernard.

The abbey had already contacted the Barry Foundation to arrange for a new Bernardus pup to be delivered next spring. It would take the monks at least a year to help train their new charge to his duties at the abbey.

7 A PAINFUL SHOWER

Clint settled into his hotel room and thought about his new detective role. Molly and Giselle had filled him in about Timothy Marcum's disappearance on the plane. His head was spinning a bit with the thought that he was an attorney, a makeshift detective, and soon to be a monk—at this rate, he'll be playing a clown in the future. It felt a bit eerie to be staying in this room where who knows what had happened.

He unpacked his things and left his computer on the desk. He had purposely gotten a new laptop for the trip so little information would be on it. He was glad he had insisted on taking his detective kit and his *So You Want to Be a Detective* e-book on a USB drive. However, he did not want Molly to see he had brought these along, so he hid them in the desk by the window.

He laid on the bed to rest his eyes, but his curiosity only allowed him a short nap. Soon, he was in full detective mode, scouring the room for clues. The room had a definite European flare, as one would expect, but there was no sign of a struggle or any obvious blood stains. He was on the first floor, and he could see getting in and out of the window would certainly be easy. The street was quiet, so it would be easy to drag someone through the window without being seen. No papers or magazines besides the typical tourist ones were on the table. He checked under the bed and mattress and in the bathroom, but found nothing.

He decided to take a shower since Molly and Giselle were picking him up soon. He left the bathroom door open just in case the girls were early so he could hear them. He noticed the curtains blowing in the room a bit more and felt that was odd since it wasn't that windy. He stepped into the shower and let the hot water pour down his back. As he reached for the shampoo he heard someone in the room.

"Molly? Is that you? I'm in the shower!" he called out. When he didn't hear a response, he peeled back the curtain. "Moll—"

A massive tattooed arm with fresh wounds encircled him, closing his throat. Then, a gun was jammed against the back of his head.

"Where is the flash drive?" his assailant said in a deep foreign accent.

Thinking quickly, though not knowing what the hell the intruder was looking for, Clint choked out, "In the desk drawer by the window."

Their rendezvous was interrupted by a knock at the door. In one swift motion, the assailant slammed the gun across the back of Clint's head and quickly disappeared.

* * *

Clint gradually came to as he heard the frantic voices of Giselle and Molly. They patted him down, trying to dry him off. He was still in the tub, and blood and water were everywhere. He wasn't sure how long he had been unconscious, but he had one hell of a headache. He tried to remember what had happened, but everything seemed hazy. He did remember the tattooed arm and the blast across his head.

Molly and Giselle yelled at him together, "Clint, what in the world happened to you? Are you okay? Did you fall in the shower?"

Clint slowly started to get up, his head pounding like a symphony. "Someone came into this room and hit me over the head. Maybe he was frightened off when you two came." Clint blearily looked around, holding a towel to his head.

The room was a disaster. Everything had been turned topsy-turvy, the mattress was flipped over and his suitcase dumped out. His computer was gone and so was his USB drive. His wallet was on the floor, minus his cash, but luckily, his ID and credit cards were still there. Relief washed over him when he remembered he had left his passport at the hotel front desk. *What a welcome to Brussels,* he thought.

Giselle had the hotel call an ambulance, and despite his protests, he was taken to the local emergency room. He needed half a dozen sutures, but the CAT scan of his brain was fine. He felt miserable, but his headache improved when a pretty young nurse took over his care. The nurse made sure Clint was as comfortable as possible, but she made Molly's blood boil when she seemed to be too concerned with his comfort.

The police asked him some questions and thought it odd that someone would break into his hotel room for a computer and a few hundred dollars in cash without taking his credit cards. None of the group said anything to the police about their detective work. Clint also neglected to tell them about his USB drive.

After a lengthy interview with the police, the group was starving. Giselle had massive amounts of food delivered from the Brasserie Horta restaurant to the emergency room, so she was very popular with the ER staff. By the time they left, they had many new friends in Brussels.

Despite his headache, Clint was anxious to get back to the hotel room and see what he could find. After the police had checked out his room, the hotel staff had cleaned up the bathroom and the rest of the room. They felt terrible that someone had broken into his room and offered to have him stay for free for the rest of the week. Clint obliged, grateful he wouldn't have to sleep out on the street.

As he sat in a hotel chair, he couldn't help but wonder why someone would have bothered to steal the USB drive to his computer. *They must have been looking for something,* Clint thought. *Boy, won't they be disappointed when they realize what they took.* Unfortunately, that mistake meant whoever assaulted him might be back to get what they were looking for.

He took out his detective kit and an ultraviolet light. He switched on the light and turned off the room's lights. The girls stood by the window as Clint traced the light on the floor and along the walls.

"There certainly was blood on the floor, but some of it could be mine," Clint said as he panned the light over the carpet.

He noticed some white powder along the baseboard in a corner that showed up with the light. He got out his penknife and pried the molding away from the wall, finding a little hole in the wall housing another USB drive.

"Bam!" he shouted. "I found something. Take that Dick Tracey! Not too shabby for my first official case."

The ladies grabbed Clint and began dancing around. Clint started to get light headed after a minute and had to sit down.

"Great work," said Molly. "Now, how do we figure out what's on it?"

"It depends if it is encrypted. If it is, it could be difficult to open, but I just may know someone in Brussels who can help us," said Giselle.

"More detective work," boasted Clint.

"We know this young man's sister, Marguerite, and if he is not too computer savvy, I bet we can figure out his password. Most people try to use something for their passwords they will remember that other people don't know. What time is it in LA? We could call her now and get a list of likely passwords," Molly chimed in.

Giselle looked at her watch. "I keep my watch at LA time so I can call my office when it's convenient. It's eleven-thirty at night here in Brussels, so it's two-thirty in the afternoon in LA. I'll call Marguerite now."

Almost immediately, Marguerite picked up, and Giselle explained their situation. They also told her that a friend, Clint, was helping them. Marguerite was excited they had made some progress, but was distressed that Clint had been attacked. She gave them a list of names and dates that her brother would likely use, noting the most probable was his dog's name Dotsy and her birthday June 10, 1990.

"Tomorrow we can try to see what is on the USB drive," said Clint. "Before I totally crash, I should probably tell you about the tattoos on the gorilla of a man who attacked me while I still remember it." Clint closed his eyes. "Let's see. He choked me with his left arm, which had two figures. On his upper arm was a black, more primitive devil with horns and teeth. On his forearm was a more detailed black panther leaping toward his wrist. He also had some significant wounds to his right forearm. The wounds looked like some type of bites or like maybe his arm had been crushed. I'll have to research the tattoos in the morning to see if they give us any more clues."

"You need to get some rest tonight," said Molly. "Are you sure you don't want one of us to keep an eye on you tonight?"

"I'll be fine. Just don't come by too early tomorrow morning."

Molly made arrangements to see Clint in the morning and take him around Brussels if his head allowed. She knew an amazing place they could go for breakfast. Clint collapsed onto the bed and was asleep before Molly and Giselle even left the room. They smiled at each other as they closed his door.

"Clint could use a little TLC after getting that nasty hit on the head. I'm just glad he wasn't hurt more," said Giselle.

"I'll try to take care of the TLC and promise not to let romance get in the way of our investigation. I think it is great Clint found the USB drive. We will have to try to read it tomorrow," Molly said as they headed out the hotel. "I am worried about Marguerite's brother. I suspect that the same people who broke into Clint's room likely took him for whatever reason. They seem quite dangerous, and who knows what they have done to him. The sooner we find him, the better."

"At least now we have a starting point. How many burly men have tattoos of a devil and a panther on one arm?" Giselle said.

"I agree. The tattoos on our assailant may help us track him down. Maybe we should have been more forthcoming with the police. I still have that detective's number if we decide we need his help."

"All things considered, we are moving forward on this case very quickly. I'll call my friend about the USB in the morning. I need a decent breakfast and to check out the main square here, the Grand Place. I hear there is a great café in one of the guildhalls. I'm long overdue for a mimosa and some steamed buttered mussels. And don't let me forget to get some chocolates and pralines at Wittamer to send home. Some people would do most anything for a box of Wittamer chocolates, and that can be very useful at times."

Molly shook her head. "Always the negotiator, but I guess there are worse things you could bargain with than a box of chocolates."

The girls left the Sabina and headed back to their Five-star Hotel.

8 TIMOTHY AT THE LOUVRE

Timothy looked across the road at the Seine and savored the last bite of his amazing Parisian lunch. Who could possibly consider fast food when one could relish food like this? He was ready for his meeting at the Louvre, but he had to first check in to his favorite Parisian hotel, the fabulous Hôtel de Crillon, built over two hundred fifty years ago for Louis XV. He could just imagine his father blowing a gasket at the cost of this little extravagance. He arranged a rental car through the concierge since he knew Paris quite well and avoided Parisian cabdrivers whenever possible. He drove to the Louvre, and despite traffic and lots of the usual tourists, he was able to park fairly close to the entrance.

Tim had been to the Louvre many times but still felt overwhelmed by its majesty and sheer magnitude. He couldn't resist taking Teri, his new watch and AI companion, to the Louvre. He had been somewhat lonely in Brussels and enjoyed a comforting female voice, even if it was an artificial one.

"Teri, what is something unusual about the Louvre?" he asked.

"Stop asking me difficult questions," she responded. "Unusual is a comparative adjective. As a computer, I might be able to evaluate that in the next ten years, but not now. You could ask me what is unique about the Louvre."

"Okay, Teri, what is unique about the Louvre?"

"First, the Louvre was built as a fortress along the Seine back in the twelfth century and was named after Napoleon for a time after he came to power. Another unique fact is that the Mona Lisa has not always been on display at the Louvre."

"Thank you, Teri," said Timothy.

"No need to thank me for my answers," Teri replied.

Timothy thought about asking Teri about her concept of beauty, but thought better of it. "Teri, how close can you come to an object in the Louvre?" he asked.

"Since there are over 680,000 artifacts on display in the main Louvre and a complicated architectural structure that is somewhat difficult to measure. I would estimate within ten meters, or roughly thirty feet," she responded.

Timothy nodded and headed into the Louvre to meet with Monsieur Gerard Malbec. He checked in at the imposing information counter and soon met a very straight-laced elegant gentleman whose shoes looked like they were polished at least every seven minutes.

"***Bonjour!***" they each exclaimed, exchanging pleasantries.

"I have been in contact with your father and his representatives and will follow his somewhat perplexing requests," the Frenchman said in a hushed voice.

"My father is usually perplexing," said Timothy. "I expect he wants you to help me find a small object among the thousands of treasures in this building. I have been told it is near the Greek statuary, and I have the GPS coordinates."

"That should be of some help, but this may still be a monumental task," said Malbec. "We should begin immediately. Your father must certainly be something if he can get the Louvre to grant you access as they have."

Timothy responded with a knowing look.

As they weaved through the crowds, Timothy was reminded of his college days when he had studied art. He knew he could easily get lost in the Greek statues, dissecting the muscles and proportions of the bodies that made them so lifelike, so he had to force himself to focus on the task at hand. He was aware that what he was looking for would likely be similar to the flash drive he had gotten from the monk. He also surmised that he couldn't actually examine objects on exhibit, so the hidden object would have to be in one of the signs, part of a barricade, a light fixture, or hardware on one of the doors or cabinets.

Timothy and Malbec spent hours going through the various exhibits to no avail. They worked late into the night, and in desperation, Tim asked Teri if the schematics of the Greek statue section showed more than what they were finding.

"I can't get great detail, but I can get a closer look than you can with your eyes," she said. "Let me hook into Malbec's computer and see what I can find."

They wandered around again in the defined area, and eventually, Teri found a wall with a hidden access behind one of the exit signs. Timothy was able to swing the sign away from the wall, revealing a keypad with six raised buttons. Malbec entered the Louvre's general password, and the wall slid open to reveal some of the Louvre's monitoring equipment in a small hidden closet with a narrow passageway. Malbec recognized it as part of a system monitoring humidity, temperature, and even oxygen levels in the Louvre.

"This is all pretty standard equipment," he said.

"Everything except for the broom in the corner," Tim noted.

"Yes, that's true since this is not a utility closet."

Timothy examined the broom carefully, and noticing the top of the broom was slightly loose, he unscrewed it. "Voilà!"

There, in the top of the broom, was another USB drive. Both Tim and Malbec were quite excited, and even Teri seemed lively. Tim plugged it into his computer, and indeed, it seemed like the second part to the drive he had gotten in Brussels. He immediately sent the info to his father in California.

"We should celebrate!" Tim said.

"Well, not just yet," said Malbec as he pointed to two large, muscular behemoths who were glaring at them from behind one of the statues.

9 BRUSSELS

Clint was relieved his world wasn't spinning anymore and his headache had dissipated when he awoke in the morning. Even still, he got up slowly and held on to the towel rack when he went to the bathroom. It was hard to believe all that had happened in the last day. He gingerly showered and rinsed the rest of the blood from his hair. The doctor in the ER had told him he could do so carefully if he applied the antibiotic salve they had given him. His arm was sore from the Tetanus shot he had gotten, but that was the least of his worries. He dressed slowly and was still straightening up when there was a knock on the door. He was happy that someone was actually knocking instead of barging in. He thought about Molly and happily opened the door to her vision.

"Now that's a vision of Brussels I would fly five thousand miles to see," Clint said as he invited a delighted Molly into the room to get a better look at her.

"My goodness, Clint, you are much more lively this morning than I expected. I was quite worried about you last night. You must heal quickly."

Clint laughed. It took all of his strength not to flirt with Molly, so he had to remind himself to stay in character. *I'm a monk. Be a monk, Clint,* he told himself. He was totally taken by her sweet smile, blond curls, perfume, and curves in all the right places.

"I thought you might just call to check on me this morning, but I'm glad you're here. I am starved since I didn't eat last night. Do you want to join me for breakfast?"

Molly gave him a quick peck on the cheek. "Monk or no monk, I am happy to see you up and about after last night. It is scary to think someone hit you because of our case. I talked to the Detective Jacobs who talked to you last night. He wants to discuss the case with us today. Let's go for breakfast now, and we can discuss this later."

Molly navigated the buses through the city and soon they were at the Grand Place, one of the world's top central squares. Clint was in a daze, but not from his head injury. The buildings around the square, dating back hundreds of years, were decorated with culture and history, a dream come true for an art enthusiast.

"Let's head over to one of my favorite restaurants," said Molly. "La Brouette, or the wheelbarrow, is right in the square. I love their lasagna, and their breakfast spread is fantastic. Plus, I love their wood-backed booths, high ceilings, and glass chandeliers, or if you'd rather, we can sit outside and admire the Grand Place."

"Let's sit outside and enjoy the summer weather and beautiful architecture and crowds," said Clint. "It's crazy to think I was just reading about the guild houses on the plane, and here we are, sitting in one of them. The magazine on the plane said the beer museum with the Cantillon brewery is across the square from here. The yeast they use is local, so they have to open the roof to get the yeast spores. I wouldn't mind sampling a Lambic beer but would have to go easy with my recent head trauma."

"We can give you a taste, but that will have to hold you for now," said Molly.

As they sat outside at La Brouette enjoying their breakfast, the square bustled with tourists and locals. Venders were selling all sorts of trinkets, Belgian treats, and flowers.

"You should see this square during a summer when they have the Flower Carpet. The locals fill the entire square with intricately designed flower arrangements. It really is an amazing sight."

"I can only imagine how beautiful the contrast between the vibrant flowers and the Gothic architecture must be," Clint said with a bit of awe.

"We could spend all day talking about this, but before I forget, I need to tell you that I called Detective Jacobs. He agreed to meet us here to show you some photos of tattoos on his laptop. I didn't mention the USB drive to him since Giselle knows someone who may be able to access that."

Almost on cue, Detective Jacobs arrived, laptop in hand. "You certainly look better than you did last night, Clint."

"Thanks for stopping by and helping out. As Molly probably told you, we are looking into the disappearance of a young man, Timothy Marcum. We have been hired by his sister to see if we can find him."

Detective Jacobs gasped. "Timothy Marcum? I was just told by Chief Detective Karven that a young monk by that name disappeared from the monastery. I must tell my superior immediately. Your client may have been kidnapped, though that would be very surprising for a monk."

Molly, also shocked by the rapid turn of events, explained, "This young man's family is extremely wealthy, though he has been distanced from them. Excuse me while I call my partner Giselle and let her know as well."

They both made quick calls and returned to discuss what to do next. Detective Jacobs brought them both up to date. "We all have to meet at the precinct this afternoon at one-thirty to meet with Detective Karven. If there's any other information you received from Timothy's sister, please bring it with you. It sounds like the people involved are dangerous, so we will need to proceed with caution."

Clint nodded in agreement. "I can understand your concern, and we will certainly keep our eyes open. Unfortunately, my friend David and I have an appointment at the Lavro Monastery this afternoon, but Molly and our partner, Giselle, can meet with you at the precinct."

"Yes, we will be sure to meet you there, detective. Until then, maybe I can show Clint a bit more of Brussels before his appointment this afternoon," Molly said as she stood up from her bistro chair.

Detective Jacobs shook both of their hands, and they parted ways.

Molly proceeded as a tour guide for Clint throughout Brussels. They saw the Manneken Pis, the little brass statue of a naked boy urinating into a fountain. They stopped off at the beer museum across the square and shared a beer. They did a bit of shopping at Les Galeries Royales Saint-Hubert, the oldest shopping mall in Europe, where Clint bought Molly a chic silk scarf and a lace kerchief. At the end of the tour, Molly returned the favor by buying Clint a few chocolates at Wittamer. Clint couldn't seem to get enough of these delectable chocolates, and if allowed, he would have bought out the store.

As one-thirty approached, Clint was disappointed to have to part ways with Molly. She reluctantly hugged him goodbye and then headed off to the precinct. Clint made his way back to the hotel to meet David before their trip to the monastery.

10 THE ABBEY MEETING

David and Clint had rented a little Fiat for their two-hour drive out to the abbey from Brussels. It was a beautiful day, so they drove with their windows down, letting the warm summer air massage their faces. Clint breathed in deeply, committing the smell of the grassy hills to memory. The lush, green Belgian countryside was idyllic. David and Clint were quiet most of the ride as both were absorbed in their thoughts. David was reminded of his previous trips across Ireland, minus the salty air of the coast. Here, the scents were much more pungent and the occasional other drivers seemed much less crazed.

As they made their way around a bend, David glanced across at Clint, and finally breaking the silence, he said, "So, you still think you can play this monk role for at least a few days? I'm not sure how receptive the head monk will be to my proposal, so I need you to commit to your role. I've already done my research."

"So then fill me in, Mr. Expert," Clint said with a laugh.

"I know, since they switched over to using a dry malt process, they must have an English firm running the brewing process. They abandoned their copper kettles and are now using stainless, and their production is capped at a maximum two million gallons a year, which they export about 15 percent of, mostly to Europe. They make one beer with a lower percentage of alcohol, essentially for the monks, and their second beer is for sales to the public. To qualify as a Trappist beer, the process has to be supervised by the monks, brewed at the monastery, and the proceeds have to support only the monastery and charity. They also sell some cheeses to help cover their costs."

Clint gave David a long look. "Okay, you've definitely done your homework. But, since this order of monks has been brewing beer for close to one hundred years, I truly doubt you will be able to convince them to work with us. I am willing to play the monk role, but only for a short time. These monks really are committed to a certain way of life, and I respect that. I don't know how long I can justify pretending to do what they do."

David nodded, but stayed silent until they arrived at the monastery grounds. The monastery and brewery were usually closed to the general public, so they walked into the museum to see about meeting with the head monk. David looked at the beer available for purchase in the museum and knew he would have to sample one before leaving.

A distinguished elderly monk approached them. "Hello. You must be David and Clint. My name is Brother Antiochus, and I am the head monk of this monastery. I hope your drive from Brussels was pleasant."

"Greetings, Your Reverence," said David. "It is a beautiful day, and our drive was inspiring, as is your monastery."

The monk laughed. "You can call me Brother Antiochus and skip some of the formality here. We monks try to live a simple life. Clint, you seem to be a bit quiet. How long have you thought about becoming a monk? As I'm sure you know, most of the monks here are quite a bit older than you."

"I've thought about this for some time but even more so recently," said Clint. "I've always been somewhat circumspect but had kind of a rough childhood. I guess I too am looking for a simpler life. I would like to at least try the monastic life to see if it is right for me."

"We certainly can try you in the novice program here," said the monk. "It is somewhat rigorous. Our diet is simple, and we focus on prayer and do regular meditation and exercise. There is no radio or TV, and the only music is from the chanting at our services. I want you to be aware that this lifestyle requires a lot of discipline and commitment. If you would still like to try this lifestyle, we can start now or you can return after thinking about it for a while."

Clint looked fairly intently at Brother Antiochus before saying, "I am ready to start my work as a novitiate now. I don't feel I need to think about this anymore before starting."

"Welcome to your training then," said the monk.

Another older monk joined them to escort Clint to parts unknown of the monastery. David and Clint said brief goodbyes before they parted. David and Brother Antiochus then sat at a large but simple desk, and the monk pulled out the folder that David had sent him. One could feel a definite shift from both David and the monk from standard pleasantries to business mode. They paused to reset the tone.

"Mr. Collins, I have reviewed your proposal in detail and admit I do find some of what you suggest interesting. As you know, we have had a monastery here for hundreds of years and have been brewing beer since 1931. We strictly follow the Trappist regimen, and our monks supervise the brewing of our beer here with a computerized system run by an English company that provides a constant product of which we can be proud. We are not motivated by a focus on profit as most businesses are since all our profit goes to cover our costs of the abbey and the rest goes to charity. I'm not sure what benefit you could provide us beyond what we have now."

David smiled and stretched. "Contrary to what you think, I am well aware of the different motivations and concerns you and your fellow monks are likely to have. I am very familiar with a number of charities and have tried to raise money to help those less fortunate. Just because I am a businessman does not mean you and I are dissimilar. I agree that improving your business simply to make more money does not support the Trappist or religious spirit I feel present in this abbey. I would not have brought my friend here to study with you if I did not feel this is a holy place. Money can be used in many ways, but certainly it can be used for the good as well as for lining the pockets of the rich. Please review the business proposal you have, and if you see fit, I can present it next week at your board meeting."

Brother Antiochus was actually impressed, which had not happened for a very long time. In speaking with David, he realized three things: these people had nothing to do with the murder of Brother Adolphus; David was an impressive individual, and though the board was unlikely to consider any new proposals for the brewery, he would let them look at the information David had brought; and finally, he felt sure that Clint had something about him he believed would help them through their current troubles. How or why he believed this, he had no idea.

"I will present your information to the board early next week. If they need more information from you before that, I will contact you directly. I will check on your friend Clint daily and keep you informed as to how he is doing. He is free to leave at any time he chooses."

David shook Brother Antiochus's hand and bowed slightly. "I deeply appreciate the courtesy you have extended to Clint and me. I look forward to hearing from you regarding both Clint and the matter at hand." David quietly left the monk.

As he headed back to his car, he wondered how Clint would fare in his role as a monk. He usually was quite adept at adapting to whatever roles he had to play, but this one was more challenging than most. David stopped at the museum store to buy several bottles of Lavro before leaving the abbey.

11 THE PRECINCT

Molly met Detective Jacobs at the precinct to discuss their case. Giselle had been talking with Chief Detective Karven on the phone and had decided to meet with him before the meeting to bring him lunch. Giselle always felt food, especially good food, could help any interaction. When they all got together, Giselle was adjusting her hair a bit as the others came into the room.

Molly eyed Giselle. "I see you and the detective have already been actively examining this case—from all angles," Molly said the last bit with a raised eyebrow.

Giselle laughed. "Yes, we have been working hard at evaluating all aspects of this case."

She then made introductions all around, and they all sat down in the detective's office. Detective Karven was a dark, handsome man in his early fifties with a forceful presence, though he seemed a bit distracted.

Detective Karven summed up the facts of the case as he understood them. He indicated that it was not common for the police to discuss cases outside the department, but he was aware that they had some information about this case that the police did not.

"So, we've established that Timothy Marcum disappeared one week ago, apparently while in Brussels, and you were hired by his sister to try to find him. He had been studying as a novitiate at the Lavro Monastery for a month before his disappearance. His family is quite wealthy, but he has been estranged from them for some time, with the exception of his sister. Last week, a senior monk at the same monastery died of uncertain causes. The monastery has not heard from the novice since then, but they may be hiding some information to try to protect him. To make matters more complex, your friend Clint stayed in Timothy's room yesterday and was attacked by a large man with distinctive tattoos who ransacked the room. Clint's computer was taken and some cash, but his credit cards were left. We believe the intruder was likely frightened off by the arrival of you ladies," Detective Karven stated, motioning to Giselle and Molly.

Giselle and Molly nodded in unison, both taken by the detective's striking looks.

Detective Karven continued, "Giselle and I have reviewed some of the information we have regarding the intruder's tattoos. The top devil tattoo looks like it was done in a Russian prison, while the black panther on his forearm is likely a professional tattoo. We believe the two together suggest the wearer's strength and evil nature.

"We believe the novice from the Lavro Monastery and your client's brother are the same person. We also were able to track Timothy's iPhone, which pinpointed his last location as Paris, but we haven't gotten a signal since then." Detective Karven paused for a brief moment before adding, "We believe the people who took Timothy Marcum and knocked out Clint are the same. They are clearly dangerous, so I suggest you leave this investigation to the police. I will try to reach my friend Detective Clousou in Paris to put out a search for Timothy's phone."

Giselle started to laugh. "I know this isn't funny, but you *actually* know the Pink Panther Inspector Clousou?"

Detective Karven frowned. "I'd advise you not call him that if you want him to help us. He is quite competent, but he gets very upset at the mention of a certain pink feline."

"In any case, Molly will leave for Paris immediately," said Giselle. "We were hired to find Timothy Marcum, and that is what we will try to do, but we will be careful. I'll keep in contact with you, detective, and I do appreciate your concern for us as well as the young man who disappeared."

Detective Karven shook his head and reluctantly shook hands with the pair as they made their way out. He was certain they would ignore his warnings, but he had hoped they wouldn't.

Molly gave Giselle a critical look. "So much for breasting our cards. Sounds like you and Detective Karven had an in-depth discussion about all aspects of this case, especially your personal qualifications."

Giselle innocently looked Molly in the eye. "Why yes, we had a very pleasant talk, though you can see he really does not want us to continue our search for Timothy. I will have my office book you a train ticket to Paris tomorrow. Do you think Clint could meet you in Paris after his stay at the abbey? It might be helpful to let him snoop around a bit at the monastery first."

Molly shrugged her shoulders. "Let's hope so. We can figure it out tonight at dinner with David."

Molly and Giselle headed back to their hotel to meet with some high-end computer experts.

"We have to get a look at that USB drive before you leave town," Giselle said. "I didn't want to let the detective know we had it until we had a chance to check it out ourselves."

They arrived back at the Hotel Warwick. Molly loved the huge four columns in front of the hotel embossed with gold on top. They gave her a sense of permanence in a changing world.

They were greeted inside the lobby by the three computer experts; actually, two were executives and one was a real computer expert. The two executives had on dark suits and ties and were in their forties, and the expert wore a sport shirt and rumpled pants; he looked barely out of school. They headed up to Giselle's suite where they began working on the USB drive.

"Hopefully, one of these passwords will work on this drive. Otherwise, it will take days to try to decrypt it," said the geek. "This is a clean computer, just in case there is a sophisticated virus on this drive." He plugged the USB in and set to work with the suggested passwords.

The rest of the group settled in for what might take a while. Giselle paced the room in her five-inch heels, the clicking noises matching the typing noise coming from the geek's keyboard.

After an hour, the geek shouted out, "Bingo! We are in! Not too sophisticated. He must not spend much time on computers."

They all rushed over, but Giselle told the suits and expert to give them some space while they looked at what was on the drive. Molly waded through what looked like a complicated chemical structure.

"My organic chemistry schooling was far too long ago, not to mention, I never had a knack for the subject. Our teaching assistant, Mr. Smith, was pretty hot, so I had a hard time focusing in class," Molly said.

"Enough about your schooling and love life," said Giselle. "What do you think that compound is?"

"I'm sure with all your office's resources you must have access to a chemist," Molly responded. "My guess, though, is that it's some kind of alcohol because it looks like it has a hydroxyl group on the end," said Molly. "Isn't there any text or other information on there?"

"There does appear to be some sort of cost breakdown, and if it's accurate, it looks very profitable," said Giselle, looking at the figures. "I am going to put this in the hotel safe while I decide if we should share this with Detective Karven, and I'll have a chemist review this formula from my office to confirm your analysis."

"I agree. Even though I'm fairly certain it is an alcohol compound, you should have it verified because my private tutoring sessions with Mr. Smith had very little to do with organic chemistry," Molly said.

"You'll have to tell me more about that tonight at dinner. We're supposed to meet David, and I think we deserve a fabulous meal before you leave for Paris. I don't think Clint will join us since he's still at the monastery—sorry, Molly," Giselle said as she eyed the computer geek who was wolfing down some snacks. "All right, men, thank you for your help, but we need some time to freshen up. Out you go," she said, shooing them out the door.

Molly stretched out on the elegant couch. "I'm not sure how much we should be telling David tonight. We really don't know him that well, and we still aren't positive why he is here."

Giselle gave Molly a dismissive look. "You leave David to me. He's here to work some deal, and I doubt it has anything to do with us, but we'll see."

"Whatever you say. Just, please be careful with that formula. Someone may already have died protecting it."

Giselle nodded. "I'll guard it carefully. Don't worry. So, how do you think Clint is doing at the monastery? I wouldn't be surprised if his prayers were interrupted by thoughts of you."

At the mention of Clint, Molly got a faraway look in her eyes and blushed a bit. "Yeah, I have been wondering what he is up to as well," she said.

"I can tell by the way you're blushing you have been thinking of him!" said Giselle. "That monk certainly has turned up the heat on your privates. After our dinner tonight, we may have to sneak out to the monastery to give you two a moment alone."

"Oh, quit it, Giselle," Molly said, but her face bore a spark of hope.

"But in all seriousness, we should ask Clint if he has heard anything yet about Timothy Marcum. I'll call David to see when we are to meet and if he knows anything about accessing the monastery. I can have the hotel arrange transportation."

Giselle then picked up the phone and called her office to make arrangements for Molly's trip to Paris and to hire a chemist to look at the formula on the USB drive. She stashed the USB drive and computer in the hotel safe, slamming the safe door shut with a clink.

Molly headed back to her room to research the Lavro Abbey to determine how best to access it at night to find Clint. Giselle took to the streets of Brussels to find equipment for the night, venturing to several electronic and detective stores.

12 CLINT THE MONK

Clint smiled as he polished the huge brass handrail leading down from the monastery's front door into the very bowels of the building below him. The rail was simple yet elegant and contrasted well with the marble stairs and ebony wooden supports. He smiled at the simplicity of the routine physical labor, which seemed completely in line with the monks' philosophy—and maybe even his own. Of all the jobs, he had had over the years, he could still enjoy unalienated work, as young Karl Marx called it. Clint certainly wasn't a Marxist, but he had a bit of liberal bent—much more than his friend David. Over the years, he had been in the military, driven cabs in LA, studied and practiced law, and now he was learning to be a detective and a monk at the same time. Life had certainly given him a few twists and turns.

As he polished the brassy handrail, he couldn't help but think about Molly and her soft blond hair brushing against him after his bludgeoning at the hands of the Russian. He knew these weren't the best thoughts for a monk, but they may be okay for a pseudo monk. He did have to be careful of the unintended rise in the front of his monk's garb, so he forced himself to focus on Timothy Marcum's case.

Clint had learned that Brother Adolphus had actually been killed and Timothy had disappeared after that. As a detective, Clint was lucky to be staying in Timothy's room, but knew it wasn't too out of the ordinary since that was where the novices stayed. He decided he'd give the room a more thorough investigation after lunch. He heard lunch would be rather simple, but he looked forward to his serving of the monks' "session," or lower alcohol beer. At this point, any beer would be welcome.

The resounding chime of the monastery's giant grandfather clock echoed through the marble hallway and interrupted his thoughts. One chime meant one o'clock and time for lunch, after which he would then participate in "private studies." Clint was already salivating, though he knew he would likely still be hungry.

He gathered in the cafeteria with about a dozen monks, and not a word was spoken. Simple hard bread, cheese, and an apple was their basic fair. He must have looked somewhat saddened since one of the monks smiled at him and quietly put his portion of cheese on Clint's plate. Clint bowed in response and smiled back at him. Clint gladly polished off every morsel of food and washed it all down with his allotment of beer, draining every last drop.

After lunch, the monks retired to the library. The walls were lined with at least five thousand books, including some texts over a thousand years old. Clint met with his tutor, Brother Lesjack. They sat at a large wooden table, and Clint prepared himself for what he assumed would be similar to a Religion 101 lecture. However, he was surprised to learn his initial studies would instead be based on what Clint found perplexing about religion. He reveled in the tutoring session, taking advantage of the library's vast resources and impressive computer access. The other monks seemed just as focused on their studies. There wasn't a sleepy eye in the group.

They studied for an hour and a half, and at three-thirty, it was time for their afternoon exercise. Despite their advanced age, the monks ran a one mile circuit around the grounds and then did yoga and stretching exercises for half an hour. Clint appreciated the change of pace and the ability to stretch his legs. He missed the speed of his bike in LA, so the chance to run made him feel even more alive.

After their exercise, they were back in one of the chapels for afternoon prayers for an hour. Clint wasn't used to spending so much time in prayer, but he did his best to fulfill his duties—even though his mind tried to drift to Molly several times.

Dinner was rice and steamed vegetables and left Clint dreaming of a porterhouse steak. His mouth filled with saliva at the thought of tender, thick steak. One of the other monks gave him a reassuring nod when he noticed Clint's faraway look. Clint nodded back and then scooped another bit of rice and broccoli onto his spoon. When he was finished, he rinsed his bowl and followed the other monks down to their sleeping quarters.

Clint was happy to retire to his room after dinner and used his secluded time to search his room. His hard work was repaid when he found a letter from Timothy that was never sent to his sister. *This detective work certainly can be rewarding*, he thought.

Suddenly, Clint felt the silent vibration of his phone that he had hidden in his pants go off. This was only to be used in case of emergency so he wondered what it could possibly be.

"Molly going to Paris tomorrow to find Timothy. Will be sneaking into monastery tonight," the text from David read.

Wow! A woman in the monastery. This certainly will be a first, thought Clint. Clint knew immediately this would be his last night at the monastery since there was no way he would let Molly chase down Timothy in Paris alone, especially not with his attacker still on the loose.

Since it was now going to be his last night, he decided he might as well check out the brewery upstairs while all the monks were asleep. He knew he probably would not have a chance to do so again.

He snuck up the five flights of stairs, and when he ran into Bernardus, he was happy he had brought his iPhone with him. He shined its flashlight on his face so as not to alarm the dog. Upon seeing it was only Clint, Bernardus settled back down onto the floor and closed his eyes.

Clint dug his hand into Brother Antiochus's coat and pulled out the keys to the brewery. He then quietly unlocked the door and let himself in. Looking around at the beautiful stainless steel brew kettles, he realized their suspicions had been right all along. Brother Adolphus could not have possibly fallen from there since the ladders were all enclosed. *If ever circumstantial evidence pointed to a criminal it does so here,* Clint thought, remembering one of his favorite *Sherlock Holmes* quotes.

As he searched through the brewery, he found the monks' private stock of beer and was forced to drink two large mugs—to ensure quality control of course. The beer was delicious and made him feel energized. He would miss this aspect of being a monk. He then heard one of the guards for the brewery coming so he headed back into the bowels of the monastery to wait for Molly.

13 DINNER WITH DAVID

Giselle and Molly met back up at six-thirty to catch a cab for dinner at Comme Chez Soi with David. They were surprised that David had already arranged a Hansom cab for them, complete with two white horses and a driver in full period costume.

"I have to admit, David has a certain style that one can't help but admire," Giselle said.

"Now don't you get your privates in an uproar just because of two white horses," said Molly as they got in. "What are the names of your horses?" she asked the driver.

"That, would be Filo and Filamina," said the driver. "I've heard the restaurant you're headed to has some of the best French cuisine in Brussels."

The horses' hooves clip-clopped on the pavement. The girls had a feeling of being back in Victorian times with the carriage and the European architecture they saw out the cab windows.

"Will I be picking you ladies up after the dinner?" asked the driver.

"No," said Giselle. "We have already made other arrangements, but this has been wonderful. Please feed Filo and Filamina well tonight." She handed the driver a very large tip.

"Thank you, miss," he said.

"And here's another five euros for calling me 'miss,'" said Giselle with a smile.

They climbed out of the cab and headed into the restaurant accompanied by a sea of tantalizing smells. The huge flowered skylight over the dining room made them sad they weren't there during the day, but the lighting was perfect for their evening repast. David waited for them at an elegant table already adorned with appetizers. He hoped he wouldn't salivate onto the table before he started gorging himself.

"*Bonsoir*," said David. "Welcome to Comme Chez Soi! By all accounts, it is supposed to be one of the best restaurants in Brussels, and that is saying something. Please sit and join me."

The girls smiled and took their seats across from him.

"Clint is ensconced at the monastery, and the head monk is supposed to keep me updated on how he is doing," David continued. "So far, I haven't had any calls for help from Clint. Molly, I understand you have plans to go to the monastery tonight to check on Clint. As I told Giselle, I'm not sure that is a great idea, but I'll leave that up to you two. Certainly, something is going on at that monastery that needs to be investigated."

Molly noticed an anxious group of American tourists next to them. They likely had never eaten in a high-end restaurant like this and were overwhelmed by all the cutlery.

Molly smiled and got their attention. "You look miserable. Relax! Just work your way in from the outside with the silverware, and if worse comes to worst, use your hands," she said with a wink. "Please enjoy your meal. I'm sure it will be wonderful!"

The tourists looked more relaxed and thanked Molly.

They all laughed. Giselle gave David a quick once-over and decided to let him in on at least part of what had been going on in their lives. She quickly updated David about their meeting with Detective Karven, but she did not tell him about what they found on the USB drive.

David shook his head at all they had going on in one day. He decided he too would be honest and told them about his meeting at the monastery. He even let them in on his plans to take over the brewing and about Clint's role in his plan. He did not feel that the monks would likely give his proposal much thought and that Clint would not last too long in the monastic life, so he no longer worried about what the women knew.

When Molly heard this, she quietly breathed a sigh of relief, knowing she no longer had to feel guilty for fantasizing about Clint.

David gave Giselle a hard, conspiring look. "So, in the interest of being honest, I should probably tell you one more thing. I once met both Timothy and his father for a business deal several years ago. Timothy seemed nice enough—actually, too nice to be involved in such negotiations, though probably more than a bit spoiled. His father was something else. He reminded me of something out of *The Godfather* movie series, a real-life Vito Corleone, including real-life muscle and guns. I quickly decided that no deal was worth my life and backed out. If there was enough money involved, I would not be surprised if Timothy's father had something to do with the killing of the monk and the kidnapping of Timothy. You ladies need to be careful. The Marcums aren't a family to get into bed with."

"Interesting," Molly said, trying to put the pieces together.

"Well, that would have been nice to know earlier, David," Giselle said sarcastically. "It's too late to back out now, though, so we will be careful."

"David, do you think you could give Clint a heads up about tonight?" Molly asked.

"It would be helpful if Clint could still play the role at the monastery for a bit longer so we could track information there. I'm sure he wants to get out of there, but our Molly can convince him to stay," Giselle said, winking at Molly.

"Already done," David said.

David and Giselle laughed, but Molly felt defensive. "Just because I find Clint sweet and attractive doesn't mean I'll hop into bed with him the moment we have a chance, which is more than I can say for you, Giselle, about a certain precinct detective."

David and Giselle exchanged glances. He raised his eyebrows, and Giselle shrugged her shoulders.

At that moment, the waiter came by with a tray filled with orange, red, purple, and green vegetables; roasted scallops; and garlic encrusted meats. All three of them now began to salivate. David, of course, had a great

Belgian beer to accompany the feast—his favorite, a St. Bernardus Abt 12. As they indulged in their eats, they decided to set aside business talk and found themselves relishing in their shared love of the French cuisine.

At about nine-thirty, Molly bid them adieu, changed into her black outfit, and then caught her ride in the parking lot. David and Giselle moved to a smaller, less cluttered table for coffee and a more intimate atmosphere. Without skipping a beat, they picked up their conversation where they had left it.

"I don't think my proposal to the monks is likely to go through," said David. "Clint and I are set to fly back to the states in a few days, but maybe we can help you in the meantime. I have some contacts in Brussels who may be able to help us find out some more information about Timothy. If Molly and Clint can find his phone in Paris, that would help a lot. At the worst, you and I could spend some time exploring Brussels before the 'kids' get back."

Giselle reached over and brushed David's hair back from his forehead while looking him straight in the eyes. "No one can ever accuse me of not being willing to mix business with pleasure. I think the rest of our discussions tonight can be at my suite, unless you have some objections."

"No," said David, putting down his coffee cup. "To your suite it is, and we can carry on our *discussions* there." He paid the bill and sent his compliments to the chef. They headed out of the restaurant, and the doorman had a cab waiting for them to whisk them back to their hotel.

"What, no more white horses?" Giselle asked.

"The horses are in bed already, dreaming of hay and playing in the noonday sun without harnesses or wagons to pull," David said. "This cab has one hundred fifty horses hiding under the hood and happy to drink gasoline and fart out exhaust emissions. They don't dream of anything except for an occasional oil change."

"How poetic, Mr. Collins," she said. "I really didn't expect such imagery from a corporate raider." She grabbed his collar and pulled him to her.

"If your expectations are low, you may be in for some surprises," he said with a smile and then kissed her.

They arrived back at the hotel and headed up to Giselle's suite, walking hand in hand.

As they got to her door, David smiled and said, "Some corporate mergers are more fun than others."

"I think we can put further business discussions to bed for the moment," said Giselle.

They closed the door quietly and put out the DO NOT DISTURB sign.

14 THE BREAK-IN

Molly tried to relax in the cab on the way to the monastery. She had thrown her "bag of tricks" from Giselle into the trunk for safekeeping. She hoped any alarm system at the monastery would not be too sophisticated. She assumed that the brewery would have a state-of-the-art security system and likely even a guard.

Luckily, she didn't need to break in there. She was happy they were able to give Clint a heads up she was coming, even though Clint's cellphone could barely transmit any information from deep inside the abbey. She told the cabdriver to drop her off at the abbey and then pick her up an hour later. The driver had a heavy Spanish accent, so Molly did her best to mix in any Spanish words she could muster.

"*Senorita*, you are very beautiful," said the cabdriver. "Where is your *novio* tonight?"

"Thank you for the compliment," said Molly. "I don't have a boyfriend, but I am meeting a likely candidate tonight. I'll let you know how it works out. We are working together at the moment."

The cabbie laughed. "Perhaps he will become your boyfriend. In any case, I'm sure he makes your work more pleasant. You are definitely making my cab more pleasant just sitting in the backseat."

Molly rolled her eyes. "You are too kind. Could you tell me a bit about the Lavro Monastery that I am about to see? Do you know anything about the monks there, especially the monk who recently died?"

"I do know the head monk there and had met Brother Adolphus once when bringing some supplies to the abbey. He was very nice and quiet elderly but seemed in impressive health for his age. I guess prayer and diet and exercise can't be all that bad for you, but I personally would like a little sex thrown in once in a while."

Molly laughed. "That does sound like a prescription for a healthy life," she said. "If he was so healthy, how did he die from a simple fall in the brewery? It just seems a bit odd if you ask me."

"Working in the brewery can be dangerous. Those stainless containers for the wort are quite tall, and a fall from there could certainly injure you. It is, however, a bit odd that any of the monks would be physically working on the brewing process. There is an English company that usually does the day-to-day operations, and the monks simply supervise," the cabbie stated.

"That is very strange. Have you ever heard of a young monk named Timothy Marcum?" she asked.

"I have not met Timothy Marcum, but that is not unusual since the novices are generally kept in the bowels of the abbey and have little interaction with the public. I think the monks are afraid the novices will be corrupted by the rest of the world, and maybe they are right."

Molly agreed. "You sound more like a philosopher than a cabdriver. Hopefully, we can figure out some of the confusion stemming from the monastery," she said as they arrived at the abbey. She stealthily took her things and headed for the back of the building.

Darkness surrounded most of the abbey buildings, but the brewery adjacent to the monastery was well lit. Music and happy voices with some singing came from the bar up the street even though it was almost a mile away. Molly tried her hand at one of the old locks on a door behind the abbey with some of the materials Giselle had sent. The lock was over one hundred years old and didn't appear to have been opened for that long either.

No go! she thought. Molly had brought a schematic drawing of the building and decided to try a door leading to the laundry. *Even monks have to wash their clothes sometime, and knowing men, they likely send them out to be cleaned*, she thought.

She opened this door within minutes. As she was feeling victorious, she turned around only to be knocked flat on the ground by a huge furry creature. Fortunately, she did not hit her head, but she had been scared out of her wits. A huge wet tongue engulfed her face, and an immense tail practically knocked Molly down again. She turned her cellphone light on and was greatly relieved to see a gigantic but very friendly Saint Bernard happily sitting next to her. He must have weighed over three hundred pounds, and the tag on his collar read BERNARDUS. Molly reached into her bag and pulled out a biscuit that Giselle had packed. *Leave it to Giselle to think of everything.*

"Here, Bernardus," Molly said, giving him the biscuit while extracting her foot from underneath the immense canine. "What a fine animal you are. Maybe you can lead me to Clint for another treat." Molly was overjoyed to see the abbey's guard dog was so friendly. She got up and petted Bernardus. "Good doggie," she said.

Bernardus seemed confused but happy for the late-night company and snack.

Molly held his huge head in her hands and looked into his eyes. "Bernardus, can you take me to Brother Clint?" she asked. David had sent along a few of Clint's clothes in case he needed them, so Molly took out one of Clint's socks and let Bernardus smell it. "Find Clint!" she ordered.

Something seemed to connect in Bernardus's memory, and he let out a soft bark. Off he went down the stairs of the monastery at a fairly good clip for such a massive creature. Molly chased after him as best she could, trying not to slip on the polished marble stairs.

She had gone down at least five flights of stairs when her guide stopped in front of a closed door marked DORTOIR, or dormitory. The door was not locked, and Molly opened it, hoping she wouldn't wake any sleeping monks. She could just imagine a celibate monk awakening in the middle of the night to see a young woman wandering through his dormitory. She held back a laugh. A flickering light at the end of the hall caught her eye, and she quietly made her way to it.

She happily found Clint in his small cubical reading some letters by candlelight. He looked up and saw Bernardus and his companion. A smile crept across his face, and he quickly stood up to greet them. Unfortunately, he hit his head on the low ceiling.

"Wow, Molly!" he said. "How did you ever find me? The monks just went to bed, and with the guards wandering around the brewery I couldn't leave one of the backdoors open to let you in. What are you doing with Bernardus?"

Molly came over and gave Clint a hug. "I met Bernardus upstairs, and he led me down to you. Pretty amazing, isn't it?"

"I wouldn't be surprised at anything Bernardus could do," said Clint. "He is very smart. The monks have kept a Saint Bernard here for hundreds of years, and Bernardus is a direct descendant of all of them. I'm glad you're here, but if the monks found out, I would certainly get thrown out of here. David sent me a message that you were coming, but he didn't say why. Is everything okay? He did say you plan on leaving for Paris tomorrow."

"We had dinner with David, and he told us all about the plans you two made and why you are posing as a monk. He admitted that he doesn't feel it's likely the monks will be interested in his offer," she explained. Molly then went on to tell Clint about their meeting with the police chief. "The police are looking for information on Timothy Marcum who was a monk at this very monastery. Have you heard anything about him?"

"Believe it or not, Timothy Marcum actually stayed right here in this very cubicle. It is specifically for novices at the abbey. I found a letter he was writing to his sister, and I was trying to read it by candlelight but without luck. Since it sounds like David is bagging his negotiations with the brewery, I can leave with you. I'll just leave the monks a note. I have to admit that while staying here has not been easy, I do feel much stronger and more focused. I haven't minded the prayers, exercise, and strict diet, and I enjoyed the solitude. I also managed to find some of the monks' private stock of beer, and even though it has a lower alcohol content, it seemed to give me more energy."

Molly took a good look at Clint. "If I didn't know better, I would think you look stronger and healthier in just the last day, but maybe it's just the candlelight or the adrenaline rush from sneaking into the monastery. The bad news is we need you to stay here a bit longer and find more information about Timothy Marcum and what happened to Brother Adolphus."

Clint shook his head. "There is no way that I would let you go to Paris on your own and risk you running into any more of these evil thugs. I will leave Brother Antiochus a note saying that there was a family emergency and I had to leave. I'm sure he already knows my true calling is not to become a monk. I am not sure why he went along with this little deception. I am going back with you tonight, and I confess that your safety is not the only reason for this." He reached over and pulled her into his arms and gave her a very un-monk-like kiss.

Molly definitely felt like melting, but was true to her detective duties. "I could get into the habit of your embraces, but we unfortunately don't have time to test that out right now. We may have time in Paris, though, to do more than track down Timothy Marcum."

Clint smiled. "Personally, I was thinking we could start such activities in Brussels tonight. We can always sleep on the plane."

"Okay, Romeo, that's a pretty dramatic change from monk to heartthrob." Molly laughed. "Write your note, and let's get out of here before I attack you or scare one of the monks."

Molly, Clint, and Bernardus quietly snuck back through the dormitory and up the stairs. Bernardus was breathing heavily by the time they got back up to the laundry area. Molly gave Bernardus another well-deserved biscuit for all his help. Bernardus went back to his colossal dog bed, and Clint and Molly locked the abbey door and headed back to the cab.

Their philosophic cabdriver was waiting exactly where Molly had left him. Clint asked them to stop by the bar up the road. He came back smiling with three bottles of Lavro for their trip back to Brussels.

"Unfortunately, you will have to wait until you are home for your beer," he said to the driver.

"I can happily wait for that," said the cabbie. "Alcohol and cab driving don't mix too well, even in Belgium."

Off they headed back to Brussels. Molly and Clint read Timothy's letter in the backseat, but chose not to discuss it until they arrived at the hotel.

After about half an hour, the driver broke the silence, saying, "I believe someone is following us. These roads are not well traveled, especially at this time of night, and it is odd that someone behind us is making the same turns and matching our speed. Should I lose them?"

"At the next turn, shut off your lights and pull off where you can so we can check them out," said Clint. He pulled out a stiletto knife from Molly's bag and put it in his pocket. It was another gift from Giselle.

After about three minutes, a dark Mercedes passed them and sped up, appearing to be searching for something. From the corner streetlight, Clint could vaguely make out the large figure driving and could almost envision the tattoos on his left arm from their last encounter.

"Wow!" said Molly. "I bet he recognized you at the bar. This is scary. Can we backtrack and take a different route back to Brussels?"

"No problem!" said the cabdriver. "It will take a bit longer, but should be safe. Do you think you know the other driver? Should I call for assistance?"

"No, we should be fine," said Clint. "I doubt he knows where we are staying in Brussels, but I don't know what he was doing watching the monastery or why he is following us. Were you able to get his license plate number, Molly?"

"Of course," she responded. "Molly, the number one female detective at your service." She took off the binoculars she had gotten from Giselle's bag of tricks and put them back. She handed Clint the license plate number.

They headed back with their lights out and started a circuitous route back into Brussels. All three were a bit on edge until they were safely back at the hotel. They put in a call to Detective Karven, alerting him of the dark Mercedes and the plate number so the police could look further into the suspicious driver.

15 THE PAIRINGS

They got up to Giselle's room and laughed when the saw the "Do Not Disturb" sign on the door. They made a bet on who the likely paramour of Giselle's might be. David was high on the list. Clint and Molly strode hand in hand back to her room and made sure their own "Do Not Disturb" sign was on their door. They made it as far as the couch before they intertwined, but managed to repeat their sexual delights in front of the fireplace on a Persian rug, on the oversized bed in the bedroom, and again in the elaborate shower their suite provided. The couch was convenient but limited their positions. The fireplace was romantic but too hot after a while. The giant bed was like a playground, but the silk sheets were slippery, and they both wound up on the floor. The shower was refreshing at first, but then their skin pruned. They finished with the "column" position they found on Molly's Kama Sutra app on her iPhone. They were standing in the shower with Clint behind and their arms intertwined. After another monumental orgasm, they both made their way back to the bed and collapsed, looking at each other and laughing.

"To think, of all the men in the world, my sexual bar has been set by a monk," said Molly. "Maybe prayer and abstinence is what we all need."

Clint held her close. "You certainly played a large part in this union. I definitely think the foreboding from this detective case added to our sexual tension," Clint said and then his stomach growled. "I am starved out of my mind. I barely ate at the monastery, and I think we burned at least five thousand calories tonight. I am calling room service to see what the kitchen can rustle up at this hour."

In less than an hour, Clint was happily gorging himself on coq au vin, Wittamer chocolates, and champagne. Molly had a bite here and there, but was happy to watch her new lover sate his culinary appetite. As Clint ate, she sent a text to David, telling him Clint had left the monastery and would be accompanying her to Paris. She also let him know about the letter Clint had found. She then crawled under the silky bedsheet and closed her eyes.

They were able to get a few hours of sleep before Giselle's loud rap on the door woke them up. Molly answered the door wearing the top from Clint's monk's robe.

Giselle roared into their hotel room carrying packages galore. She gave Molly a knowing smile. "You must be one of those monkettes I've heard about—sort of like the monk's version of a groupie. I bought your groper some more clothes."

Molly actually blushed a bit, surprising both she and Giselle. "I'll have you know I'm a woman in lust or something. I'm no groupie. Though, I might have trouble keeping my hands off Justin Timberlake. Thanks for all the clothes. As usual, you are amazing! Speaking of which, who was your escort into the midnight hours last night?"

On cue, David walked into the open door dressed as usual to the nines. He too came in carrying bags and boxes and added to the pile. As if to answer Molly's question, he gave Giselle a peck on the cheek. Clint came out of the bedroom wearing his monk's pants and little else.

Giselle laughed, pointing to all the scratches on Clint's back. "I know at least one of us had a run-in with a real tiger last night. Clint, dear boy, all these packages are your new clothes, and you best get dressed and meet us downstairs for breakfast. You and Molly are scheduled to leave for Paris on the 1:20 p.m. train today. We have a lot to discuss so we need to get moving. Be sure to bring the letter that Molly texted me about. You know, the one from Timothy Marcum to his sister."

This was a lot for Clint to process on three hours sleep. "Give me fifteen minutes to shower and dress, and I'll meet you downstairs. I'll need to borrow a suitcase from one of you for the trip. Molly, what did I hear about Justin Timberlake?"

Molly laughed. "Just that I'm a big fan. Better get moving so we can talk before catching that train."

Giselle and David left to get some coffee while they waited for their friends to change and join them. In the elevator, they even held hands for a moment.

16 TIMOTHY AND THE GOONS

Timothy was frightened for the first time since the abbey. As the two goons approached him, he had little doubt as to who had tipped them off.

Malbec quickly jumped into the narrow corridor with the equipment and pulled the wall closed. "So sorry!" Timothy heard from him as the wall closed.

The goons approached him and easily lifted him off the ground. They took his equipment, finding his prized USB drive.

"Do not make a single sound as we are leaving the Louvre," one of them said. "We have the information we need, so breaking your neck would be, as you Americans say, 'easy as pie.' I don't know why pie is easy, but breaking your neck would be. Do you understand?"

Timothy nodded. His feet were barely touching the ground. As they reached the exit, one of the guards approached them, and Timothy could feel added pressure across the back of his neck.

"Mr. Marcum," the guard said. "I hope you were able to find what you were looking for."

Tim feigned a smile and said, "Yes I did, and thanks for all your help."

They headed out the door with Timothy's neck intact. It was already getting dark, and Timothy could see these goons were not going to let him escape. They asked him where he had parked and took him to his car.

The talkative goon looked at Timothy and said, "We have to make sure you understand how serious we are. We also have a message from our friend Sergio in Brussels."

Hidden by the darkness and cars, they struck Timothy in the abdomen, back, and chest. He had never been in a fight before let alone suffered a beating like this. Despite their warnings, he cried out, which only made them hit him harder. He usually had bodyguards to protect him, but where were they now? His assailants were quite methodical and left him with several broken ribs and multiple bruises. They avoided bruises to his face so as not to raise concern when they took him back to his hotel to search his room and decide what to do with him. The thugs fought back the urge to kill him, knowing they were supposed to keep him alive in case they needed him for leverage with his father.

They took the car keys and threw him in the backseat whimpering. Then, they took his cellphone, wallet, and passport and threw them into the glove compartment.

I'm going to die, Timothy thought.

Over and over, the two asked where Timothy kept the first USB drive he had gotten from the monk. He tried to tell them that he did not have that drive, that he had left it in Brussels, but the Russians didn't believe him. They headed to his hotel to search his room for it. They would have to call Sergio to decide what to do with Timothy. Timothy's prospects did not sound good. They tied his wrists and then both got into the front seat. They pulled his wallet from the glove compartment and found his hotel key, which told them where he was staying.

Despite his rib pain, trouble breathing, and multiple bruises, an idea dawned on Timothy as he lay in the backseat while they drove away. The thugs had not noticed his tech watch, and since his phone was still in the car, he could try to text his father for help. Despite his hands being tied, he was able to access the controls with his right thumb. He silently texted his father back in California.

"Kidnapped. Going to hotel. Send help ASAP," he wrote.

He was not sure what sort of help the elder Marcum would have in Paris or how soon he could mobilize any help, but he hoped for the best. The twists and turns of the car combined with his injuries caused him to become woozy and pass out.

They arrived back at Timothy's hotel and his captors assisted him into the lobby. They explained to the hotel clerk that Timothy had been drinking and was not feeling well. The hotel clerk asked if they needed a doctor, but Timothy's Russian "friends" said that wouldn't be necessary. They held a knife in his left armpit aimed at his heart, which kept Timothy cooperative.

They brought him up to his room and threw him on the couch. For fun, one of them threw a few more punches at Timothy while the other began systematically dismantling the room, looking for the first USB drive. When Timothy yelped, they covered his mouth with duct tape.

When his search turned up nothing, the more senior goon grew impatient.

"You're going to call your father! If he wants you back alive, he needs give us the information we want! In the meantime, your friend Sergio would like a souvenir from this outing. He seems particularly fond of your right thumb, wants to affix it to a tennis ball for his mantle," the thug said with a sneer.

As his captor took out a much larger knife, Timothy experienced true terror. He sprung from the couch, trying to escape, but both large men grabbed him and forced his right hand onto the table in the kitchenette of Timothy's suite. He screamed behind the duct tape when they made an incision just below the first knuckle of his right thumb. Then, the senior goon raised the knife high into the air, ready to deliver the blow that would chop of Timothy's thumb.

Suddenly, there was a knock at the door. Both Russians assumed a fighting stance, and one silently made his way to door to look through the peephole.

"Maid service!" a maid on the other side of the door happily said.

"Go away," the Russian said forcefully. "We don't need service today!"

"I have to at least give you some new towels, and there is a message for you, Mr. Marcum, from your father."

"Just leave the towels and the message by the door," said the Russian.

"No problem," said the maid as she left.

The Russian opened the door to check the message and, despite his size, was knocked off his feet by three heavily armed agents from Tim's father. Even though they were clearly outmanned and certainly out gunned, Tim's captors tried to resist. One of the goons threw a punch, landing it on a messenger's chin. The messenger responded by pistol-whipping the goon, knocking him out. The other goon struggled as two other messengers restrained him on the ground, one holding the goon's hands behind his back while the other kicked him relentlessly in the ribs.

Tim was only half aware of what was going on, but vaguely realized he was not about to die. As one of Tim's helpers removed his duct tape, despite his injuries, he managed to smile. He recognized one of his saviors.

"Jeffrey, thank you and please thank my father," he managed to squeak out before passing out.

17 FINDING TIMOTHY

Molly and Clint dressed quickly and headed down to the lobby. Clint was delighted to actually be wearing real clothes for a change instead of his monk's outfit. They met up with Giselle and David and headed for the coffee shop.

Giselle winked at Molly. "So, how did your monking go with Clint last night?"

Molly rolled her eyes. "It went quite well, thank you. I also presume your debriefing with David went well."

Giselle smiled a coy smile. "Yes, you know how we lawyers love to focus on the details. Now we better settle down to work and go over Timothy's letter while we have breakfast. Clint, you clean up nicely. Although, I miss the monk's clothes."

Clint returned the compliment. "You and David are also looking very sharp this morning," he said, nudging his friend. "I have the letter here and made copies at the hotel front desk for all of us."

They all sipped their various coffees while they scoured over the letter. Timothy Marcum's letter to his sister was brief but informative.

Dear Sis,

Sorry I haven't contacted you sooner. As I will explain, I don't have a phone, and correspondence is not easy here. I am fine, and as I mentioned to you, I am on a great adventure. I am outside Brussels and am soon going to Paris. As strange as this may sound, Dad has hired me to do a project that could have a tremendous impact on humanity (as Dad put it). Unfortunately, he has not been more specific than that, but he did promise to pay me one million dollars if I follow through with this and an extra million if I am successful. That may not sound like much coming from a billionaire, but it certainly would make my life easier. I don't know how he treats you with your allowance, but ever since he had to pay Mom twenty million in the divorce, he's been quite stingy with me.

I am currently playing the role of a novice monk at a monastery. Imagine me as a monk! I can't tell you more as I have been sworn to secrecy, and honestly, I don't know much more. I'll try to call as soon as I can. Don't push Dad for details.

Love,
Tim

"Wow!" all four at the table exclaimed in unison.

"I thought his father might be involved in this, but I had no idea he actually set his son up to go on a dangerous mission without even telling him why. That does sound like the Cornwell Marcum I know though," said David.

"We could try calling Mr. Marcum directly, but I doubt he would even take our call or discuss his son, and he certainly wouldn't discuss the details of this project," said Clint.

"Yeah, what the hell did he even mean by a 'tremendous impact on humanity'?" Giselle asked. "What a jerk to send his son off totally unprepared to deal with criminals and murderers. No wonder Tim's sister was worried about him! I hope Timothy survives this and we are able to find him. I personally feel like calling Mr. Marcum now and screaming at him." Giselle began to fan her face with a menu to slow the reddening of her face. "The sooner you two get to Paris and track him down, the better. I am glad you are leaving this afternoon. Go find that boy!"

Their meals arrived, interrupting their discussion. As usual, they were greeted with the scents of traditional Belgian food. The Frites and steamed mussels melted in their mouths.

David brought them back from their gustatory ecstasy. "So, Clint, what do you think you will do first in Paris to find Timothy?"

Clint paused to wash down the last morsel of his crepe. "I'll start by calling his phone again—though, so far, he hasn't been answering my calls, texts, or emails. Then, we'll try to use the 'Find My Phone' app, but if his battery still isn't charged, we'll have to contact the police in Paris. I'm not eager to involve them, but it may be necessary. If all else fails, I suppose we can try to contact Tim's father to see if he will help us."

"Sounds like a good plan," said Molly. "Giselle, maybe you and David can find out more information about Tim's father and the Russian who has been tailing us."

"We're on it!" said Giselle. "I'll put my office staff to work on this right away to see what we can find."

"I have my own resources as well," said David. "We should be able to come up with something. We best be on our way to the train station to get you two off to Paris. Too bad we can't join you."

Giselle laughed. "Yes, there is always something about traveling on a train that gets my juices flowing. I think it has something to do with the clickety-clack and back and forth motions of the train. Maybe you and I should take a quick train ride around Brussels today, David, just to check out the scenery," Giselle said with a wink.

Clint and Molly took that as their cue to leave and went back up to the room to grab their bags. As they stood in the doorway, they held each other for a moment. They were excited about going to Paris together, but they definitely had work to do.

They met Giselle and David downstairs where they all headed off to the train station in a cab. It was raining, and Clint was not sad to be bidding adieu to Brussels. The smell of Molly's perfume next to him sent his emotions skyrocketing as they drove through the city. He had the sudden sensation that he could accomplish just about anything with his newfound love.

Blah, blah, blah, he thought. *What sleep-deprived, sex-addled ravings of an ex-monk. Time to focus on the job at hand—finding Timothy. You can enjoy the blessing of Molly later.* He leaned back and fell asleep for the rest of the ride to the train station.

* * *

Molly and Clint said their goodbyes to David and Giselle and climbed into the first class coach to Paris. It was only one hour and twenty minutes from Brussels to the Gare du Nord Station in Paris. They held hands and instantly fell asleep for the entire ride to Paris.

When they arrived in Paris, they both felt a bit refreshed. They took a cab to the swanky Four Seasons Hotel George V that Giselle had booked for them. The old-world charm, polished beauty, and attentive staff simply enveloped them on entering the lobby. Of course, this came at a price, but that was the trade-off. Leave it to Giselle to pick out the ritziest hotel in the city right on the Champs-Elysees.

Their suite was comparable to Louis XIV's style, even though this was the refurbished George V. For a moment, Molly and Clint sat on the elegant couch and looked at each other, shaking their heads. They felt they should be in period costumes just to blend in.

"I'm going to take a shower. I hope I don't get lost in the bathroom," said Molly. "If you don't hear from me in an hour, you better come looking for me." She went off in search of the bathroom.

Clint smiled. "Well, I think it's time I tried calling Timothy's phone again." He again dialed the number and was startled when someone actually answered the phone.

"*Bonjour,*" a pleasant male answered the phone.

Since Clint knew that Timothy did not speak French, he figured this was not likely him. "*Bonjour*," Clint responded. Do you speak English? Who am I speaking to?"

"Yes, I do speak English, and this is Monsieur Pierre at the Avis car rental agency. I am answering a phone left here by a customer. And with whom am I speaking?"

Clint was excited and felt like getting Molly out of the shower. "This is Clint Daniels. I am looking for a Mr. Timothy Marcum."

"This is Mr. Marcum's phone," the clerk replied. "I have been trying to reach Mr. Marcum since he left his phone and some other personal effects in a car that he rented from us. I have been unable to reach him and was thinking of notifying the police."

"I don't think that will be necessary since I am a detective hired by Mr. Marcum's sister to help find him. His sister has power of attorney and can send that to you with a release so I can return his phone and other effects to him. Please text me your company information, and I will have his sister send you these documents ASAP. I would greatly appreciate your texting me back at this number when you get them."

"I will have to talk with my manager, but that sounds like something we can do. I will text you as soon as I get the documents from his sister. We are open another three hours, but I will stay a bit longer if need be. I have been quite concerned for him," said the clerk.

Clint wondered what the clerk's concern was about. "Thank you so much. I know his sister has been worried about him as well."

They said their goodbyes, and Clint ran into the bathroom. He slipped on the wet floor but caught himself before throwing his arms around a delightfully clean and frisky Molly.

"I have some great news," he said. "An employee at a car rental agency found Timothy's phone and will give it to us after we get his sister to release it."

Molly was ecstatic and started jumping up and down, accidentally losing her towel. This was not lost on Clint, who decided opportunities are what you make of them, and he began licking Molly in the most opportune places.

"Wait, you amorous ex-monk," she said. "You still have to call Timothy's sister so she can forward her information to the car company. Make your call while I dry my hair, and then we can proceed with our romantic overtures."

Clint reluctantly let her go and went back into the bedroom to call Marguerite. She, of course, was overjoyed and promised to send a copy of her power of attorney for Timothy and a release to the rental company. Clint gave her David's number in case she had trouble writing the release. He then called David and Giselle to let them know the good news. They were having lunch on the square in Brussels.

"Sounds great," said David. "I would be happy to help Marguerite if she needs advice. We're having another great meal here. Amazing sex, food, and travel, it's what I live for these days." Clint heard Giselle laughing in the background. "We'll start researching the elder Marcum and the Russians this afternoon. Call us when you have more info on the phone and Timothy."

Clint ended the call and cleared his voice. He sang out in his best Little Richard voice, "Good Golly, Miss Molly, get your bottom in here."

Molly could be heard laughing from the bathroom. "Yes, sir, Monsieur Clint. I'm coming as asked." She came into the room sporting her sexiest lingerie and jumped into his arms while throwing both legs around Clint's waist.

He lifted her easily into the immense four-poster bed and kissed her. "Did you look up the next five positions on your Kama Sutra app?" he asked.

"Oh yes, Monsieur Clint, I did. Do you think we will get through all sixty-four positions while we are in Paris?" she asked.

Clint began nibbling on her ear. "Easy, grasshopper. We are not in a race. This is a sexual journey of discovery. There is no need to rush."

They proceeded to discover each other's sexual delights for the next hour until they both fell back in the bed sated and pleasured. They looked at each other and began laughing.

"Pleasant afternoon delights," said Clint. "I am starved. You do make me work for my meals."

"One would think after a couple of orgasms you would describe our interactions as more like rapturous or amazing but not simply pleasant," Molly said.

"I stand corrected. Rapturous afternoon delights," he said. "Let's get dressed and hit one of those outdoor cafés along the Champs-Elysees. Hopefully, we will hear from the car rental agency soon so we can get Tim's phone."

Clint took a quick shower, and then they both dressed and headed down to the lobby.

18 HOSPITAL ENCOUNTERS

Timothy gradually awoke with the vague sensation that he was in a field of lavender in the south of France. As he became more focused, he could see a beautiful dark-haired woman hovering near him. It was definitely her lavender perfume that he smelled. He gradually realized some pain in the right side of his chest, right hand, and head. He realized he was in a hospital bed and had tubes coming out of everywhere, even his penis. It dawned on him that the vision next to him must be a nurse.

Timothy cleared his throat before saying, "Excuse me, miss, but where am I, and who are you?"

"Ah, Mr. Nelson, it is good to see that you are awake," she said with a definite French accent. "You are in the American Hospital of Paris and have been unconscious for the last two days. I am very happy to see that you are back with us. I will have to let your physician know you're awake." Her smile caught Timothy by surprise. "My name is Jolene, and I am your nurse. You suffered some injuries, including multiple rib fractures and a partially collapsed right lung. I will let your doctor describe them to you in more detail. We have a pain patch on you, but I can give you something more for the pain if you need it."

"Thank you for your help, but I must tell you, my name is not Mr. Nelson. I am Timothy Marcum," he said.

"I had suspected that might not be your real name since your friends have set up a pleasant but rather large guard outside your room who limits who can come in to visit you," said Jolene. "Your family must have significant influence to have the administration agree to a change in their usual policies. Since your oxygen has been quite good for the last twelve hours, I will take you off the oxygen so at least you will have one less annoyance to deal with. Your doctor should be in shortly."

Sadly, Jolene had to leave but was soon replaced by a young, very officious man who clearly was his doctor. He had a French accent as well but spoke impeccable English.

"Good morning, Mr. Marcum. I will dispense with the charade of your fictitious name since I am hopeful we can get you out of here by tomorrow. My name is Dr. Carson, and I have been supervising your care. As you undoubtedly know, you were beaten two days ago and brought here for treatment. You have multiple contusions on your head and neck. You have at least three fractured ribs on your right side and a partially collapsed lung. You have a bruise to your right kidney and a deep laceration to your right thumb. We feel you should not have any nerve or tendon injury, but we will have to see. You have a chest tube in the right side of your chest, but I feel I can take that out today. Since you are now awake and the blood is clearing from your urine, we should be able to remove your Foley catheter from your bladder as well. Even though you have had substantial injuries, I feel you should heal completely after some time. I would recommend you go to a rehab center or arrange for home-care for the next two weeks. You should not travel for the next two weeks while you allow your body to heal. Do you have any questions?"

"Wow," said Timothy. "That is a lot to digest. I will certainly be happy to get rid of all these tubes, especially the one in my penis. I was really worried about my thumb, so I'm happy to hear you think it will be okay. Do you know if my family has been notified and if my phone and wallet were recovered?"

"I spoke with your father directly, but I am not sure about your possessions," Dr. Carson responded. "Nurse Jolene will help me take out your chest tube and Foley, and then you can speak with your friend Jeffrey who has been waiting outside. I know he has been most anxious to speak with you."

Jolene came back in with a tray for the doctor and another sensual reminder of lavender. Timothy was surprised that removing his tubes was not too painful but suspected he was medicated more than he was aware. When Dr. Carson and Nurse Jolene left, Jeffrey came into his room and smiled.

"Boy, you sure looked like shit back at the hotel when we found you," he said. "We were really worried, but now you look like shit that has been cleaned up a bit. How are you doing?"

Tim started to cry. "Thank you, Jeffrey, for saving my life. I am certain I would not be alive if not for your and the others' help. I will make sure my father knows that. To be honest, I don't feel too badly, what with the pain meds and now that the tubes have been removed. Do you have my cellphone, wallet, and passport? Those goons put them in the glove box. What did you do with the goons by the way?"

Jeffrey paused before saying, "It may be best you don't know a lot about what happened to those goons, but I am told they were found by the Paris police with a large quantity of cocaine and are now guests of the gendarmes. We are still looking for your phone and possessions but should get them soon. I understand you will probably be discharged tomorrow, and I talked with Nurse Jolene about who we could get to help care for you. She does private duty nursing on the side and would be willing to help you for the next week if you'd like."

Timothy immediately perked up. "That would be great. I can't imagine anyone not healing quickly with her around."

Jeffrey nodded and then excused himself since the staff had advised him not to spend too much time talking with Tim. He went back to sitting outside Tim's door, guarding his employer's son. Timothy immediately fell back asleep, dreaming of lavender.

19 REUNITING WITH TIMOTHY

Clint and Molly left the hotel, walking the block hand in hand, and headed toward one of the iconic symbols of Paris, the Arc de Triomphe. The sidewalk was busy with shoppers and tourists who were window-shopping the high-end stores. There were a number of bustling cafés along the street, and Molly suggested one to her liking. Their maître d' was very personable and helpful, unlike the stereotype of ill-mannered and aloof Parisian waiters. The café au lait and food were superb, of course, and sitting watching the flow of humanity was inspiring.

Their meal was interrupted by Clint's phone. "Monsieur Daniels," he heard. "This is Pierre at the car agency. We received the information from Mr. Marcum's sister and can release his belongings to you. She speaks French quite well, and that was helpful. I texted you our contact information, and if you get here shortly, we will still be open."

Clint and Molly were overjoyed. "We will be right over, and thank you so much for your help," Clint said.

They quickly paid their bill, including a generous tip. They caught a cab and were soon circling the Arc de Triomphe with a multitude of other vehicles of every size and type. They were able to see the arc up close as they went around it. It was only a fifteen-minute drive to the car agency, so before they knew it, they were meeting Pierre.

"*Bonjour*, Mr. Daniels," the clerk said. "Here is Mr. Marcum's phone, his wallet, and his passport. I do need to see your passport as well and have you sign this release. I should warn you, there was a fair amount of blood in the backseat of his rental car."

Molly let out a gasp.

"Thank you for letting us know. We need to find him as soon as possible. Do you know who returned the car?" Clint asked while he showed his passport and signed the release.

"I did not see the man myself but was told by my coworker that he was a large English-speaking man named Jeffrey, who seemed very friendly. Unfortunately, he did not give us a forwarding phone number."

Clint and Molly thanked Pierre and immediately started going through the texts in Timothy's phone. Marguerite had given them his password earlier. They saw his pleas to his father and that he was staying at the Crillon Hotel. They caught an Uber this time and were quickly on their way to the hotel.

"Timothy certainly does travel in style," said Molly. "The Crillon may be the top hotel in Paris. I sure hope he is okay. I can't imagine he left his things in the car just by accident, but I guess we will find out soon."

Clint agreed. "Hopefully, our hunt is almost over. I do hope our quarry is safe."

After they arrived at the Crillon, they dashed into the imposing lobby. They asked to speak to the manager and were soon in a large audacious office seated across from a stylish elderly gentleman. They explained their situation, and Clint produced Timothy's passport, wallet, and the letter from Timothy's sister stating they were employed by her to find her brother.

The manager reviewed the information. "Your documents look appropriate, but I will need to contact this gentleman's sister to confirm before giving you any information."

He went into the adjacent office, and Clint and Molly could hear him having a lengthy conversation in French. Clint could get the gist of it and knew Marguerite was confirming what they had told the manager.

"I spoke with Mr. Marcum's sister and was able to confirm what you have told me. We like to keep our client's information private, but I feel it is appropriate to let you know what happened to Mr. Marcum. He has been a guest of our hotel for the last several days and suffered an accident two days ago. We do not know how this happened, but it occurred outside the hotel. He was brought back here with significant injuries and was taken to the American Hospital and, from what I can gather, has been recovering. We are keeping his room available for him as it sounds like he should be returning here shortly."

Clint and Molly both let out a long breath. "Thank you for your help," Clint told the manager. "We will head over to the hospital to check on Timothy right away."

"Please give Mr. Marcum my regards and my wishes for a speedy recovery," said the manager.

Clint and Molly looked at each other and shook their heads in disbelief. They couldn't believe they were finally so close to actually seeing Timothy. They caught another cab and were soon on their way to the hospital.

"I hope he is okay," said Molly. "I wonder what happened to him. Do you think your Russian had anything to do with this?"

"Customs would likely have stopped him if he tried to fly out of Brussels," said Clint. "But it sounds like someone beat up Tim pretty badly if he wound up in the hospital. Thankfully, we'll find out in a few minutes."

They pulled up to the hospital and jumped out of the car before the driver even came to a full stop. They ran to the front desk and were greeted with a friendly smile. When they inquired about Mr. Marcum, however, they were given a blank stare. Clint could tell this was a subterfuge and asked to speak with the manager on duty. They were told the manager was not available, but there was someone else they could speak to. They were introduced to a rather larger American man who looked like he could play as a linebacker for the Pittsburgh Steelers. The linebacker kept a poker face as he drilled them with questions about their connection to Timothy and their intentions with finding him. They once again explained their rather long story and showed him Timothy's cellphone, wallet, and passport. They were shocked when their inquisitor threw his arms around them and embraced them.

"My name is Jeffrey, and I have been asked to look after the younger Mr. Marcum by his father. I'll let him tell you most of his story, but in summary, he was beaten badly by two Russians and has been recovering since. The nursing staff thinks he will be discharged tomorrow, but that is not for sure. We have been looking for his phone, wallet, and passport, so I am pleased to hear you have found them. I know Tim's sister well, and I'm sure she will be happy to know he is doing better."

Clint was still recovering from the linebacker's embrace when he choked out, "She doesn't even know he has been in the hospital. We will need to call her as soon as we see Timothy."

"I am surprised her father didn't tell her since we have been in contact with him," said Jeffrey.

"I have heard the elder Marcum is not the most communicative person, but I'm sure his daughter may have a few words for him when she finds out he knew where Tim was," said Molly. "Can we go in to see Timothy?"

"Let me check with his nurse, Jolene, to see if it is okay," said Jeffrey.

Within minutes, Molly and Clint were face-to-face with their client, Timothy Marcum, who they were seeing for the first time. They could recognize him from his pictures, but he looked sickly. His right hand was splinted, and multiple tubes ran from his IV to his wrist. Timothy tried to smile, but with some difficulty.

"Jeffrey told me you were hired by my sister to find me. Well, here I am, though not exactly in shape for my *GQ* photoshoot. Thanks for your efforts. Can you put me in touch with my sister? I need to let her know I'm doing okay," Timothy said.

"I'm Molly, and this is Clint," Molly said, pointing to herself first and then to Clint. "From what the nurses say, you have been doing quite well, all things considered," said Molly. "It has been an adventure for Clint and me to find you. We will need to ask you some questions to find out exactly what has been going on with you and why those thugs beat you up so badly."

"Maybe it would be best to call your sister first," said Clint. "She has been very worried about you. Then, if you're comfortable, you can tell us your story."

"Yes, I agree I should talk with Marguerite first, but then I would be happy to tell you at least most of my tale," said Timothy. "I have been sworn to secrecy by my father on some of the details, but I can let you in on most of what has happened."

Clint called Marguerite on Tim's phone and handed it to him. They could all hear Marguerite's excited shouting when she realized she was talking with her brother.

"Tim, thank God you are alive! I have been so worried about you. Are you okay? Are you with Clint and Molly now?"

"Hey, Marg. I'm kind of beat up now, but I will be okay," Tim said with a sigh. "Your friends are with me now and have been helpful. It's a long story, but I'm safe now. In fact, Jeffrey, Dad's bodyguard, is sitting outside the door right now."

"Why in the world would Jeffrey be with you?" Marguerite asked. "Is Dad somehow involved in all this? He hasn't told me a thing, and I may have to strangle him for that. And what do you mean you were beat up?"

"I know you have lots of questions," Tim said. "Yes, I have been working for Dad. He sent Jeffrey here to help protect me. I was beaten up by some thugs here in Paris and wound up in the hospital. I am doing better and should be discharged tomorrow."

"I'm flying out tomorrow after I inflict some serious bodily harm on our father," she said. "Sounds like you need to rest up, so I'll get the rest of the details from Molly and Jeffrey. No more running Dad's errands! I should be in Paris by tomorrow night. Get some rest, and let me talk with Molly."

They said their goodbyes, and Tim gave Molly the phone. Marguerite thanked Molly and Clint for their help in finding her brother. She told Molly she would have her father double their salary for their work. Molly told Marguerite that she and Clint could meet her at the airport when she flew in to take her to the Crillon where Tim would be staying. Molly told her she would update her later on what Tim had been up to.

After Molly hung up with Marguerite, Tim outlined his adventures and horror in his quest for information for his father. He told them he was able to find two pieces of a puzzle his father desperately wanted, but he did not know why he needed this information or why the Russian goons had been after him. However, Timothy knew that, since the Russians were willing to kill for it and that his father would risk a significant amount of money and his wellbeing, whatever it was, it was quite valuable.

"Well, Tim, I have to agree with Marguerite. I think it's time to end this quest you're on for your father," Clint said.

"Let's discuss this more after I get some rest," Timothy said with a nod.

Molly and Clint left Timothy to rest and meandered their way out of the hospital. Although they were relieved to have found their subject, they both felt somewhat disappointed their quest was over and they no longer had an excuse to spend so much time together.

Clint winked at Molly. "I think it is time for a bit of celebration since our job is over. I'm going to book us on a dinner cruise on the Seine, and I don't want any objections. A little dinner, wine, and touring the City of Lights with you is just what I need."

Molly gave Clint a hug. "I've been to Paris a number of times, but I have never gone on a dinner cruise. I've heard the lights, especially over the Eiffel Tower, are gorgeous at night. What a perfect way to end our little jaunt. We should call David and Giselle to give them a heads up on our success and arrange to meet them so we can all head back to the US."

The two then headed back to their hotel to change. Molly had just enough time to whisk into Chanel to buy an amazing little black chiffon dinner dress for the occasion. When she tried it on in their room, Clint whistled.

"Wow, you look like Paris Hilton," Clint said, eyeing her up and down.

"Thanks. I'm happy to look like her, but I try to keep my sex life a bit more private than she does," Molly said with a laugh.

As they walked to the door to head out, Molly's phone rang. It was Marguerite, and she began by apologizing profusely.

"Molly, I am so sorry to disturb you after everything you did for my brother, and I remain truly grateful, but there is bit of a complication. After confronting my father about all that has been going on, he agreed he can no longer use Timothy as his errand boy. I'm grateful he no longer wants to use him, but now my dad wants to have a meeting with you and Clint. He's convinced you two could complete the quest that Timothy was on. Honestly, it sounds ridiculous to me, but there is no reasoning with my father once he has set his mind to something. He wants to set up a phone meeting tomorrow afternoon at four, Paris time. He won't tell me the specifics about what he wants you to do, but it would involve traveling outside Paris for some sort of negotiation."

Clint was listening on speakerphone. "If there are negotiations involved, our friend David is the man for this job. Maybe we could get him in on a conference call if your father is agreeable. We obviously need more information to see if this is feasible and if it is something we want to do. We would also need some protection, given who Timothy was up against. Molly and I are going on a Seine cruise, so we will call you back after the cruise and after we talk to David."

"Thank you, Clint and Molly. Again, I'm so sorry to get you mixed up in all of this," Marguerite said, and then she hung up the phone.

Molly and Clint headed out into the brisk summer night air. Molly was happy she had brought along her wrap as her shoulders were covered in tiny goosebumps. She was almost as tall as Clint in her four-inch Jimmy Choo black heels. She loved the way they looked with her new Chanel dress, but they slowed her down a bit.

Molly and Clint caught the boat just in time to be seated for their meal. A sexy jazz singer was doing her best to emulate a French Billie Holiday. The duo popped a bottle of champagne to celebrate their success in finding Timothy.

Lord only knows what Tim's father has in mind for us to do next, Clint thought. It seemed forever since he had been back in LA practicing law, but looking across at Molly, he had to admit these adventures with David did have an upside.

"You certainly look deep in thought for someone who is supposed to be celebrating," said Molly. "I can't imagine anything more beautiful than the lights of Paris reflected in the river. What are you thinking about?"

"I am just comparing your beauty to these lights," said Clint.

"I suspect Paris would win hands down, unless you're referring to Paris Hilton again." Molly laughed.

"Paris Hilton or Paris, France, you still would win," said Clint.

"Although I enjoy the compliment, I don't think we need any bologna with this fine meal. Let's call David and Giselle to see if they want to come to Paris."

Clint chuckled at Molly's modesty. *She really doesn't understand just how beautiful she is,* he thought.

As they came around a bend in the river, they took a moment to be in awe of the Eiffel Tower lit at night.

"Yes, I suppose we should call David," Clint finally said. He then pulled out his cellphone and dialed his friend's number.

David answered, and Clint and Molly could hear loud music and the sounds of a flamenco guitar and castanets.

Clint laughed. "David, only you and Giselle would find flamenco music in Brussels. What are you two up to?"

"Just taking in a bit of the local culture," said David. "I can hear jazz in the background. What are you two up to?"

"Same," Clint said with a laugh.

Molly and Clint proceeded to give David and Giselle a synopsis of their recent events, including finding Timothy and their upcoming meeting with Mr. Marcum the next day. David and Giselle immediately agreed to take the train to Paris in the morning. David was interested in hearing Mr. Marcum's proposal, and Giselle couldn't resist the idea of shopping with Molly in Paris.

The two couples made arrangements to meet at about noon the next day.

Clint then texted Marguerite, stating that they all would be in Paris the next afternoon and were able to take her father's call. He sat back and enjoyed his dessert of crème brûlée and café au lait.

"I'm glad our business is done for the moment and we can get back to enjoying the food and beauty around us," he said. "I still have a couple of surprises for you tonight."

Molly licked the last of her crème brûlée from her spoon and said, "More surprises, Monsieur Clint? You certainly can be a mystery, but I guess I should expect as much from a makeshift detective."

They disembarked back at Pier 3 near the Eiffel Tower.

"Can you and those stilettos handle a half-mile walk, or should we catch an Uber?" Clint asked.

"Well, I think Jimmy Choo and I can manage half of a mile, but any longer than that would be pushing it," Molly replied. "Fashion statements and exercise certainly can coexist, but four-inch heels do set some limits."

They crossed the Seine at Pont d'Iéna and headed into the Trocadero Gardens.

"Why are we going into these gardens at night?" Molly asked. "I am a bit confused, Clint."

"I have been told these gardens have the best view of the Eiffel Tower at night," said Clint. "I want to take your picture in front of it."

"Okay," said Molly. "I guess no reason we can't play tourists for a moment, as long as I can take your picture as well."

They joined the late-night group of Eiffel Tower aficionados and were rewarded with spectacular views and photos to remember the whole experience.

"We better catch an Uber and get to our last destination," said Clint after some time. "We need to hurry since our show starts in half an hour."

"What type of show are we going to see at ten-thirty at night?" asked Molly.

"What else but the late show at the Crazy Horse Cabaret," Clint responded just as their Uber pulled up.

Molly started laughing. "Well, I can see where your mind is tonight. Too bad David and Giselle can't come with us."

They were soon deposited into a throng of people in front of the cabaret. They quickly found themselves inside the theater sharing another bottle of champagne while they waited for the performance.

The show was rousing—and arousing to say the least. Some of the most beautiful women in Paris were adorned in little or no costumes and danced in well-choreographed routines, playing out little vignettes at times.

At the intermission, Clint had to put some of the ice from the champagne bucket on his neck.

Molly laughed. "I thought you might need to put that ice a bit lower after watching that performance."

"There probably isn't enough ice to help with that," Clint replied.

The second act of the show was just as spectacular. The lighting and music helped coordinate with the dancers' gyrations. The crowd was on their feet at the end, calling for more. Clint and Molly joined the rest in a standing ovation.

"What a night it has been," Molly said as she grabbed Clint's arm on their way out.

"It's definitely been one to remember," Clint said as he flagged down a taxi.

They wearily made their way back to their hotel, thankful for their Parisian cabdriver, despite the madness of his driving. Molly kicked off her four-inch heels as they walked up the elaborate steps of their hotel. Clint fumbled with the doorknob, almost too tired to function. As they made their way across the room, Molly slinked out of her dress and fell into the bed. Clint followed closely behind, and before they knew it, they both gave way to deep breathing and snores. Molly's last thought was of Giselle descending on an unsuspecting Paris.

20 MR. MARCUM'S PROPOSAL

Clint had gotten up early for a little cardio and weightlifting in the hotel's gym. On his return, he could hear Molly in the shower. He quickly disrobed and joined her in the shower for a little unfinished business.

"Nice way to start the day. If I had known I was going to get this much cardio, I wouldn't have gone to the gym," said Clint.

"Well, you're not done yet. How about a brisk walk before we meet David and Giselle for some lunch?"

"Works for me," said Clint.

"That sunshine out there looks inviting, and for a change, I wouldn't mind my Nikes instead of these heels. Let's head over to the Luxembourg Gardens and back along the Seine," Molly said. "I think that should be about ten kilometers there and back."

"Sounds good to me," said Clint. "By then, we both will be as hungry as wolves."

They joined the Parisian swirl of people and soon were lost in their thoughts as they quickly strode along. Their strides seemed to be naturally in sync, and they held hands. Molly and Clint were both very quiet, each thinking about where their romantic relationship was going. They could be heading back to the states as early as the next day or two, unless Mr. Marcum arranged otherwise.

Molly eyed the man she'd grown to significantly care for over the past few days. *Is this just a fling? What does all of this mean?* Molly wondered. They paused as they got to the center fountain, joining a host of other romantic couples and families with children, some who played in the pond.

Clint looked at Molly. "So, my dear Molly, I'm sure you've been thinking about the same thing that I have. What happens with us now that we are likely heading back to our homes and reality? I am not the most romantic guy on the planet, but I'm not foolish enough to want to pull the plug on whatever this is."

Molly pulled Clint to her and kissed him. "Paris is one of the most romantic places, so I think I have to agree with you that ending things at this moment would be ill advised. Let's give it at least another a day or two and see where the world spins us."

Clint nodded and then spun Molly around before kissing her cheek. They laughed and headed back along the Seine. Before long, they were back at the hotel.

They changed into slightly more formal clothing since Lord knows where David and Giselle would drag them. At twelve-thirty, Clint's phone rang announcing their friends' arrival.

There was no mistaking Giselle's voice. "Well, you French detectives, I am half-starved since the food on the train was *les misérable*. We're in room 707, just below you. You better not keep us up tonight with all your thumping! Meet us out front. I know just the place for lunch, Restaurant Citrus Etoile near the Eiffel Tower."

Molly laughed, happy to hear her friend's voice. "We saw the Eiffel Tower all lit up last night. It was amazing! I have to tell you what else we did, but it can wait until we meet. I'm starved myself. We went on a ten kilometer adventure this morning, and I need food."

"I won't argue about lunch," Clint chimed in.

The four reunited outside the hotel and caught a cab to the restaurant. Of course, the maître d' Louis at Citrus Etoile instantly recognized Giselle and threw his arms around her, kissing her on both cheeks.

"Miss Giselle," he said in his best English, "it has been far too long since you have been here. I will tell the chef Armon. Coco, your favorite showgirl, is here eating lunch. I'm sure she will be excited to see you as well."

"It is good to see you too, but please know my friends and I are starved and would love some café au lait, mimosas, and crepes," Giselle responded. "They can then get whatever else they want for lunch."

"It will be as you wish," Louis replied. "Please sit here, and your food will be ready in a moment."

Giselle thanked him, and the group settled at a table near the front. Giselle grabbed Molly. "I want you to meet someone I have known here for some time."

They went to the back of the restaurant and saw an elegant black woman sitting and reading *Le Monde*. Molly thought she recognized her from the Crazy Horse show she had seen the night before. When the woman saw Giselle, she threw her paper down and embraced her.

A good deal of French was exchanged, little of which Molly understood.

"Sorry, Molly," said Giselle. "This is Coco, a dear friend who dances in the show at the Crazy Horse and helps direct parts of the show. Coco, this is my friend Molly."

"Clint and I saw the show last night," said Molly. "It was amazing!" She shook hands with Coco. "You certainly are beautiful, and you move like a goddess."

Coco laughed. "You are beautiful yourself. If you can move with any grace across a stage, I'm sure we could use you. I have known Giselle for the last ten years. We met when she was studying at the Sorbonne, and she even filled in at times for our show. Did you know she had formal ballet training but chose a business career instead?"

"I would probably trip moving five feet across the stage, so no Crazy Horse for me," Molly responded. "And, Giselle, you devil, you never mentioned you used to perform at the Crazy Horse!"

"She not only performed, but over the years, she has helped a number of the dancers financially, including myself. She has beauty inside and out. She is well respected in our community. Although, I sure wouldn't want to be sitting opposite her in a court room."

Giselle saw their food was arriving and bid adieu to her friend, promising to get together before she left Paris. They rejoined David and Clint as mountains of delicious food arrived. Louis had improvised a bit, knowing Giselle's favorites. The four dug in, and for the next fifteen minutes, all that could be heard at the table was the clicking of knives and forks, occasional chewing, and periodic sighs of satisfaction.

"I have to get back to Paris more often. Maybe I need a vacation home here," said David, finally breaking the silence. "There is simply nothing back in the states that could even touch this food."

Giselle eyed him. "With all your real estate connections and a few dollars, I'm sure you could find a little *maison* in Paris. With that blazing intellect of yours, I bet learning French would even be within your grasp."

Molly let out a gasp. "Giselle, you actually complimented David on his intelligence! I'm not sure I've ever heard an actual compliment to a member of the opposite sex from you. Very interesting!"

"I'll try not to let it happen again," said Giselle dryly.

David laughed. "Living in Paris part of the year might be something to think about, even without learning French. But that can be discussed later. Now that we've tended to our stomachs, let's get down to business. We need to discuss our upcoming phone call with Mr. Marcum and any strategies we might want to use."

Clint sighed. "It just makes me feel all warm inside to hear David switch to his lawyer mode," Clint said sarcastically. "But I do agree, it is time to get down to business. Now that you two have had some time to digest what Molly and I told you last night, what are we going to do about the Russian stalkers?"

"Those Russians are certainly nasty characters. Were you able to find out anything about them, Giselle?" Molly asked.

Simultaneously, Giselle's and Clint's phones rang.

Clint looked at his caller ID and said, "The plot thickens."

David raised an eyebrow as the two each took their calls outside. When they returned to their friends, Clint had an odd look on his face.

"That was Timothy. He has been discharged from the hospital and is back at the Crillon Hotel with his nurse Jolene. We are to meet him there at four this afternoon for our phone meeting with his father. You will all be interested to know that the place Tim's father wants us to go next is not London, Madrid, or Athens, but Mongolia! Not my first choice for a little light travel."

Giselle laughed. "Well, my call was from my poor secretary back in California. It's the middle of the night for her. She advised me not to leave Paris as my firm has some work for me here for the next two weeks. They even advised me to hire an assistant to help take testimony we will need. As much as I would love living in a yurt in Mongolia, I will have to stay here in dull Paris at the Ritz. Molly, you are welcome to be my assistant if Clint can manage without you—that's assuming David and Clint want to become some of Marcum's minions."

"If Clint really needs me, I would consider Mongolia, but working with you in Paris would be a dream," Molly responded.

David took the floor. "I have actually considered going to Mongolia in the past and its northern neighbor Tyva, once known as Tuva. Mongolia is huge, but sparsely populated. Because it is very rugged outside its capital city Ulaanbaatar, almost half the population lives in the capital. The rest of the country is home to many nomad tribes. Mongolians are known as the best horsemen in the world, which I'm sure helped Genghis Khan conquer a major part of the known world some eight hundred years ago. I've always enjoyed Mongolia's history. In fact, following Marco Polo's route through Mongolia or fly-fishing for the largest trout in the world has been on my bucket list. I don't know what Mr. Marcum has in mind, but there would be worse places to go to than Mongolia."

Giselle and Molly exchanged looks. "Giselle, maybe you weren't too far off complimenting your new playboy on his intelligence," Molly said teasingly.

Clint shook his head. "Thank you for the far eastern travelogue, Mr. Collins. I am not so sure, though, that I want to follow Marco Polo or Genghis Khan through Mongolia, especially with a pack of evil Russians chasing us. I am willing to hear Mr. Marcum out, but this could be more danger than I want to sign up for. Giselle, were you able to find out more about the Russian who killed the monk and nearly clubbed me to death?"

Giselle got out her notebook. "The information about a Mongolian connection certainly answers some questions about the Russian interest in this case. Our Russian monk killer and Clint's attacker is Sergio

Gremlin. The Brussel police force is still looking for him. He is Russian ex-military and part of a criminal organization based in southern Russia. Who is in charge of the group at this point, I don't know. Whoever it is though seems to be after whatever Mr. Marcum is and has no problem being ruthless to obtain it."

All four were quiet for a moment.

Clint finally spoke, "I guess I am lucky to still be alive. Maybe it's time to let the professionals duke it out with the Russians. David, what did you find out about Mr. Marcum and why he sent his son on this chase knowing he might be in danger?"

David nodded. "Cornwell Marcum was born in 1946 in Los Angeles, California and has remained there all his life. His father, Calvin Marcum, left him with a tidy fortune of one hundred million dollars from shipping and importing before he passed away. Cornwell was always more interested in real estate than trade. He currently owns a good deal of it in San Francisco and the Southwest. Pushing seventy, he now has broadened his interests and recently has purchased some IT companies and shares in genetic engineering corporations. His net worth is around $2.5 billion, making him the 357th richest man on our planet. Despite his wealth, he felt his wife of twenty years was not welcome to the twenty million dollars granted to her in their divorce.

"I'm not sure what Mr. Cornwell is up to but I'm sure it is high stakes, considering the Russians are after it as well. However, that Cornwell would risk his son's well-being for his own self-interest does not surprise me, but

I'd like to think he was unaware of all the dangers Timothy would face."

"Not the sort of man I would invite to my tea party," said Giselle. "Speaking of which, we need to end ours. It's almost time to head to Timothy's for our phone call from the man himself."

"I doubt you would ever have a 'tea party,' unless mimosas were being served," said Molly. "I do agree we better get going. I need to powder my nose or whatever one says these days to politely go to the bathroom."

"In this group, I think you could say 'I need to go to the bathroom' and leave powdering one's nose to whomever," said Clint.

They all got up and thanked Louis for a wonderful meal. Giselle let him know she would be back since she was going to be in Paris for the next two weeks.

Molly and Clint decided to walk back to their hotel after their big lunch. She had split the difference between fashion and practicality and had worn stylish walking shoes. Walking along the Seine was always an unforgettable experience. Both Clint and Molly were lost in their own thoughts about their upcoming phone call with Mr. Marcum. Clint wondered if the reason they all called him Mr. Marcum was because he was a billionaire or that his age made them all think of him as a father figure. Clint decided that, whatever the reason, he was much happier with his own father, despite his meager financial status.

When they arrived at the hotel, David and Giselle were already there, talking with a rejuvenated Timothy and Nurse Jolene. Timothy seemed to be healing quickly; the swelling of his face had gone down, and his movements were much better. Certainly, some of his recovery seemed related to a definite fondness he showed toward his nurse. As usual, Jeffrey the bodyguard stationed himself outside Timothy's door, reminding them all of possible threats they might face.

At precisely four o'clock, Clint's phone rang, and he placed the call on speakerphone.

"Cornwell Marcum here," the voice on the phone announced.

The group then went around, stating their names to show who was present.

"Thank you all for coming to this meeting and for helping my son Timothy. My daughter Marguerite has been quite upset with me for involving Timothy in this affair, but I was not aware it would turn out to be this dangerous. I felt a certain degree of secrecy would be helpful and knew I could depend on Timothy's silence. I regret his injuries and the death of his friend Brother Adolphus. I am impressed, however, that, despite the circumstances, Timothy was able to acquire the first two pieces of a puzzle I have been trying to solve. The results of which could be earth-shattering. I am hopeful that Timothy can become a more important part of my company once all this is over.

"I realize Timothy is not able to continue getting the last piece of information because of his injuries—and since his sister would probably disown me. This task will require the ability to negotiate and the fortitude to travel to the nomadic regions of Mongolia. I do understand my daughter hired you, Molly and Giselle, to find my son, and you both enlisted David and Clint to help you accomplish that. I suspect David and Clint would be up to the new task, and I would, of course, send along Jeffrey, my trusted bodyguard to help you. Molly and Giselle, you could accompany the men, but since this will be quite rigorous, I am not sure you will want to go."

"Unfortunately, Molly and I will not be able to go to Mongolia as we have other business to tend to in Paris," Giselle said.

"Very well," Mr. Marcum said. "Clint and David, if you two are interested in my proposition, you would need to leave for Mongolia in two days as there is a ceremony outside Mongolia's capitol you will need to attend. Since Mongolia does not require a visa for US citizens, you would simply need your passports. I am willing to offer both of you one million dollars each if you can accomplish getting the information I want. If you are interested in continuing our relationship beyond this, it could lead to a great deal more money, but I cannot make any promises until I have seen your work. I will need to know your answer tonight since we have to book flights. If things work out as planned, you will be back in Paris in a week. Any questions?"

David and Clint looked at each other. David was the first to speak. "Clearly, our biggest concern for this venture would be our safety. A mere one million dollars for my heirs does not excite me much. Do you have other resources in Mongolia? In order for me to sign on, I need to know what we are negotiating for and why it is so valuable."

Mr. Marcum let out a sigh and then responded, "We have a guide arranged in the Ulaanbaatar as well as 'helping hands' along the way. I have even spoken to the Mongolian army, and they have agreed to help if needed. Jeffrey also is very resourceful and dependable. What you are negotiating for is the last element of a serum to increase strength and limit aging. I know this sounds absurd, but I have verified information that this serum works, although not on everyone. I believe it could still change a great deal of lives both in longevity and financially."

Giselle's eyes grew wide at the mention of an age-defying serum. *To think, I could keep this body for years to come,* she thought.

Clint covered the mouthpiece and whispered to David, "Do you really want to be involved in this?"

David nodded his head and said to Clint, "Does a bear shit in the woods?"

Giselle laughed. "I prefer the rhetorical question 'Does the Tin Man have a metal dick?'"

Clint uncovered the mouthpiece and asked, "So, where exactly would we need to go?"

Mr. Marcum replied, "You would fly into the capital, Ulaanbaatar, and go by truck and then possibly horseback some five hundred miles to the largest lake in Mongolia, Khövsgöl Nuur. There, you will meet with nomad herders and a chieftain to get the information I want."

David answered. "The four of us will need to discuss this more in-depth, but we will get back to you tonight with an answer. We promised to pick your daughter up at the airport and bring her here. We will call you back at ten tonight our time."

They said their goodbyes and ended the call. They all looked at one another.

"Wow!" said Molly. "That is a lot to digest and respond to in six hours. I can do fairly well on horseback, but I wonder just how many mosquitoes there might be at a high alpine lake in Central Asia and what diseases they might carry. Sorry, Clint, but this is more than I want to attempt. I'm not sure even you guys should do this."

Clint shook his head. "This is certainly more than I signed on for. A bit more intimidating than being a monk. David, I can't blame you for wanting in on this adventure, but this would certainly take the cake. I do better on a Harley than a horse, but I could probably keep from falling off. What do you think?"

David was shaking his head as well. "I have to agree. This would be our most ambitious foray, but you know I like a challenge. One million dollars for a week. How much an hour would that be? I wonder what the nomads eat. Probably mutton and anything else they can get their hands on. If Ponce de León could cross the Atlantic on a sailboat and struggle through Florida swamps to find the Fountain of Youth, how bad can Mongolia be?"

"You know, he never did find the Fountain of Youth. Although, I understand some older New Yorkers who moved to Florida feel they have," said Giselle. "If you go, please bring back a bottle of eau de Mongolia for me. You never know if the stuff may actually work."

"I think we need a couple of decent beers to sort this out," said David. "Giselle, you know everything about Paris. Can you find us a couple of brews to jumble our brains around to give us a better perspective?"

"Of course," she said. "We can hit the Académie de la bière in Montparnasse after we drop off Marguerite. They have decent food and the Belgian beers I know you like."

"Perfect," David said. "Let's call a car and pick up Marguerite at the airport. I'm getting hungry again and thirsty. I wonder what the beers are like in Mongolia."

They met a very tired but happy Marguerite. She threw her arms around Molly and Giselle when she saw them.

"I can't thank you two enough for all your help. When I found out about my father's role in all of this I almost put him in the hospital. I haven't been able to sleep thinking of those thugs beating up my poor Tim," Marguerite said.

Molly held Marguerite's hand in her hands. "I think Tim is doing quite well, and the doctor assured us he thinks he will make a full recovery. I think your being here will help him a lot."

Molly introduced Marguerite to the guys and then told their driver to take them back to the hotel so they could meet up with Timothy. She then rolled up the window between their seats and the driver's for more privacy. On the ride, they filled Marguerite in about their conversation with her father. She was fascinated with the information they uncovered, but understood their uncertainty about what to do.

When they arrived at the hotel, Marguerite was delighted to be reunited with her brother, but not quite so delighted to see a possible budding romance between him and Jolene. She was too tired to go with them to dinner, so she ordered room service for herself, Tim, and Jolene. They said good night, and the four headed out in search of beer and a final decision.

The restaurant was busy, but the beer and food were great. After a couple of beers and some of the best scallops they had eaten, it was getting close to show time. They had to decide whether or not to head to Mongolia in search of the last ingredient of the serum. Clint and David looked at each other.

"I know you want to do this," said Clint, shaking his head. "This is like honey for a bee. This is the ultimate negotiation—the art of the deal in Northern Mongolia with the future of the world's youth possibly at stake. I'll only get on board if this is our last adventure of this sort. And you owe me another beer tonight. Lord knows what we will be drinking in Mongolia."

David sheepishly ordered them another beer. He raised his glass for a toast. "My dear friend, Clint, may we share one more adventure to end all adventures."

They all clinked their glasses and then drank.

"I'll call Mr. Marcum and draw up a contract tonight," said David. "I'm sure he has at least half a dozen attorneys at his disposal to look at it tonight. Let's call it an early evening and head out clothes shopping tomorrow. We need to get outfitted for whatever is to come."

They headed back to their hotel and settled in for the night. Too many thoughts and too much alcohol did not encourage love-making or sleep, but eventually, oblivion caught up with them all.

* * *

Sure enough, when they awoke there was a slightly revised contract on David's computer with generally acceptable terms. After a quick breakfast in their rooms, they joined forces to attack Paris's sporting goods stores. For shoes and simple clothes, they went to Nike on the Champs-Élysées, and for jeans and sweatshirts, they went to the local department stores. For more specialized clothing, they headed to Patagonia. Giselle, of course, was the lead and able to direct them all tirelessly.

They soon felt ready to survive at least ten days in a potentially hostile environment. Timothy even gave Clint the AI watch his father's company had developed with its new solar battery. By the afternoon, they had to send a cab full of packages of every sort back to the hotel while they continued their last efforts.

That evening, after naps and showers, they managed to regroup for their final Parisian meal before taking off for Mongolia. As usual, Giselle had the honors of picking out their dining establishment, but David and Clint requested a steakhouse. Restaurant Bien Élevé proved to be just the ticket. The food was delicious and the service reasonable for a French restaurant. Molly couldn't stop eating the fries; she even caught herself reaching over to Clint's plate for some of his.

"Giselle, you have outdone yourself," said Molly. "You need to come out with *Giselle's Guide to Paris*. I'll help you research the restaurants and clothing stores. Just think, we could do the best shopping and eating, and it could all be tax deductible!"

"Molly, I think you and I are going to have a great time in Paris," said Giselle. "I wish our young studs could accompany us, but *c'est la vie*. They have another mission in life to achieve."

Clint sighed. "I feel like a soldier going off to war—but at least they are armed."

"Oh, Clint," said Molly worriedly.

"I know. I have to keep a positive view on all this and realize it may be the experience of a lifetime."

David again raised his glass for a parting toast. "To dear friends and lovers, here's to the nights we'll never remember with the friends we'll never forget."

They all grinned and clinked their glasses before sipping their sweet champagne.

"I have to agree with Clint that this may well be a life changing experience. Hopefully, we'll be having dinner here again and celebrating our success together soon," David added.

They downed the last of their champagne and headed out into the night. They returned to the hotel, but this time, with a buzz from the champagne, nothing could interrupt their amorous activities.

21 MONGOLIA – THE FLIGHT

Morning in Paris brought a muddled collage of thoughts to Clint. He was up early and down in the exercise room at the hotel trying to wake up his muscles. He knew he had a long flight today and was trying to help his body adjust to that. Molly was just waking up when he got back to the room. They both could feel a sense of uncertainty from their anticipated separation. Suddenly, their relationship seemed so complicated. They exchanged a morning kiss and showered, forgoing intimacy in favor of expediency.

Clint and David's flight was going to be chartered by Mr. Marcum, so their departure from the airport would be simplified, but there was still the usual last minute chores.

"Giselle dropped off an emergency kit this morning for the two of you," Molly said. "Hopefully, you won't need to use it. She even put in sleeping pills, pain meds, water purification tabs, and activated charcoal in case of poisoning. A knife or gun might have been more practical but would likely not allow you to get through the airport. We argued about her last little gift from one of her contacts in Paris. Please be very careful with this. It looks like a standard USB drive, but it actually contains an explosive device. When you plug it into a computer, it sets a timer and will explode in thirty minutes. I think

Jeffrey should be in charge of this little package. It's currently missing a necessary explosive component so he can sneak it through airport security. I hope you don't need it, but be sure to obtain the missing component for this when you reach Mongolia in case you have to use it. Mr. Marcum assured Giselle he has a contact in Mongolia who can assist with this."

"Wow," said Clint. "I'll talk with David and Jeffrey about this and give it back to you for safekeeping if they think it is too dangerous. Giselle certainly is something."

Molly embraced Clint. "You know I will miss you."

Clint nodded. "I will definitely miss you as well. I should be back soon—and one million dollars richer. We will have one hell of a celebration."

They embraced harder.

"Well, I will certainly look forward to that," said Molly. "No doubt Giselle could put together a celebration that would make Bastille Day look like a kindergarten party."

"We should get down to meet David and Giselle for breakfast," said Clint. "I'm all packed. Jeffrey and our Mongolian guide, Uri, are going to meet us at the airport."

"Uri? Isn't that a Russian name? Are you sure you should trust him after all we've been through lately with the Russians?"

Clint gave her a sweet look. He liked that she felt concerned for him. "Don't worry. I asked Uri about his Russian name, and he told me his father was Russian and his real name is about fourteen characters long in Mongolian, so Uri was much easier to go by."

"Okay, I trust him if you do."

The two headed down and met David and Giselle in the café outside the hotel.

Giselle lifted her glass and toasted David and Clint with her mimosa. "To new adventures and happy reunions!"

They all pensively agreed.

Clint raised his croissant and said a prayer of thanks to the French pastry gods. "The thought of coming back to one of these croissants is enough to keep me alive."

"I'm sure Mongolia will offer us some unique treats, though probably no croissants," said David. "Let's head out, troops. We have a plane to catch."

Marguerite had come to meet them and again thanked them for their help with Timothy. She reported he was doing very well and had surprised the doctors with the speed of his recovery. She brought the instructions to Tim's AI watch and a note from Timothy wishing them well. She hoped the watch would prove as useful to Clint as it did for Tim. She wished them well, and they headed off to Charles de Gaulle Airport for their chartered flight on Elite World Airways.

The foursome remained quiet, except for Giselle's queries to the Uber driver in French. In typical Giselle fashion, she asked his thoughts on the best Taiwanese restaurants for dinner.

When they arrived at the airport, they made their way to the international terminal and the charter counter. They couldn't mistake Jeffrey since he was head and shoulders above the rest of the crowd. He introduced them to a smiling yet somewhat weathered Mongolian man with a jangled scar on his left cheek, Uri.

Giselle was never one for extended goodbyes but did exchange a brief but passionate kiss with David. Molly and Clint had to be pulled apart or the men would have missed their flight. David and Clint checked in for their flight to Ulaanbaatar, Mongolia both a bit distracted. Even David was not used to such opulence on seeing their plane. To fly from Paris to Ulaanbaatar, a distance of over seven thousand kilometers, Mr. Marcum had chartered a Gulfstream G500, a truly magnificent plane. Few planes in the world could match its speed and distance capabilities. It could carry eight passengers in ultimate luxury.

Jeffrey, Uri, David, and Clint settled into their spacious leather seats, seats that even accommodated Jeffrey's massive size. Marie, their spicy French flight attendant, could have stepped out of *Playboy*, complete with her low-cut top, ample breasts, short heels, and even shorter skirt. She filled them in on some of the facts about their plane and the usual preflight instructions.

"Gentleman, welcome to one of Gulfstream's finest planes, the G500," Marie said. "Though this looks like you are flying in your living room, it is still a plane, and you have to follow routine airline precautions. Our pilots today are Captain James Stark and his copilot Roy

Cross. Our flying time should be about eleven hours, depending on wind speed. Please keep in mind we will lose seven hours because of time zone changes. We should arrive in Ulaanbaatar, or UB as we call it, at roughly eight in the morning tomorrow. There is water and drinks in a fridge here in the cabin. I will serve dinner at six o'clock Paris time and breakfast at six-thirty tomorrow morning Ulaanbaatar time. Help yourself to any snacks you want in the meantime. Please keep your seat belt on for takeoff, but after that, you can roam around as much as you'd like. Your seats transform into beds, and I would suggest you keep hydrated and get some sleep tonight. Any questions?"

"Any videos or info on Mongolia you have would be helpful," said David.

Uri injected, "I have a half-hour video about Mongolia and can talk as long as you are interested about the capital and where we are going. I also have pamphlets about the Naadam athletic games you are going to the day after tomorrow. I had planned on starting once we were airborne, but could oblige now."

"Sounds good to me," said Jeffrey and then turned to Marie. "Please start bringing me mass quantities of food once we take off. I am starved since I missed lunch, and I don't think you want me munching on any of your leather furniture."

Marie laughed. "We would prefer you leave the furniture as it is. I can help you cook something, or you are welcome to cook for yourself if you prefer. I need to take my seat now to take off. Once we are at ten thousand feet, I'll bring you something."

Jeffrey thanked her, and they all settled in for an uneventful takeoff.

"This plane has more power than a Saturn rocket," said Clint. "I think we could be flying to Mars, not Mongolia."

David eyed him. "I think it might take us a bit more than eleven hours to fly to Mars."

As requested, Marie showed up with some snacks for the group. Jeffrey was very appreciative. When the seat belt sign was off, Uri turned on the video screen at the end of the cabin. He fiddled with the controls and was soon showing them a half-hour video that introduced them to Mongolia. Once they had absorbed a bit of Mongolian "propaganda," as Uri referred to it, it was time to educate the group on the *real* Mongolia.

"I was born and raised in Mongolia in Ulaanbaatar, and I love it dearly," said Uri. "Most people have a definite misconception about Mongolia. They picture us as uncivilized and blood thirsty, not the descendants of the great Genghis Khan who ruled the largest empire the world has ever known. He developed trade routes from Europe to Asia and was the first to develop a centralized mail system. It is true that, since the Mongolian empire fell, our country was mainly controlled by China and more recently was under Russian control from after WWI until 1990. Under Stalin, a lot of the monasteries were destroyed and, even as recently as the 1980s, some of our leaders were imprisoned for creating a stamp that celebrated the eight hundred years since the birth of Genghis Khan. We thankfully have been self-governed since 1990, and our economy has since flourished.

"You will see that Ulaanbaatar is undergoing tremendous changes. Half the population of our country lives there, which is a blessing, but brings about its own challenges. The last ten to fifteen years have seen a definite modernization of our downtown area. Gone or refurbished are the old Russian block buildings, and many tall buildings now dot the landscape. The other 1.3 million people in our country live as nomads or in small cities, but even the nomad lifestyle has been declining. You will often hear the slogan that Mongolia is the land of eternal blue sky. This is not merely some tourism gimmick, but rather is a genuine feeling we Mongolians have for our country."

"Wow, I thought David was an expert on Mongolia, but you take the cake," Clint said in amazement.

"Thank you, Clint. I take pride in my country's history. So, in the video you saw the different areas of Mongolia. We are going to head to the northwest, one of the most beautiful areas of the country. We will be in the capital tomorrow and can visit some of the sights. The next day, we will go to the central stadium to see the yearly athletic tournament called the Naadam. You will see wrestling, archery, and horseback riding. Two of the sons of the chieftain we need to meet are competing in the Naadam, and I think it might be helpful for you to meet them there."

David laughed. "Clint, I know you have been pretty interested in archery. Maybe we could have you compete."

"Don't mock me, David. You might be surprised at how good I'm getting at archery. I have been working with my daughter to get her interested in it," said Clint.

"All right, all right, Robin Hood. I believe you," David said with a grin.

Uri laughed at their banter and then went on to describe in more detail some of his favorite hidden gems of Mongolia. He answered as many questions as he could before leaving them to their thoughts.

After Uri had left, David turned to Jeffrey. "So, Jeffrey, I think it's time you told us why the big rush on meeting with this chieftain and just what are we in for. I'm sure Mr. Marcum has some reason for whisking us across Asia in his private plane."

As usual, Jeffrey did not mince words. "You would need to talk directly with Mr. Marcum about his thoughts. I know he wants you to meet the chieftain's children as a way of gaining some favor. The Mongols do business differently than we do back in the US. They value honesty, family values, and tradition as much as pure monetary gain in their negotiations. In the US, you might be able to negotiate a deal through an attorney or on the phone. Here, you will have to travel five hundred miles by Jeep and horseback and use whatever cunning you have with the chieftain. I have met him, and he is something else!

"I will tell you that we are in a hurry also because of the Russians. They would very much like to get their hands on this formula, and they would gladly resort to violence and foul actions if necessary. We will need to be on our guard."

David looked deep in thought and then said, "I'm not surprised that negotiations with the Mongol chieftain might be challenging. Clearly, Mr. Marcum did not send us thousands of miles at no small cost if it weren't so. I will need to spend more time getting to know the Mongolian idiosyncrasies."

Clint got up and patted David on the back. "Personally, I think I would like to get to know the Russian idiosyncrasies a bit more, just to keep us alive. I think I'll take a stroll about the plane before reading more about our next stomping ground." He headed to the pantry, more for something to do than to find something to eat.

Marie was in the processing area of the plane preparing dinner. She gracefully flipped the crepe she was frying while deciding on which filling to stuff it with.

Clint whistled in appreciation. "Nutella was always my favorite, but you know what they say, so many flavors, so little time."

Marie happily grabbed the Nutella and handed her latest creation to Clint for his gratification. "Monsieur Clint, you are just in time to help me make the crepes. As payment, you get to try the first."

Clint happily stuffed the warm crepe in his mouth. "*Merci*," he garbled, trying not to dribble too much of the Nutella out of the corner of his mouth.

"So, what brings you to Mongolia?" she asked. "Are you here for the Naadam Festival or for business?"

"I guess I am here to try to change the world a bit," said Clint.

"That is an interesting response," said Marie. "Are you trying to change it for the better or for the worse?"

"I guess I would hope for the better, but the answer to that would depend on your point of view. I suppose it's like choosing which filling to have for your crepe, but on a global scale. Future historians could say 'he chose the Nutella, but in retrospect, the apple filling would likely have changed the planet in a better way.' I say, though, we just make the crepes and leave interpretations to the philosophers."

"Wow," said Marie. "I will certainly agree to that. Please pass me the apple filling."

They continued making the crepes in silence and brought their stack with fresh whipped cream back into the cabin for all to enjoy.

22 ULAANBAATAR, MONGOLIA

The four travelers ate and tried to keep busy while awaiting their arrival in Mongolia. Before long, they touched down in Ulaanbaatar, Mongolia. They were all bit jet-lagged from the trip, but they were anxious to explore their new surroundings. The airport itself looked similar to most, but the array of people and their different dress were startling. There were those with western-styled clothes who could have fit in walking down Wall Street or Fifth Avenue in New York. Next to them strode a proud Mongolian nomad with his traditional long coat, or *deel*, with a large colorful silk sash around his waist. Mixed in the crowd were various monks in their traditional robes. All sorts of languages permeated the scene before them.

Going through customs was surprisingly easy as the officials there spoke English, and Uri helped expedite the process. As they waited to pick up their luggage, they watched the diverse press of humanity.

Once their bags arrived, they met their driver, Sardeepa. He apologized for their vehicle to the hotel since they would be riding in an old Russian truck for their first journey in Mongolia. David negotiated riding inside while Clint, Jeffrey, and Uri rode al fresco in the back with the suitcases and gear. Though not the most comfortable, it did offer them a great view of the countryside and eventually the city.

The warm, seventy-degree air was invigorating, contrary to the stories of thick polluted air Ulaanbaatar was often subject to. The brown-green pastureland of the steppes was dotted by infrequent sheep munching happily on the dried grasses. They saw occasional white domed *gers*, or yurts—the traditional, portable homes the nomads used when traveling from place to place. They also saw short, powerful Mongolian horses ridden by the nomads and sometimes children as young as five or six years old.

The grasslands transitioned into the city with little to no warning, other than some mounds of garbage with plastic left at intervals. There was little to distinguish the Mongolian capital from many Western cities except for the throngs of people with quite varied dress, just like in the airport. The variety of cars was also a bit bewildering. Clint's jaw dropped at the sight of a new Mercedes next to an oxcart. The streets were littered with old Russian vehicles of varying ages and repair.

Sardeepa honked his horn as a pedestrian walked across the street in front of their car, pulling them all out their thoughts.

"Crossing the street in some parts of the city can be a real challenge. You must be careful," Uri noted.

As they came to the center of the city, Chinggis Square, Uri pointed out this area would serve as the center of the Naadam events, which would be starting the next day. It also housed their hotel. The Best Western Premier Tuushin Hotel was Ullanbaatar's newest high-end hotel and included refinements like a spa and two restaurants.

David and Clint were impressed by the stylish lobby and pleasant English-speaking staff. They headed up to their modern rooms and both took showers before resting a bit. Even though it was three in the morning in Paris, Clint had promised Molly he would call when he arrived. As expected, Clint woke up Molly, but she was happy to hear his voice.

"Hey, good looking. Have you been able to keep up with Giselle?" Clint asked.

"Hey yourself. No one can keep up with Giselle. Shopping with her is like trying to keep up with the Energizer Bunny," Molly said in a groggy voice. "How was your flight?"

"We had a great flight and even got some rest. We are going out to see the main square and some of the museums soon. So far, the capital looks like most big cities but with a strong Russian influence combined with many cultures."

"I'm glad you got there okay," said Molly. "I'm going back to bed. Call me when you can."

They said their goodbyes, and then Clint headed down to the lobby to meet with David and Uri. Jeffrey decided he had had enough of the capital's culture from past trips and slept in. They headed out into Chinggis Square. Even though it was a large physical area, it was already jammed with people of every nationality and dress. From the air, it would have looked like a huge jar of colorful and different shaped beads dumped onto a counter. In the center of the square stood a huge statue of Genghis Khan on horseback with his four companions. On the south end of the square was a statue of Sükhbaatar, the hero of Mongolia's revolution against China in 1921, on horseback.

David, Clint, and Uri wandered through the square and over to the National Museum of Mongolia. Though it was fairly busy, they were able to make their way through exhibits from the Stone Age to the Gold Treasure area, which held a remarkable golden tiara. Uri was particularly proud of all the archeological finds in Mongolia. He was less excited by the costumes and jewelry on the second floor. All three were fascinated by the armor and relics from the Mongols of the twelfth century and the rise of Genghis Khan on the third floor.

They were somewhat disappointed with the newly opened Museum of Dinosaurs nearby simply because it did not yet have many exhibits, but they enjoyed the displays that were there. Clint could easily envision himself and Molly on a dig in Mongolia. Who knows what relic from the distant past they would unearth?

After getting their tourist fill, the three headed back to the hotel for lunch. At the restaurant, Clint tried a more traditional Mongolian food called *buuz*. It consisted of steamed dumplings with mutton, onions, and garlic.

As Clint devoured the dumplings, he said between bites, "Forget croissants! I could eat these every day."

David had chosen a more American dish, the Mongolian idea of a hamburger, but watching his friend inhale the dumplings made him believe Clint had taken the right approach. Both Clint and David tried some Mongolian beers while Uri stuck to vodka.

"This afternoon, we are going to see the Gandantegchinlen Monastery, one of the few the Mongolian Buddhist monasteries the Russians did not totally destroy," Uri said. "Our last venture this afternoon will be a private session with one of the most respected shamans at the Shaman Centre. I can tell from the looks you two are giving me that you are skeptical, but all I ask is that you keep an open mind and see what he has to say."

"I'm always one to keep an open mind with regards to religion. I even did a stint as a monk," said Clint. "My partner here, however, has been known to be a bit more unbending in his views on many things."

"I admit my first reaction to shamanism is to be skeptical, but I will try not to be too judgmental," said David.

They finished their drinks and lunch and headed out into the hot Mongolian afternoon. Uri had arranged for a somewhat upgraded transportation in the form of a Jeep, and they all piled in. Maneuvering across town with the Naadam traffic took patience mixed with a degree of vehicular madness. They did manage to get to the Buddhist monastery in one piece.

Uri explained that the monastery was one of the biggest tourist destinations in the capital. Over half the people in Mongolia are Buddhists, although almost as many have no specified religion. The Russians, especially under Stalin, did their best to wipe out Buddhism. Many monks were killed and monasteries destroyed. Since Mongolian independence in 1990, there had been a resurgence of Buddhism in Mongolia.

The three wandered through the temples and were especially enchanted by the white images of the Buddha of longevity and the twenty-six-meter gold-plated statue of Megjid janraisig, a sage who leads men to truth. Uri loved to tell the tale of the original statue at this site that was taken by the Soviets allegedly to melt down into ammunition. Despite the press of people, there was certainly a sense of peace about the monastery. They did not encounter any of the six hundred monks who lived there.

"Onward to the Shaman Centre and hopefully a rewarding experience for you both," said Uri.

"I'm okay as long as they don't whip us or ask us to eat any bizarre thing," said Clint.

"I have been through some cross-examinations that might make anything the shamans dish out a piece of cake," said David.

Uri shrugged his shoulders. "Remember, try to keep an open mind please."

Without further delay, they arrived back at the Shaman Centre, a series of somewhat ramshackle buildings with a fair number of people milling about. They were immediately taken into one of the buildings and asked to change into white robes and remove their shoes and socks.

"I feel like I'm getting ready for a massage," said David.

Clint laughed. "I think they are just going to massage your brain a bit."

Uri waited behind with the clothes while David and Clint were escorted down a dark corridor and into a very spiritual room. There was a strong odor of incense, and the only light in the room was from multiple candles. One could hear drumming coming through the walls in a soothing beat. Multiple pillows lay about the floor, and a washbasin sat in the corner with towels. Their escort did not speak, but indicated to them to wash their face, hands, and feet. They did so and sat down on the pillows, wondering what would come next.

After a few minutes, a small, somewhat weathered man in white robes, wearing dark glasses, and carrying a cane wheeled in a cart with a simple tea service. Surprisingly, his features did not look Asian, and from his gait and cane, he appeared to be blind. He poured tea for all three of them and sat on the pillows in front of them. He took a sip of his tea and motioned for Clint and David to do the same.

"Everything looks better after starting with a cup of tea, even if one is blind," he said with a definite Brooklyn accent. "I understand you both are lawyers from LA. What are you doing in Mongolia?"

David and Clint were startled to realize their shaman was likely from the US.

David almost spilled his tea. "Excuse us, Your Worship, but are you from the United States?" asked David. "We were not expecting a shaman from America."

"You can call me Max if you'd like," the shaman said. "Yes, I am from Brooklyn, but I have been a practicing shaman for the last nine years here in Ulaanbaatar. The universe holds little distinction between Mongolia and the US. My former name was Max Fromstein. My associates here call me Mah Jongg. It is private joke since it is the name of a popular Chinese game supposedly named by Confucius after a bird. It has another, more subtle meaning involving a certain craftiness. The head of our order felt I needed an occasional reminder to remain spiritual and avoid trying to be too clever. I might point out that is one issue I frequently find with clients who are lawyers—they often are too clever for their own good. I can tell just sitting here that both of you have the strong spirit of the fox. As with many things in life, it can be a good thing and a bad thing."

David and Clint tried to absorb all of this. David took another sip of tea and made a bowing motion that Clint copied.

"Max, or Mah Jongg, thank you for sharing your story and insight. It is a pleasure to officially meet you. I am David, and this is my friend Clint. We have been sent here by a powerful person in the US on a quest. We have some adversaries who would like to prevent this. Any of your suggestions would be well received."

The shaman took another drink of tea and sat pensively. "I have no definite opinion about your quest. A long life may be a goal for many, but the quality of each life is the heart of the question. As I have said, you both have qualities of the fox, but Clint also has those of the wild horse. You will need to focus on these traits to succeed in your quest. I can tell you that I sense danger for you and your associates tonight and recommend you heed this counsel. Peace be with you, go Dodgers, and l'chaim."

The shaman got up and bowed to them, and they bowed to him in return. He exited the room, leaving them to their thoughts. After some contemplation, their escort arrived and led them to change back into their clothes.

David and Clint looked at each other and started laughing. They certainly had not expected to see a Jewish shaman from Brooklyn, but his words still rang true. They couldn't shake the eerie feeling that his warning for tonight might come true. They felt they needed to talk with Jeffrey as soon as possible. They told Uri a bit about their meeting with the shaman, but decided not to tell him everything.

They walked back to their hotel, noticing the crowds were getting thicker in anticipation of tomorrow's festivities. They excused themselves from Uri and met up with Jeffrey. He was very concerned when they told him what the shaman had said about that evening. They were supposed to meet with the two sons of the nomad chieftain for dinner at a Western-styled restaurant called Millie's. The two sons had requested to go to the restaurant as they had hoped to try hamburgers and fries since much of their daily food consisted of mutton.

"I certainly don't want to get the chieftain's sons involved in any of our issues," said Jeffrey, clearing off his hotel bed to give Clint and David a place to sit. "Maybe we ought to cancel meeting with them and just see them tomorrow at the games."

"It's hard to say if it would be better or worse for the boys to meet with us," said Clint. "At least we know that if something were to happen tonight, we would be better prepared. Since we don't know their family, it would be difficult to let them know why we are concerned. I think we should still meet them, but maybe a change of scenery will change our luck."

David agreed and called Uri to try to change the restaurant. He used the excuse that he and Clint wanted to try an authentic Mongolian restaurant. Unfortunately, Uri said he couldn't reach the family of the boys so quickly, so they would have to meet at Millie's.

"Well," said Jeffrey, "I think the old proverb 'forewarned is forearmed' applies. No one best mess with these boys while I am around!"

The three split up to rest a bit before going out to eat. David and Clint knew that Jeffrey was psyching himself up for battle. They were a bit concerned they would be unleashing such a force in the restaurant, almost like igniting a spark in a hydrogen-filled space.

Clint, David, and Jeffrey met back up with Uri in the lobby at six that evening, and they all headed over to the Millie's. The warm night was made even warmer with the throngs of people wandering about. The bright reds and oranges of their clothing made the people look like large flowers. Some families were sitting in small groups under trees or next to buildings eating their dinners. Everyone seemed in a festive spirit.

The four made their way across the square to Millie's and were surprised at how westernized it looked. The decor reminded them of a Denny's or IHOP back in the states, though the furniture was made of heavy wood and not cheap plastic. Jeffrey was pleased his mass was easily supported by the well-constructed chairs.

Shortly after they were seated, they were met by their guests, the brother to the chieftain and his two nephews. Clint and David were pleased that they all spoke surprisingly good English. They all introduced themselves, bowing with their introductions.

"Our names may be a bit difficult for you to pronounce, but generally American names seem so short to us," the uncle said. "I am Ganzorig, and these are my nephews. Ganbaatar, which means steel hero, is our fierce wrestler who just turned sixteen. This is his brother Otgonbayar, which means youngest joy. He is our amazing eight-year-old rider. Both will compete in the Naadam tomorrow, and we are extremely proud they are representing our region. I know American names have meanings as well, but they seem not to carry the importance we believe names do here. I have left the rest of the men we have brought along outside since I don't think this restaurant could accommodate another dozen hungry Mongols. They have plenty of food that we brought with us from our camp, so don't feel sorry for them."

David, as usual, led the introductions of their group. "I am David, and my friends are Clint and Jeffrey. The name David is Hebrew for beloved. Although, I'm not sure too many of my associates would describe me as that. Our Mongolian guide is Uri, and he can translate anything you do not understand." David and the rest exchanged bows with their guests.

The boys were practically drooling over their hamburgers, French fries, and Cokes. These were not an everyday occurrence back on the steppes, but American food was becoming more common with Mongolia's leap into the twenty-first century.

Clint watched the boys devour their meals, and he couldn't help but smile at their excitement. Ganbaatar seemed older than sixteen with his muscular build. His dark brown eyes, black wavy hair, and quick smile surely must have caught the eye of a few Mongolian teen girls. His brother Otgonbayar was much quieter and had a more, wiry build. Being in the big city for the Naadam was clearly a major event for both of them.

As they ate, Ganzorig boasted about his nephews. He told them how Ganbaatar had wrestled last year and did fairly well for his age, and this year, he was favored to do quite well. He also told them how fearless Otgonbayar was as he would be racing twenty-five kilometers on horseback against boys almost twice his age. David thought he seemed too small for such a feat, but because the race was so long, he realized there was a definite advantage for a lighter rider.

The boys had wolfed down their food and slurped their Cokes, but the chocolate cake with ice cream really put them over the top. They would have ordered seconds, but their uncle was worried about them overeating since they had to compete the next day.

The adults sat back, sipping their Mongolian tea. They made arrangements to meet the next night after the competitions before David and Clint would take off to head to Northwest Mongolia for the meeting with the boys' father.

As they all leisurely got up to leave, a scarred disheveled man at the next table bumped into Ganbaatar and grabbed him by the arm, brandishing a knife. Jeffrey was a blur of motion. In one fell swoop, he grabbed the knife before it struck the boy and slammed it into the wooden table, burying the blade at least three inches into the wood. He then threw the aggressor against the wall and grabbed him by the neck. The boys' uncle started screaming at him in Mongolian and loudly called for help from his family waiting outside the restaurant. Soon, the restaurant was filled with a jumble of Mongolian men all yelling at the assailant. The assailant choked out a few pleas in Mongolian. Without missing a beat, the men took the assailant outside, leaving David, Clint, Jeffrey, and Uri with the boys. Jeffrey put his arm around the younger boy to comfort him.

In a few minutes, Ganzorig came back in and bowed to Jeffrey. "Thank you so much for your help," he said. "These boys are precious to me and my family, and we are indebted to you for your actions."

"I was only doing my job, sir," said Jeffrey. "I am glad no harm came to your nephews. Do you have any idea why someone would want to harm them?"

"We questioned the assailant, and he works for one of the betting dealers who handles wagers on the Naadam. Since Ganbaatar is one of the favorites, they were trying to hedge their bets by injuring him so he couldn't compete."

"Wow, that's pathetic! Who would want to win that way?" David said. "Your country seems so spiritual. I'm shocked something like this would happen."

"You are right. We are very spiritual people," said Ganzorig. "But just like everywhere else, we have nasty people here as well who are willing to make money any way possible."

The boys were fascinated with the knife embedded in the table and tried to pull it out. Jeffrey asked Ganzorig if he wanted it removed or left for the police.

"Oh no," he responded. "We won't be needing the police since no one was hurt. I am confused, though, as to how this man knew we were going to be here. Did anyone else know we would be eating at this restaurant?"

"Not that I know of, but we did have Uri try to reach you to see if you wanted to meet somewhere else. He said he couldn't get ahold of you," said Clint.

An angry expression washed over Ganzorig's face, and he rose to his feet while shouting at Uri. Uri then took off running out of the bar and was gone.

"Ganzorig, are you okay? What was that all about?" asked David.

"I have a cellphone. Uri could have easily reached me, so he must have been in on this little game. I am afraid we will have to get you another guide. Uri won't be doing much talking after my family is through with him."

"I'm sorry, Ganzorig. We had no idea," David said.

"It is not yours to worry about. I will introduce you to my nephew Saltar. He is a fishing guide and knows Mongolia very well. He will be a great guide. He does have one small weakness that could be a problem though. He is a bit obsessed—I think that is the right term—with the singer Bob Dylan. You might have to listen to a good deal of his music."

David and Clint looked at each other.

"Well, it could be worse," said David. "He could be into heavy metal or rap music. I think we can handle Dylan for the next week."

The waiter came over and again expressed his apologies in Mongolian and English for the attack on Ganbaatar. They all looked at the knife driven several inches into the middle of the wooden table. Jeffrey offered again to pull it out, but the waiter said there was no need as the owner was going to break off the blade and pound it through the table. Ganzorig thanked the staff for their help and then signaled to the boys it was time to leave.

"We have to be up early tomorrow for the events. We better get back to our camp to get some sleep. I hope to see you tomorrow, but if not, I will certainly see you at my brother's *ger* in Northwest Mongolia." He again bowed to Jeffrey. "You will always be welcome in my camp. I view you as kin for your heroism. We will have a celebration in your honor when we meet next. I sense the gods have brought you to us."

Jeffrey was moved by Ganzorig's words. "I am fond of your nephews and wish them well in their competitions tomorrow."

Jeffrey, Clint, and David each shook the boys' hands before heading out into the night. The rest of the boys' family bowed in respect as Jeffrey waved goodbye to them.

As they crossed the square to their hotel, David dodged a large determined woman pushing a cart with every type of basket imaginable.

"I think we need to thank Shaman Max for the heads-up in the restaurant tonight. Jeffrey, you sure made short work of that creep with the knife. I'm glad the boys are okay, and even happier that your bravery will surely help my negotiations with their father."

"I'm just happy that creep didn't hurt the boy," said Jeffrey. "I might have seriously injured him if he had."

Clint sighed. "I can't believe someone would actually be willing to injure one of the boys just to improve their betting odds. I guess we can never be too careful. As we learned from Timothy, we best keep our eyes open."

When they got back to their hotel, the three turned in for the night. Clint decided to call Molly—this time at a more reasonable hour than on their arrival. They caught up on their recent experiences. Molly was amused by the shaman from Brooklyn and shocked about the attack on the boy. She had difficulty conveying the bizarre journey involved with being Giselle's "secretary." Clint wondered how working for Giselle could be more peculiar than traveling through Mongolia, but he would take Molly at her word. He fell asleep dreaming of foxes and wild horses.

23 THE NAADAM

After his morning workout, Clint met David and Jeffrey for breakfast. They were accompanied by an interesting young Mongolian man who was clearly different from most. He was tall and thin and had obviously dyed blond hair. He was almost as animated as Giselle. When Clint approached the table, the young man had jumped up and thrown his arms around him.

"Clint, dear Clint, I am Saltar, the cousin of the boys you met last night and who you helped protect. You can call me Sal. I am delighted to take you to the Naadam games today and ferry you three across Mongolia. I studied political science and animal husbandry at UCLA for two years, which is why my English is pretty good. I know my uncle already warned you about my love for Bob Dylan, but I will try to keep it under control."

Clint was a bit overwhelmed but amused as well. "Nice to meet you, Sal. I am looking forward to seeing the events today and hope the boys do well. I'm not sure how poli-sci and animal husbandry go together, but knowing some of our politicians in the US, I guess that might explain some things."

David laughed. "I think most of our politicians belong in a barn more than our Capitol. I suspect your father chose your courses in animal science and you elected to take political science. Hopefully, you found both studies rewarding."

Sal spread his arms wide in a communal gesture. "All learning helps develop the mind, but I confess the California girls taught me more than all my professors combined."

They all laughed and settled into a fairly American breakfast with a few Mongolian touches. They had all given up on drinking coffee here and settled for the ubiquitous tea that most Mongolians drank.

While they ate, Sal gave them a briefing on the Naadam games they were going to see along with a history lesson. "The athletic games we are going to see date back before the time of Christ some seven thousand years ago, well before the Olympics ever existed. Stone tablets from the Bronze Age show wrestlers fighting and the three main events of the games. Our beloved leader and conqueror Genghis Khan is known to have had his troops wrestling to help maintain their strength.

"The current games consist of three sports, wrestling, archery, and horse racing. The first modern games started in 1921 after our separation from China and have continued until now. Regional Naadams are held around the country, but the main event is held here in Ulaanbataar on July 11 through July 13. We will be able to see the opening ceremony, the wrestling with my cousin Ganbaatar, and the archery. We can see the celebrations tonight, but unfortunately, we'll have to head out tomorrow to see my uncle so we may miss Otgonbayar riding. Since he is riding a two-year-old horse for fifteen kilometers, they may race later today, but we will have to see. You are probably tired of my talking, so

I will let you finish eating." He turned on his iPod and, with his earphones in place, closed his eyes to listen to Bobbie D. The rest of the group could faintly hear "Like a Rolling Stone" filtering across the table.

Clint laughed. "That seems like an appropriate song for the next part of our adventure."

"I would have thought with the winds across the steppes 'Blowing in the Wind' would be more appropriate," said David.

They finished their breakfast and headed out to the Naadam stadium along with flocks of people. With all the colors, the stadium looked like a giant kaleidoscope with a green field in the middle. There was a definite festive atmosphere and a palpable feeling of pride from both the spectators and participants. The stadium started to fill up by nine-thirty before the traditional honor guard, composed of nine riders with horsetail banners, opened the ceremony. The athletes began to file in, and at eleven, the ceremony began with a speech form the Mongolian president. Sal did his best to translate, but they could tell this certainly wasn't his favorite part of the program. The program began in earnest with singing, dancing, and traditional Mongolian music and horseback riders. Clint was impressed by the lack of pretense and commercialization of their simple ceremony and the joy that the performers and crowd shared.

Sal turned to his charges excitedly. "This is my favorite part of the Naadam—the wrestling. There are no weight classes or age divisions. The combatants are picked by lottery, though this was not always so and often leads to major disputes. They wear a traditional wrestling outfit composed of a short-sleeved jacket, or *jodag*, which is usually red or blue. This exposes their breasts to eliminate the possibility of a woman infiltrating the competition, which supposedly happened once in the distant past. They wear tight-fitting briefs, or *shuudag*, and leather boots."

"I bet we can get you one of these outfits, Clint. I'm sure Molly would find it quite alluring," David teased.

"We should get one of those outfits for Giselle," said Clint. "I'm sure you would find it interesting as well."

Sal continued, "The matches used to last for hours but are now limited to thirty minutes and take place on the grass you see in front of you. Each wrestler tries to get the other wrestler to touch the ground with some part of his body other than his feet or palms. There are many moves and strategies involved, and it is not always the biggest or strongest contestant who wins. Ganbaatar is one of the lightest wrestlers and probably the youngest, but he is very fast and has been training hard. I even practiced against him and was on the ground in less than fifteen seconds.

"The other thing I like about the competition is that each wrestler does an eagle dance before and after competing. I confess that I still like an element of spiritualism in our culture, even though most of my family probably thinks I have been 'over westernized.' I think Dylan has an element of spirituality in his music, and it may be why I like him. But enough of my musings—my cousin is up next. I brought some binoculars for all of us."

Sure enough, they could see young Ganbaatar in traditional costume doing his eagle dance. He certainly looked more graceful than his opponent, but no points were given for grace in this competition. The other man was definitely older and at least twenty-five pounds heavier than Ganbaatar. At the signal, both men began circling each other and shortly were in a bear embrace. With a deft kick, Ganbaatar hit one of his opponent's legs out from under him and threw him onto his back. In less than a minute, Ganbaatar had won his first match. The crowd went wild as he did his celebratory eagle dance. Sal and the rest of his family clearly were the loudest in the stadium.

"That was impressive!" shouted Clint. "Your cousin certainly is fast and strong."

"Very impressive indeed!" said Jeffrey. "Now it is time for food and drink before his next contest."

"You are a man after my own heart, Jeffrey," said Sal. "It is time to introduce you all to *khuushuur* and *airag*, mutton sandwiches and fermented mare's milk. The airag is somewhat of an acquired taste and can be a bit hard on the stomach. Beer or vodka might be more your style."

"Mongolian beer and mutton sandwiches it is, Sal," said David. "We need to toast your cousin for his first victory."

They strolled to the tents and found the lines were not too long since it was still early in the event. Sal helped them with their purchases and soon they were back in the stands enjoying their food and drink. The sandwiches were quite tasty, but Clint wondered how much lamb he would have to eat over the next week.

The matches went fairly quickly in the early going. They started with 512 contestants, and each wrestler who lost was eliminated from the competition.

Ganbaatar was able to win his next two matches due to his amazing speed. His third match was more difficult since his opponent outweighed him by at least fifty pounds. In the fourth round, his luck ran out. He was matched against a former champion who outweighed him by at least seventy pounds. Even against such a brute, Ganbaatar was able to hang on for over fifteen minutes and even came close to knocking the giant off his feet once. The champion was able to ultimately force Ganbaatar to the ground. Even though he lost, the crowd went wild cheering his performance. In recent years, no one less than eighteen had ever made it to the fourth round. After the match, the champion bowed to Ganbaatar in respect for his efforts.

The competition continued for another two hours, becoming a battle of wills, strategy, strength, and pure body mass. It was like watching ten championship wrestling matches back to back. The winner, reaching the class of Giant, did his eagle dance around the entire group of wrestlers. The crowd rose as one and bowed to him, shouting praises.

Sal took out his earplugs and let them know the wrestler who had beaten Ganbaatar came in third overall. He explained that the highest- ranking wrestlers carry their rank forever and have a great deal of respect. Some have even been elected to the Mongolian Parliament.

Clint looked up and was surprised to see Ganbaatar in a dark blue deel with a golden silk sash climbing up into the stands toward them. The spectators applauded him and bowed as he passed by. He seemed quite embarrassed. He and Sal embraced, and David, Clint, and Jeffrey all congratulated him. There was a remarkable change in his demeanor. The boy they had met yesterday was gone, and in front of them stood a young man, eager to find his place in the world. Sal explained this change to his charges, stating the crowd now looked at Ganbaatar as likely one of the next grand champions and possibly the youngest ever to get that title.

David, Clint, and Jeffrey quizzed Ganbaatar on his matches, while Sal went to get him some food. Jeffrey was especially interested in some of the holds that he had used. Ganbaatar humbly explained his tactics, but their conversation was cut short as the next event began.

The archery events commenced with both men and women in teams shooting with composite bows at leather targets. These targets were placed at sixty-five meters for women and seventy-five meters for men. Some of the archers were amazing, and Clint was truly impressed, considering his past experience with the bow.

Sal returned with food and vodka, and they enjoyed another meal in the stands. He confirmed that the general talk at the event was about Ganbaatar and how well he did for his weight and age. His father would be very proud. Unfortunately, the riding events were going to be the next day, so they wouldn't be able to watch Otgonbayar ride. They would, however, be able to see the fireworks and festivities later that night in the square.

Sal had made arrangements for their trip to Northwest Mongolia. He had a Jeep set up for their 425-mile drive from Ulaanbaatar to Moron.

"The highway is better than it used to be, but the journey will still take nine to ten hours," Sal said. "Fortunately, we can take Dylan along with us for the ride. We should get you some leather satchels and flatter bags for your clothes instead of the suitcases you brought for our horses to carry."

"Couldn't we fly to Moron?" asked David. "I heard there is an airport there now."

"My uncle feels you should get a better feel of Mongolia by making the drive," explained Sal. "I'm also not too crazy about the old Russian airliners they use on that route. We may take a Russian chopper from Lake Khövsgöl Nuur to our camp, but we can discuss that on our way to Moron. Unless you want to watch more of the archery, I think we should head out to complete our errands before we get stuck in the crowds when exiting. I'm sure since we are with my dear cousin we will cause a definite roadblock."

"To be honest, it is a whole lot more interesting to do archery than to watch it," said Clint. "We should celebrate Ganbaatar's win however he wants."

"Actually, I have to get back to my brother and our uncle for the award ceremony after the archery events," said Ganbaatar. "Honestly, I am more excited to see my brother race than celebrate my wins. I may not get a chance to see all of you again until we are back home. Goodbye and thanks for coming to see the Naadam."

"It has been our pleasure," said David. "It was an honor to watch you wrestle. We will enjoy seeing you back at your home."

They climbed back out of the stands and exited the stadium. Some of the shops outside the stadium were open, so they were able to buy sturdy bags to hold their clothes. Then, they headed back to the hotel and arranged to meet for the festivities that night.

* * *

That evening there was a major celebration in Ulaanbaatar, as was customary for the first day of Naadam. The booms and bursts of fireworks shone over a crowd of tipsy patrons who oohed and aahed over the colorful lights and echoes of cannon-like eruptions. Clint, David, and Jeffrey looked forward to contributing to the general mayhem. They met Sal, who wore his newly embroidered Ganbaatar T-shirt, and headed to one of the better- known brewpubs, the Chinggis Club. A long line of hungry customers packed the place. Sal winked at his group and disappeared inside. Within a few minutes, he returned with the manager, who shook their hands, and led them to a table in the back.

"Okay, Sal," said David, "how many of our firstborn children did you have to promise to the manager to get us a table?"

Sal laughed. "I just told him that I was Ganbaatar's cousin and would get him an autograph on today's program to give to his son if we were seated. We probably could have had five tables if we wanted them. I just have to drop off the program for him tomorrow before we take off. Speaking of which, we will need to leave early tomorrow—say six in the morning—to avoid the traffic from the Naadam and to get too Moron before dark. I have been instructed by my uncle to tell you about Northern Mongolia and give you a bit of history about Genghis Khan, our most illustrious ancestor. It is only reasonable that we start this in a brewpub named after him."

Their waiter arrived, and within minutes, they were sampling an official Chinggis beer on tap in the appropriate glass. Clint and David agreed Mongolian beer was worthy of its ancestry. Of course, they had to follow up with bottles of Khar Khorum and Golden Gobi. The latter had even won a grand gold medal from the Monde Institute in Belgium in 2007. They happily dove into their German food prepared by the in-house German chef. Eating bratwurst and Wiener schnitzel and drinking beer in Mongolia was a bit surreal, but no more so than some of their other recent adventures.

After dinner, they headed back to the hotel, stopping at the square to watch some of the fireworks. The night was still warm, and smells of the many small barbecues would have made them hungry if they hadn't recently feasted. Navigating across the square was a challenge given their recent imbibing and the masses of people everywhere. Most were congenial, so frequent bumps and a shoulder here of there was not a problem. Even still, by the time they made it back to their hotel, they felt as if they had just survived their own wrestling tournament. They headed up to their rooms for a shortened night given their early departure.

David and Clint met in David's room for a long overdue strategy session. David had brought a couple of bottles of Khar Khorum to help their thoughts flow a bit more easily. David opened the bottles, and he and Clint toasted one another.

"So, Brother Clint, what do you think of Mongolia so far?" David asked.

"Well," said Clint, "I can't speak much about Mongolia in general, since we have only seen Ulaanbaatar, but I get the sense that the people here have a certain innocence, spirituality, and graciousness that one does not find elsewhere. I find this to be interesting since the rest of the world often remembers Genghis Khan and Mongolians as blood thirsty. I'm starting to feel as though that is a misconception, but I guess the spirituality aspect may be more from the nomads we have met rather than the general population in the city."

"I agree with you. We have certainly seen another side to Mongolians. The nomads seem to have a spirituality about them, and they also have a sense of resilience or independence that they may well need with the evolution of their country," David said. "I'm grateful we've had the nomad chieftain and Mr. Marcum to orchestrate our trip so far, but I think we may eventually need to direct our own path. My negotiations with the chieftain should prove interesting if nothing else."

Clint sighed. "Let's hope our negotiations are left at interesting and nothing else. We've already been threatened once on this trip, and that's enough for me."

David laughed. "Come on, old man, nothing like a knife fight to keep us young and on our toes! Though, we probably should keep Jeffrey around just in case. Since we both have an early start tomorrow, we better get our beauty rest," David teased and then headed to the bathroom to get ready for bed.

After his ablutions, David had to admit he missed his feisty little whirlwind, Giselle. In the wink of an eye she exploded into his cell phone despite being thousands of miles away.

"So, you Jewish miscreant, how are you doing with those Mongolian wenches?" She laughed.

David sighed. "There is only one wench I'm interested in at the moment, and she's back in Paris."

Giselle was surprised. "I just may have to double our usual amorous activities on your return."

"I don't know if I can handle Giselle times two."

The two carried on talking late into the night.

24 DRIVING ACROSS MONGOLIA WITH BOBBY D

David and Clint groaned in the morning at the sound of their alarms. Still bleary-eyed, they met up with Jeffrey and a very excited Sal in front of the hotel. Sal was loading a red Jeep Wrangler with their luggage and supplies they would need for their trip.

"Most of the vehicles one can get to travel to Moron are old Russian trucks or Japanese cars," said Sal. "I was able to score a Jeep from the car agency using my newest negotiation technique, telling them I am Ganbaatar's cousin and will send them a picture of him. You can bet I'm going to ride this out while it lasts." Sal laughed. "Oh, and check out the beverages I got for you three!"

Jeffrey opened the cooler in the back of the car and proudly showed them the case of Mongolian beer Sal had gotten them.

"Goodness, Sal," said Clint. "You have been busy. If you keep this up, you'll have American travelers beating down your door for your services, maybe even your share of foreign women."

Sal laughed. "I would love that, but I have to admit, I find Mongolian women more appealing despite their less free-spirited sexual mores."

The men all laughed at Sal's honesty as they finished loading the Jeep. It was quiet on the square when they headed out, but some of the vendors were already setting up for another crazy day of Naadam doings. A large cadre of cleaners was sweeping up after last night's mayhem.

As they left Ulaanbaatar, they experienced the same abrupt transition from city to country they had on their arrival. It still struck them as odd that fifteen minutes after leaving the downtown of a large city all one could see was a strip of highway surrounded by an endless vista of high prairie with short grasses and low brush punctuated by an occasional tree.

The highway, as explained by Sal, had been upgraded, allowing them to drive on a paved road for most of their trip. Sal asked Jeffrey to pass around cups, a thermos with hot Mongolian tea, and some biscuits he acquired from the hotel kitchen. The highway was virtually empty, and soon David, Clint, and Jeffrey were dozing off to the sounds of the road and muffled Bob Dylan music pulsing from Sal's earphones.

They woke with a start when Sal stopped fairly suddenly for a group of nomads herding their sheep across the road. Clint was awestruck by children as young as five or six riding horses next to their parents with an ease that could only have been born from years of riding.

When they continued on, Sal took off his earphones and spoke in a more serious tone. "As I mentioned yesterday, my uncle requested I 'educate' you three about our great ancestor Genghis Khan. I know you three are well-read, and I'm sure you already know some of his history, but I must follow his orders. To most Mongolians, even though he lived eight hundred years ago, Genghis Khan is more revered than George Washington, Abraham Lincoln, and John F. Kennedy rolled into one for Americans. It is incomprehensible to many how he was able to conquer most of the known world of his day starting at age forty. He incorporated military strategy unknown prior to his methods, like his 'flash warfare,' which caught opposing armies off guard and allowed him to defeat much larger forces. He drove villagers adjacent to fortified cities into these cities to disrupt their ability to fight. He organized his warriors into units of ten, then one hundred, and then one thousand so they could fight together more effectively. He attacked from unexpected directions and often at several points at once, all the while, using materials found at their battle sites.

"He united various warring tribes across Mongolia, and he changed the basic structure of how soldiers were rewarded and how the people were ruled. He did not discriminate based on religion and allowed foreigners to practice their own religions. Some of these ideas now don't sound so unique, but many were quite innovative eight hundred years ago."

David chimed in, "I know Genghis Khan was a great warrior and is important in Mongolian history, but I'm not sure why your uncle feels we need a history lesson about him. I'm not trying to be rude. I'm just curious about his reasons."

"You will be able to ask my uncle directly when we meet with him," said Sal. "But I think he feels it is an important part of who we are and might explain some of our motivations and why they might be different from yours. I think the biggest lesson from the Great Khan was his strategy in using limited resources to overcome what seemed like insurmountable obstacles. That could be as important today as it was eight hundred years ago."

David clapped Sal on the shoulder, almost causing him to drive off the road. "I like how you cut to the chase. When things are settled here, I may have to make you an offer and steal you away from that uncle of yours. In the meantime, I would like to hear a bit about your uncle. I suspect he may have inherited more than a nomad's interest in sheepherding from the Great Khan. What do you say we crack open some of those beers as we continue this conversation, unless that would be violating some Mongolian law against driving with open liquor containers in the car."

"Considering the closest thing to a highway patrolman is likely more than two hundred kilometers away, I don't think that would be a problem," said Sal. "Please, help yourself. As for your offer, I suppose I would be open to it once I deliver you three to my uncle. If you are serious, I confess if I were to take a job outside of Mongolia, I would need to return here at least six months out of the year however. Like I said, I like the US, but Mongolia is my home."

Uncle Shugam has inherited a good deal from the Great Khan as you suggested. He is in his early fifties and has typical Mongolian features. He is as strong as a yak and as sharp as an eagle. My uncle is the head of five families who travel together and is in charge of about one hundred people. He speaks Mongolian, English, Mandarin, and Russian. He trades with a number of cities and other nomadic tribes. Currently, he is training a group of young men in a Mongolian version of martial arts, but I don't completely know what that is about. He goes hunting for small game with my father using an eagle to catch prey, but is just as comfortable playing huzur, a Mongolian card game."

Clint laughed. "I can't imagine using an eagle to hunt, maybe a drone but not an eagle."

The sleeping giant Jeffrey stretched and broke his silence. "Enough about Mongolia and Genghis Khan. It is time to stop and eat, or you will have a cranky bodyguard on your hands. I would advise avoiding that if possible."

"We should be close to Erdenet," said Sal. "We can get gas and something to eat there. They have a great little vegetarian restaurant in the city, but I can find a meat and potatoes place if you prefer."

"Do I look like a vegetarian kind of guy?" Jeffrey asked. "Bring on the meat, Mr. Sal."

"Your wish is my command," said Sal. "No need to call me mister."

When they pulled into Erdenet, they found two restaurants side by side. David, Clint, and Sal ate at a great vegetarian restaurant and bakery, Eternal Springs, and Jeffrey happily munched on meat and potatoes at the bar next door. They all gorged themselves on baked goods, which they washed down with cold beer, before they got gas and headed on to Moron.

When they got back in the car, Jeffrey took over driving, and Sal tried to teach David and Clint Mongolian card games.

The countryside gradually transformed from high steppes to more forested foothills. It was late morning, but even in the midday sun, they could feel a slight drop in temperature and change in the grasses and livestock they saw at the nomad camps they passed. David was a quick study and already was starting to beat Sal at their card games. Although, he wondered if Sal was letting him win on purpose in hopes of further securing a job.

"Okay, Sal," David said. "Please remind me why we are driving across your beautiful country when we could have flown to Moron in ninety minutes instead."

"This journey is a pictorial essay about the heart of Central and Northern Mongolia, which is not something you can get by flying over it," said Sal. "The chieftain wants you to get a real sense of our country. Why? I cannot say, but you will meet him shortly and can ask him yourself. He also wants you to see Lake Khövsgöl, which is north of Moron. The lake is such a deep blue that I think it even puts some oceans to shame. It holds 1-2 percent of the world's fresh water. It is a spiritual place and great for boating, fishing, and horseback riding. Surrounded by lush forests, it is one of the most beautiful places I have seen in this world."

David put down his cards. "I understand your uncle's desire to give us a sense of Mongolia, but I am concerned that there are some dangers related to a leisurely stroll through your fair country. I am sure Lake Khövsgöl is beautiful, but we can get a sense of this in a helicopter heading from Moron to your uncle's camp. Driving to Lake Khövsgöl and then horseback riding a couple of days to your uncle's camp sounds like fun, but we are not here for fun. Please set up a helicopter for tomorrow, and either Mr. Marcum or I will pay for it."

Sal was a bit distressed by David's direct manor but was a true guide. "We will be near Bulgan soon and should have cellphone service. I will call and arrange the helicopter for tomorrow morning, and we should be at my uncle's camp by noon tomorrow."

Jeffrey was very excited. "I love chopper rides almost as much as eating a good meal. There is no better way to cover difficult terrain in a hurry. The military appreciates a helicopter's use, but it is underutilized for civilians."

Clint had some reservations. "I would much rather take a motorcycle on rugged terrain than a chopper. Maybe I can meet you there tomorrow night and get a cycle to use in Moron."

David gave Clint his usual stare. "Considering all the other things the two of us have done together, I would think a helicopter ride would be the least of your worries. Jeffrey, any words of wisdom about our ride tomorrow?"

Jeffrey thought a moment. "Always pee before you fly in a chopper if you can. There are no bathrooms. Otherwise, sit back and enjoy the ride."

"Sage advice from the big man," said David, picking up his cards.

The rest of the ride to Moron was quiet, and Sal was able to book their helicopter for the next morning. They arrived before dark and checked into the 50°100° Hotel. Sal had always liked that it was named for being close to fifty Degrees north latitude and one hundred Degrees east longitude. It didn't hurt that the staff was friendly and the food was the best in town either. They ate and polished off the rest of their beers before settling down for the night.

Clint's phone was ringing when he got back to his room. He thought this a bit odd, especially since the number was not his daughter's or Molly's. He was surprised to hear Timothy's anxious voice when he connected the call.

"Clint, for God's sake, I have been trying to get hold of you for the last hour. Those damned Russians have kidnapped Molly and my sister. I'm scared out of my mind, and my dad's bodyguards have been buzzing around here trying to figure out what to do. My dad wants to hold off on calling the police since the message we got said they would be released if we forwarded the info I got on the first USB drive. I think I still have that on my computer. What do you think I should do?"

Clint tried not to freak out. He set down the phone and paced back and forth in his room a few times before finally responding. "Holy shit."

"I know, but I need you to help," Tim tried to say calmly.

"I'm stuck five thousand miles away from Paris when Molly needs me most. I have to get David and Jeffrey so we can make some sort of plan. Stay on the phone while I run down to get them. In the meantime, I need you to think of anything else you know about the girls' situation."

Clint ran down the hall and pounded on both Jeffrey's and David's doors. "Come to my room immediately!" he yelled.

Without asking a single question, the two men followed Clint back to his room.

Clint picked the phone back up, placed it on speaker, and then asked, "Did they let you talk to either of them?"

"The girls went shopping today, while Giselle was working, and the bodyguards stayed here with me since we did not think the girls would be in danger. Then, they didn't show up for dinner, and I get a call from these goons telling me they have the girls and will happily return them in exchange for the info I got in Brussels. They put Marguerite on briefly. She was hysterical and a bit hard to understand, but it was definitely her. She said they weren't hurt, but that's all she said. One of the goons got back on and said they had no desire to hurt the girls. I'm supposed to leave an envelope with the USB in it an hour from now in the middle of the Pont Neuf next to an artist with a large blue easel. I am to keep walking, and the girls will be released in front of the main gate of Notre Dame shortly after. They claim that the girls will be taken out of France tonight if we call the police or do not follow their instructions."

Clint did his best to control himself. "Did you get to talk to Molly at all?"

"No," said Timothy. "The goons just let me talk briefly to my sister. Do you think I should go ahead and give them the info despite my dad's wishes? Should I call the police? Tell me what to do."

"It's time to be your own man, Timothy," said David. "You need to put on your big boy pants. I say you give them the info. Hold off on calling the police until you get the girls or if they are not released. I really don't think they want to bother transporting the girls and doubt they would kill them knowing Marguerite's father and the three of us would follow them to the ends of the earth to get revenge."

"I agree," said Clint. "You only have fifty-five minutes to get the info to the drop point. You need to get moving. Don't go alone. Take your bodyguards with you, and they can get advice from Jeffrey here on where to position themselves."

"I agree with this plan," said Jeffrey. "Get going, and let me talk with my cohorts while you are on the move."

The trio in Mongolia felt a surge of adrenaline, but there was nothing they could do for the next hour.

They agreed on the Russian answer to such situations—vodka. They settled into David's room and began pouring shots of the local favorite, Chinggis Khan Vodka, and watching the minute hand of the clock in the room. Snails climbing a ten-thousand-foot mountain could have easily outpaced the lethargic movement of that clock.

25 THE CAPTIVES

Molly and Marguerite sat fuming in a surprisingly well-appointed room, considering they were hostages taken in broad daylight in downtown Paris. Their two big captors basically ignored them and were in a heated discussion, likely about what was going to be their fate. Escape seemed unlikely considering the size of their opponents, who were armed with guns and knives. *At least we aren't restrained*, thought Molly. She considered her tai chi classes and just how much power she could muster with one of her leg kicks. Her musings were interrupted by a loud knock at the door. *Perhaps the Parisian police have arrived for our rescue*, she thought.

Her hopes were crushed as a well-dressed elderly man came in and started screaming at their abductors in what sounded like Russian. With his high-end Versace suit and Fendi shoes, he looked more like a wealthy businessman and not someone who would be involved in a kidnapping. He made his way over to the two ladies.

"I am Viktor Krashenko, and unfortunately, I must decide what to do with you two young ladies. Marguerite, your father and I are in a form of competition to obtain some valuable information, and it seems you two are pawns that have fallen into our little chess match."

"We don't know anything about that, so why don't you let the two of us go, and you two can play your silly game without us," said Molly.

Viktor shook his head. "Unfortunately, Molly, that is not how this particular game is being played. I did not ask my employees to detain you, but they saw an opportunity and here you are. I may lack a bit of the finesse that Mr. Marcum has, but I still know how to get the job done."

"No matter what is at stake, my father would never have someone beaten or killed, and he certainly wouldn't kidnap innocent women. That doesn't sound like a game to me, and I am sure the French authorities would agree!" Marguerite was shouting, and Molly didn't try to quiet her down.

Viktor started to raise his voice as well. "Your father is not as innocent as you picture him. There is reason that there are so few billionaires in the world. A man of that stature is required to be ruthless at times, and both your father and I have had to play that part along the way."

Marguerite looked directly at Viktor. "So just how ruthless would you expect my father to be with someone who kidnapped his only daughter and had his son beaten? I would advise you to let Molly and me go as quickly as possible to limit the retribution that you know is coming your way."

Viktor laughed. "I can certainly see some of your father's vinegar in you. Your father's move in our little match is due any minute, and if he gives me the information I want, you will be walking out of here without a scratch. Now, please excuse me while I talk with my men for a bit."

Viktor went over to his men and gave them instructions in Russian. Shortly after, one of the men holstered his weapon and headed out the door. He was back within ten minutes with a large manila envelope, which they eagerly opened. A USB drive fell onto the table, and Viktor quickly put it in one of the computers. The men boasted, and Viktor triumphantly patted one of his guards on the shoulder.

Molly whispered to Marguerite, "Looks like they got whatever info they wanted. I wish I could speak Russian to hear what they are going to do with us."

Marguerite whispered back, "Me too. The only Russian I know is from a soap opera I used to watch. My guess, though, is that they're going to hold us to see what else they can get from my father."

"Assholes," said Molly as she felt her blood pressure rise. She then shouted, "Hey, Viktor! Marguerite has diabetes and will need her insulin if we have to stay much longer."

Viktor gave them an annoyed glance. He quickly crossed the room and smacked Molly in the face with the back of his hand. "I suspect you're lying and just trying to manipulate me. Lie to me again and you'll be met with my fist, not just a little love tap."

Molly was furious and began to act hysterical, shouting, "Whatever you say, but remember I warned you when she passes out and her breathing starts to get fast and she smells like nail polish! When that happens, you'll have to take us to the hospital, and I'm sure the authorities will have a lot of questions."

"All right." Viktor said with irritation. "You can drop the act. My plan all along was to let you go, but I did enjoy your pathetic attempt to trick me. Please, Marguerite, tell your father I was a real gentleman to you both."

"I doubt a gentleman goes around kidnapping and abusing young women," said Molly.

"You don't think I'm a gentleman?" Viktor's tone turned angry. "Let me help you with that sharp tongue." Viktor then raised his hand again. His henchmen drew their guns, pointing them at the girls. The girls froze in place, afraid to move. Seeing the fear in the faces, Viktor waved off the guns and lowered his hand, regaining his composure and laughing with delight at his ability to invoke fear. He straightened his suit and said, "I suggest you learn some manners, Molly. Not many are as forgiving as I am. Now, get these girls out of my sight."

Marguerite rushed to Molly's side, but before she could say anything, Viktor's henchmen covered the girls' eyes and dragged them out of the room.

The girls bounced around in the back of what felt like a van. They clung to each other, not knowing what would happen to them next. *Why couldn't I just keep my mouth shut?* Molly wondered worriedly. The van then came to a sudden stop, tossing the girls forward. They heard the back door open and were then thrown onto a cement sidewalk.

As the van peeled away, Marguerite could hear her brother calling to her. At the sound of Timothy's voice, she and Molly ripped away their blindfolds.

Timothy rushed to his sister, scooping her and Molly into his arms. "Are you okay? Are you hurt? Did they hurt you?" Timothy repeated.

"I'm fine. We're fine," Marguerite said, trying to calm her brother. "They hit Molly, but we're alive. I can't believe we're alive!"

Timothy examined Molly's face, noticing the welt across her cheek. "Oh, Molly. I'm sorry. Let's get out of the street. There's a café across the way where we can get some ice and call Clint."

They went across the street to a nearby café and made a host of phone calls. Molly pressed a towel full of ice onto her aching cheek as she assured Clint she was okay. Aside from his initial reaction to hunt down Viktor to kill him for hitting Molly, Clint and the others were overjoyed the girls were safe. Even Mr. Marcum breathed a sigh of relief that his daughter had remained unharmed. After apologizing to Molly for her run-in, he made both Marguerite and Timothy promise to fly back to the states as soon as they could.

"Now that the Russians have the USB, I fear their next stop will be Mongolia," Timothy confessed to the group.

Molly was not excited to hear that Clint was headed for a showdown in Mongolia with the same Russians who had kidnapped her, but at least they would have a heads-up on what was headed their way.

"Don't worry, Timothy. If Mongolia is their next stop, we'll be ready," Jeffrey said.

26 CHOPPERS AND CHIEFTAIN SHUGAM

Clint, David, and Jeffrey were all foggy from too much vodka, too much excitement, and too little sleep. They weren't prepared for a way too exuberant Sal at seven in the morning. A general wave of euphoria was mixed with the realization that an upcoming battle with their Russian counterparts was inevitable. Jeffrey, however, caught some of Sal's enthusiasm about their helicopter journey after downing a dozen eggs. The rest sat quietly drinking their tea after breakfast until Sal could no longer stand it.

"What in the world happened to you all last night?" he finally asked. "I know you must have been drinking, but something has you three distracted as a teen with a new video game. Please remember we are seeing one of the world's most majestic bodies of water today, Lake Khövsgöl. I just may have to dive out of the chopper to get your attention."

David did not want to tell Sal about the girls' abduction, so he simply said that they heard their Russian counterparts were headed to the same nomad camp that they were visiting. "You can understand our concern for your family's safety," said David.

"I'm sure Uncle Shugam can handle almost any situation headed our way," said Sal. "He has more resources than you can imagine."

"Even still, we will need to prepare for some sort of onslaught. I will be happy to coordinate such efforts," Jeffrey said.

"Sounds good to me," said Sal. "Onward to the lake, the blue pearl of Mongolia, and then on to my uncle's camp. Prepare yourselves, gentlemen, for some spectacular views. I love helicopters."

Jeffrey laughed. "Reminds me of the scene from *Apocalypse Now* when they say, 'I love the smell of Napalm in the morning' as the choppers dive over the jungle."

Clint was slightly shocked. "Boy, Jeffrey, you sure tend to put a military spin on things."

Jeffrey mused, "When your father was a general, your first toy you can remember was GI Joe, you went to military school, and you served three tours in the marines, it does tend to make you look at things from a military perspective. I am quite capable of appreciating pure beauty however, and that is what I am looking forward to today."

"Sorry, Jeffrey," said Clint. "Just the thought of Napalm seemed so incongruous to the pictorial setting we are about to see."

They all headed out, and after a brief pee stop, they scrambled aboard a waiting helicopter. Jeffrey, of course, had to check out the blades and gears and the pilot's credentials before they took off. Soon, they were over the lake, and the deep cobalt blue seemed surreal.

"How would you describe the blue below us?" asked Sal.

"Dark blue," said Jeffrey.

"I'd call it astronaut blue, like the kind they see from space," said David

"Like the blue of Molly's eyes," said Clint dreamily.

"Okay, my dear friend Clint," said David. "I do believe you and Molly are crossing into a more serious relationship, you old sap, but I have to agree with you. We can officially call the blue from Lake Khövsgöl 'Molly's eyes blue.'"

They watched the boaters and kayakers as they eventually headed east along the shore and then over the dense larch forests. Clint was sorry he didn't have the time to ride a horse or his Harley through the trails. When they passed over the fairly large rivers, he thought about how amazing it would be to go fly-fishing for the huge taimen, the giant trout that swam in these waters.

Within a few hours they could see a large clearing in the dense forest and the familiar white gers dotting the landscape with flocks of sheep and teams of horses. Children started pouring out of the gers, running to a staked out area that was obviously their landing spot. Some jumped on their horses and rode around the area.

"Okay," said Sal. "A few last minute suggestions. Mongolians are very gracious and accommodating, but we have some quirks as all cultures do. Try not to step on the threshold of the ger as you enter. Circle the ger in a clockwise manor upon entering. Watch your hosts and try to emulate their actions. Lastly, tonight there will be a special ceremony for Jeffrey for his help protecting Ganbaatar. They will prepare a sheep as the main course in the traditional manner. Jeffrey, be aware we eat all of the sheep to honor it for giving us this meal. You, as the special guest, will be offered parts of the head you might not normally eat."

Jeffrey laughed. "I have never been known to refuse food offered in my direction, no matter what. I don't think that will be a problem."

The chopper swept in fairly easily into the landing area. The blades struggled a bit because of the altitude, but with little fanfare, they were on the ground with hordes of cheerful Mongolian children wrapped around the helicopter.

Sal yelled out in Mongolian for them to stay away and threw handfuls of candy he had brought for the occasion. With the engine off, the four passengers jumped out, keeping their heads down, though Jeffrey was really the only one who had any real reason for concern. Each of them instantly had one or more little set of Mongolian hands grabbing theirs and guiding them to the ger of what must be Chieftain Shugam.

The children stayed outside and David, Clint, and Jeffrey were surprised at the quiet, homey feel inside the ger. Chieftain Shugam looked up from a book he was reading and greeted his visitors. He looked quite vigorous despite being fifty-some years old, and his intense walnut eyes scanned each of them in turn. His stoic presence gave little doubt that he was totally in charge and they were his guests subject to his authority.

He greeted his nephew first. "Sal, or should I say Dylan, it is good to see you again. I am pleased you were able to get our guests here without incident."

Sal smiled. "It was my pleasure, Uncle Shugam. I think it was a learning experience for all of us. Allow me to introduce my new friends David, Clint, and Jeffrey."

Uncle Shugam rose and gripped each of their arms in turn, and they responded in kind. On meeting Jeffrey, the chieftain bowed his head slightly.

"Thank you, Jeffrey, for protecting my son during the Naadam," Shugam began in nearly perfect English. "Because of your efforts, he was able to participate in the wrestling tournament and with some success. We will have a special celebration tonight in your and his honor."

Jeffrey bowed his head in return. "That is very kind of you, sir. I like your son, and it was my privilege to come to his aid."

Shugam turned to David and Clint. "It is my pleasure to meet you two as well. I know you have come far to discuss some issues. I have no desire to delay these negotiations. Living a nomad's existence, I prefer to be direct in my business dealings. You may have some lunch and tour our grounds here with Sal, and we can meet back here at two in the afternoon to begin our discussions."

David was pleased at such a direct approach to their negotiations. "It is Clint's and my pleasure to be invited to your home, and we'd also like to thank Sal for his gracious help in our getting here as well as for his cultural tips along the way. I agree entirely that a direct approach to business saves time and leads to better results."

In less than ten minutes, the group was back outside and once again the center of attention for a group of cute Mongolian children. From their energy and activity, one could see these children were not captive to video games or TV. Sal took the group around to see the sheep and the short muscular horses. The children showed off their riding.

Sal then brought them to meet his parents and shy younger brother. It was difficult to imagine that the two were related. His parents had prepared a simple lunch of cheeses and whey. Sal was happy that none of them were lactose intolerant.

After eating, they met some of the other adults in the camp, each working on a specific task. One group of seven fit young men practiced modified exercises and military-like maneuvers. Jeffrey tried to talk with them through Sal, but they were quite evasive. The group then followed Sal down to a small dock on a pristine river and could see several boats with fly fishermen happily tossing huge flies with definite expertise in search of the giant local trout.

At two, they were back at Shugam's ger. Sal advised there was no need to knock. He suggested instead yelling in Mongolian "Please hold the dog" if entering a strange ger. The four entered and found Shugam back at his desk reading. Sal was surprised to see only three chairs set out in front of the desk and realized this was an accommodation for their guests and did not include him.

Sal was somewhat hurt, but Uncle Shugam was not to be questioned. Shugam thanked Sal for his help and advised him that he would not be needed for this meeting.

"I know the three of you represent Cornwell Marcum, a wealthy man from San Francisco," said Shugam. "He would like to buy from me and my family an ancient recipe for long life and strength. You may think this is nonsense, but I doubt Mr. Marcum would have sent you halfway around the world if he didn't believe this to be true. Our negotiation, however, is complicated by my disinterest in significant monetary gain from any sale and my general concern regarding the use of our recipe. I know you are also aware of a counter proposal from a Russian investor, though that does come with certain risks. You can understand why this is not your typical negotiation."

"We are aware of this counter proposal," David said with a nod.

"I apologize in advance for sharing a bit more of Mongolian history but feel you will appreciate its significance as it relates to our current surroundings in Mongolia and our negotiations. I know Sal has discussed briefly with you our beloved ancestor Genghis Khan and his exploits eight hundred years ago. A sidebar to his story happened when one of his trusted shamans Dayan Derkh made off with the youngest wife of the Khan. Genghis and his men eventually caught up with them near here at a spiritual cave. Rather than be captured, the shaman turned himself to stone, according to legend. The Dalai Lama convinced the stone shaman to convert to

Buddhism, and Genghis left appeased. A Buddhist monastery was built nearby in memory of this episode and, at times, had upward of one thousand monks. It is known as the Dayan Derkh Monastery.

"About seven hundred fifty years later, the communists under Stalin took over Mongolia in the 1930s. They had a particular aversion to Buddhists and destroyed over one thousand Buddhist shrines, including the Dayan Derkh, and killed over 30,000 monks. With the fall of the Communist Empire twenty-five years ago, there have been vast changes in Mongolia. Some of these are wonderful, and some, as you can see in our capital, are perplexing. Unfortunately, this area has seen a rise in the mining industry and poaching of our beloved trout, the taimen. These amazing fish, often called the River God's daughters, once existed across Asia but are now limited to the rivers near here, which are the Üür and the Eg. There is a valiant effort being made to save them brought about by a wonderful group of people. A group of scientists from two universities from the US at the University of Wisconsin and the University of Nevada, Reno, along with the local Buddhists, a fishing guide enterprise, and funding from at least two sources have rebuilt part of the local Buddhist monastery. They have set up a catch and release program and are working to limit poaching of these fish and to monitor them. It is truly and amazing collaboration.

"I see the taimen as a metaphor for the nomad way of life in Mongolia. We too are at the top of the food chain, but though we treasure our independence and strength, we are as fragile as they are when pitted against changes in our environment we cannot control. Mining, though part of the fuel that is evolving our country along with technology, will leave us struggling like our dear taimen." The chieftain paused, and his soft-spoken and charming wife brought them all some Mongolian tea.

All three of the guests were not quite sure the direction Shugam was going to take with his speech. However, they courteously listened and marveled at his knowledge of English as if they were listening to an Oxford professor and not a nomad chieftain in a ger in the middle of Mongolia.

"Time to discuss why you gentlemen are here," he said. "Some of what I will tell you is documented, but a good deal of this is speculation. Most foreigners find it difficult to understand how our dear ancestor Genghis was able to conquer most of the known world of his time. Clearly, the biggest part of his success came from his intellect and military strategy. However, I believe, after reading some of the ancient texts, he may have had a slight edge. I found a reference to a special potion his mother made from the standard airag, which Genghis and the males in his family drank. The drink seemed to help augment their strength and was used for at least several generations of the Khans, but it eventually was lost to the ages. Based on my reading, I believe it may have helped with aging as well. In fact, there is even some speculation that Genghis did not die as reported since his grave has never been found."

"What do you mean? If he didn't die as they said, what happened to him?" David asked.

"Perhaps he tired of the role of conqueror and lived out a hidden life to a ripe old age," Shugam responded as he sipped from his cup. "A number of years ago, my brother Ganzorig found an ancient manuscript while helping to clean up the sacred cave near here. We weren't able to make much sense out of it until my daughter Bolormaa studied it while home from her studies in chemical engineering. I will let her tell her part of the story."

With that, his wife went out and came back with a beautiful Mongolian woman with dark eyes and a radiant smile. Jeffrey literally fell off his chair and, for the first time in a great while, felt foolish.

Bolormaa smiled even more and tried to put Jeffrey at ease. "You must be Jeffrey, and I am sorry if I startled you with my entrance. I know my father's monologues can put people to sleep at times. I do want to thank you for helping my brother, and hopefully, we can talk at the celebration tonight." She turned to the rest and introduced herself. "I am Bolormaa, which means crystal mother in Mongolian. The meaning behind my name encouraged me to pursue science, specifically chemical engineering. I currently have my master's degree from the National University of Mongolia and enjoy the chemistry of rare earth metals. About five years ago, my father brought me a manuscript to try to decipher. If you're wondering why he'd give this to a chemical engineer, you should know I enjoy studying languages. I am familiar with some older Mongolian after having read some of the old texts about Genghis Khan in the ancient Uyghur script from *The Secret History of the Mongols.* I was stunned to think that some of what I was reading might actually have been from Hoelun, Genghis Khan's mother! The document seemed to describe a chemical process to obtain a compound from airag that could enhance her son's strength and possible longevity.

"My father was excited and wanted me to try to derive this mixture. At first, I was reluctant since I was busy with my studies and was concerned such a compound might have serious side effects. Eventually, curiosity got the best of me, and I signed on with the promise we would do animal studies first. Three years ago, I did our first chemical extraction, and we ran tests on our local animals without obvious effects. Eventually, we tried low doses on several volunteers and saw dramatic results in some but no effect in others. Those who—"

"Wait. What do you mean by 'effects'?" Clint interrupted.

"As I was saying, those who responded showed improved muscle strength and endurance and seemed generally healthier with no apparent negative side effects. We have no women who have shown any effects from this chemical other than a lessening of facial wrinkles when applied topically. My father has assembled his private army of seven young men with impressive abilities, all of who ingested the formula. I am the only one who knows how to make this compound. I do have some serious concerns about the idea of marketing it to the rest of the world however. Now, do you have any questions?"

Clint, still skeptical, began, "How hard is this mixture to make, and do you have to use mare's milk? Not to say that wasn't an impressive bit of history and chemistry. I'm sure your father is proud of your achievements. I'm still just wrapping my head around this."

"The short answer is no, this compound is not easy to make," said Bolormaa. "I am amazed that anyone could have come up with it eight hundred years ago. I have not tried making it with cow's or goat's milk. Mare's milk has more lactose, which is fermented when making airag."

"I have some questions too," David stated. "How is the beer formula involved here, and how did Mr. Marcum find out about all this?"

"I think I will let my father explain that to you," Bolormaa responded.

"Another wrinkle in this tale is that my dear cousin Antiochus is the head monk at the monastery outside Brussels that Timothy and you, Clint, were staying at. You might ask how I would have a cousin in Belgium. My aunt Altantseteg participated in the first Olympics after World War II in 1948 in London. She was a beautiful platform diver and had to compete with the Russian team since Mongolia was not in the Olympics at that time. While in London for the games, she met a dashing Belgian gymnast who stole her heart, and the two escaped from the clutches of the Russian team officials. It was a bit of scandal, but they married and moved back to Belgium where my cousin was born. I have only seen him twice, but we have stayed in touch.

"Two years ago Cousin Antiochus happened to mention to me that the beer at the monastery the monks usually drank seemed to have some longevity properties for some of the monks. I, of course, mentioned our little secret potion we had been working on and decided to see what the combination of the potion and beer would do. He has been shipping their beer here since, and I have to admit, it does seem to have a positive effect on the young men we have been training. Although, two years is too short to show much of an effect on aging."

Shugam took a sip of his tea and then continued, "Mr. Marcum found out about the beer properties through Brother Antiochus. The monastery needed a new roof and other repairs, and Brother Antiochus and my cousin felt little harm could come from selling the recipe of their beer. They had no idea the impact this would have, especially when the Russians got involved. Poor Brother Adolphus was killed for it."

Bolormaa stretched, and then she noticed Jeffrey was staring at her intently. "Jeffrey, you have been awfully quiet. Do you have anything you would like to ask?"

Jeffrey stammered a bit. "W-w-would you like to take a walk with me down by the Üür River? I'd like to hear more about fly-fishing for these huge fish you have been talking about."

Bolormaa laughed. "Best question of the day. Yes, I think a walk would be great idea."

The two took their leave of the rest of the group. Jeffrey did not feel the need be present for any negotiations and was drawn to Bolormaa, a woman with the beauty of a Mongolian flower and the wisdom of Madame Curie.

"Well, gentlemen," said Shugam, "it seems one issue I have been concerned about—Bolormaa's safety—may have resolved itself. It seems she now has her own private bodyguard looking after her. I don't think I was mistaken about the looks those two were exchanging."

David laughed. "It may be a bit premature to assume anything about their relationship, but stranger things have been known to happen. Isn't that right, Clint?"

"Given your daughter's expertise in chemistry, I'd have to say they did exhibit a definite chemical attraction," said Clint. "So, what other concerns do we need to address?"

"As you can see, I'm not a materialistic man, but I may need a significant financial commitment in order to stabilize my family's lifestyle and even existence. As you people say 'the cat is out of the bag,' and I suspect soon there will be those who would be very interested in obtaining greater strength and longer life. I recognize your employer is proceeding in a civilized manner to achieve his goals, but I understand there are those who would be happy to use whatever means necessary to obtain their goals. I know the nomadic way of life will not continue forever, but I don't want to be the one to engineer its demise, which is why a financial agreement is necessary."

"I can understand your concerns," said David. "Fortunately, we have access to significant capital and your isolation here does help. This will require a good deal of thought though, so I will have to think about this tonight to see what I can come up with. I will need a list of any other bargaining points and concerns you might have. We can meet tomorrow morning to discuss this further."

Chieftain Shugam pulled out a folder and handed it to David. "Some light reading for you tonight. Inside are a few other points that need to be worked out in our negotiations. My sons should be coming back shortly, and we have planned a celebration for them and Jeffrey tonight. We nomads have to live a challenging life, so we like to punctuate that with a bit of competition as you have seen with the Naadam. In order to help you better understand our ways, I would like to suggest a challenge to each of you in the next day. We can work out the details tonight."

Both David and Clint looked at him warily. "We will try our best to meet your challenges," said David. "In the meantime, we best get back to our ger so I can review this information and prepare for tonight."

Shugam nodded, and as David and Clint went to leave, he pulled Clint aside. "I might have an interesting proposition for you, Clint. My cousin, Brother Antiochus at the Lavro Monastery knows you are visiting here. He contacted me to tell me he has your DNA profile from your brief stay at the monastery. He thinks that you might respond to our formula as my nomads have. If you want, we could try starting you on a low dose of the formula to see if you exhibit any positive effects."

Clint thought for a moment and then agreed. "Why not try a little better living through chemistry?"

"As you wish," Shugam said and then bowed to the two men.

David and Clint bowed to the chieftain and then met Sal outside, who was doing card tricks for the children. He took them to their ger and managed to find them each a bottle of Mongolian beer, which was much appreciated. They thanked Sal and then headed into their ger to relax a bit after such a busy day. They couldn't help but feel anxious as they wondered what challenges the chieftain had in mind for them.

Sal sat with a smile on his face as he listened to Bob Dylan.

David unhooked one of Sal's earphones and said, "I suspect you had an ear to the ger when we were talking. What do you think your uncle has in mind for us with these competitions? You know him better than most, so any insight would be appreciated."

Sal turned off his iPod. "Well, I can tell he is fond of Jeffrey and is already sizing him up to see if he is son-in-law material. I suspect all he would want from him would be some sort of show of strength."

"Son-in-law material? Don't you think you might be exaggerating the attraction between Jeffrey and Bolormaa a bit?" asked Clint.

"Well, they are walking hand in hand down by the river as we speak," said Sal. "My scouts tell me the current odds of them kissing for the first time on the bench under the larch tree is 2:1, and I have put some money down in favor of that."

"Your family is spying on them while they take a walk?" Clint asked.

"Of course they are, but I would prefer to call it scouting," said Sal. "A budding romantic relationship between Jeffrey and Bolormaa is major news in our camp. Anyway, I am less certain what Uncle Shugam has in mind for you two in the competition. Clint mentioned he likes archery, so that could be a possibility. And I suspect he would come up with some intellectual challenge for David."

"I could probably handle an intellectual challenge," said David before he yawned. "I think a nap may be in order, and then I'll work on the negotiation with Chieftain Shugam."

27 LIFE IN THE NOMAD CAMP

Ganbaatar and Otgonbayar arrived back from their journey from the Naadam in the late afternoon and were greeted with much fanfare. The tribe set off fireworks, and children rode their horses, hooting and howling in excitement. Most of the adults were a bit more subdued, but they danced and played music even before the official party began.

The official celebration began at sunset with the slaughter and roasting of a sheep in standard nomadic fashion. The intestines were cleaned, stuffed with the lamb's blood, and then cooked in the cavity of the lamb with hot coals. Alcohol was generously enjoyed by most of the adults. David and Clint managed to keep up with the nomads, downing a few beers before the onslaught of vodka. The boys and Jeffrey were treated as celebrities. The three of them were definitely forming a special bond that Bolormaa was pleased to see. Even David and Clint had multiple toasts in their honor. Ganzorig directed all activities and was a happy conductor of the controlled mayhem. Chieftain Shugam kept a close eye on Jeffrey and Bolormaa cuddling in the back of the room, and when he stood, the room immediately became quiet.

"Jeffrey, our dear friend, would you be kind enough to show us a bit of your strength this evening?"

Jeffrey was somewhat embarrassed, but knew better than to refuse this request, so he nodded his head. The center of the celebratory area was cleared, and the seven enhanced warriors brought out heavy steel plates and placed them on a platform with a bar across it.

"Our strongest warrior can dead lift two hundred kilos, or about 440 pounds, of these iron plates," said Shugam. "Do you think you can match that?"

"Yes," said Jeffrey. "It is easier to lift with a weight belt and hand grips, but I should be able to lift more than that."

"I respect your confidence. Could you lift three hundred kilos?" asked Shugam.

"Sure," said Jeffrey. "I'll give it a go."

The men brought out more steel plates and added them to the others. Jeffrey got up on the platform and took off his shirt for effect. He wrapped the bar with a few leather strips and focused his energy with intense concentration. The silence was palpable as he gripped the iron bar. With a shout, he braced his muscular frame and lifted the massive weight off the ground and to his waist. The entire crowd exploded into shouts and cheers. The pandemonium lasted for several minutes, during which time Bolormaa jumped on the platform and threw her arms around him. Their lips met for the first time. At the sight of them kissing, the crowd roared even louder. Adrenaline pumped through Jeffrey's body, fueled by the noise from the crowd and the beautiful girl in his arms.

Sal, though disappointed to lose his bet, felt overwhelmed with joy for the couple.

Clint and David gave Jeffrey a thumbs-up as they chuckled over his triumphant grin. They hoped their challenges would result in the same amount of success.

Clint's challenge, as Sal had guessed, was archery. He was matched against three of the enhanced warriors, and each of them had thirty arrows to shoot at targets placed seventy-five meters away. The warriors were like robots, missing only one out of thirty shots. Clint had never seen such accuracy. His skills were nowhere near as polished as theirs, but he was able to hit six out of ten targets, which was twice what anyone else in the camp could do at that distance. It was enough to impress the chieftain, and Clint was pleased.

After the archery challenge, the celebration began to die down, and David and Clint retired to their ger for the night. David, aware he still needed to prepare for the negotiations the next day, pulled out a notepad and began outlining the terms.

* * *

David and Clint woke early the next morning and made their way over to the chieftain's quarters. David wasted no time getting to business.

"I spent most of the night reviewing your requests and have compiled a list of terms I believe will benefit both parties. First and foremost, we need to formally increase the protection of your camp. Your warriors, though strong, need to be better trained and equipped. I believe Jeffrey is just the man to help with that. Secondly, we can no longer manufacture the formula for strength and longevity in your camp. We need to move this process to another more secure site. Bolormaa will need to be relocated to this new site to ensure effective production and for her safety as well. Thirdly, in order to provide continued freedom for your people, we will need to enter into an agreement with the Mongolian government to either lease, own, or formalize an extensive national park in the north central area. This agreement would have to ensure limits on mining and prevent efforts on poaching. Next, we will need to set up or modify an existing brewery to produce the beer for our product. Both the formula for the beer and Bolormaa's formula have already been established, but we'll need a location to concoct both. Then, we need to enlist a scientific entity to better study the effects of the formula and why certain people are responsive to it and others are not. Although the beer can be sold as is, if we want to eventually sell the formula as a supplement or medication, we will need to have a great deal more of medical testing, at least in the US. Lastly, we will need to eventually address the issue of Viktor, the Russian businessman who is intent on getting his hands on your formula. Actually, this may be the most pressing matter to address since I suspect he may be on his way here now," David said.

Shugam thought for a bit before responding. "So, how much money do you think it would take to assure a large enough piece of land for our use as well as other nomads in the area?"

"It would depend on how we acquired the land and what the stipulations were to control it," said David. "But I would guess at a minimum we're likely looking in the ballpark of five hundred million dollars to buy land that is big enough for your needs. I assume most of the land that large is owned by the Mongolian government, so we will have to be open to negotiating with them. I may be able to convince them to agree to a one-hundred-year lease for substantially less money if we can ensure a long-term income for the country. However, this level of negotiations would require involvement from Mr. Marcum."

"That is a lot of money. Do you truly believe Mr. Marcum would be willing to come up with that much money for this formula?" asked Shugam.

"From what I have gathered, Mr. Marcum is not one to get involved unless he is sure he can make a pretty penny off of his investment. I'm sure he is well aware of just how many people in the world can be helped by your formula. Let's say, for example, your formula can help one million people. If he charges only five hundred dollars per month for the treatment, he would earn six billion dollars a year. Aside from some fairly hefty startup expenses, he stands to make quite a bit of money on this deal."

"I see. Like you, I am concerned for my daughter's safety and can understand the necessity of moving her to a secure location, but I couldn't stand not being able to see her regularly," the chieftain said.

"That is not something to worry about. I'm sure we can work something out so you can see your daughter," said David.

Shugam nodded and then frowned. "That still leaves the problem of Viktor. I was told he is flying in tomorrow by helicopter. I have already alerted my men, but I worry he will not take no for an answer, and I fear we will be no match for his reinforcements."

"The short answer to that problem is Jeffrey," said Clint. "We'll recapture him from your daughter and put him back to work. He will know how to prepare for someone like Viktor."

Shugam nodded graciously and motioned for David and Clint to see themselves out. As David and Clint went in search of their bodyguard, they found him already meeting with the nomad soldiers. Sal served as the translator and mirrored Jeffrey's unhappiness as he examined their weaponry. The seven soldiers were each armed with a set of Mongolian bow and arrows. For greater fire power, they had three Russian AK 47 rifles, or Kalashnikovs, that were still quite serviceable despite being over fifty years old. The only handguns they had were three Russian semiautomatic Makarovs, which were used by most Russian police. There was no body armor, night vision scopes, gas masks, or shotguns, and the amount of ammunition was less than overwhelming for Jeffrey.

He had to remind himself they were out in the middle of Mongolia and not in a military zone. Jeffrey could not fully guess whether Viktor would approach this as a military operation or a standard negotiation, but he knew either way force was likely to be used or at least implied. In order to protect as many nomads as possible, he decided, with Shugam's approval, it would be best to send most of the women and children to another camping area located about ten miles away. The children, unaware of the possible looming danger, were excited about the trip and happily rode their horses to the new site.

Jeffrey, already feeling outmatched in terms of weaponry, encouraged the soldiers to look at this engagement from the eyes of their forerunner Genghis Khan. Though they had fewer forces and were less armed, they could use the element of surprise and attack from multiple fronts if necessary. They knew when the Russians were arriving and had the benefit of knowing their surroundings much better. Jeffrey was also quick to tell the men that, though he would work with them to plan effective strategies, Chieftain Shugam was still in charge. It would be up to the chief when and if any force was to be employed. After receiving a visual sign of agreement and understanding from all the soldiers, he left them to practice their potential moves.

Jeffrey then headed with David and Clint to meet with Bolormaa, Sal, and Shugam for a light dinner. They were all somewhat nervous about the scheduled Russian onslaught the next day. Sal seemed to be the most distraught as he listened to some traditional Mongolian music on his iPod rather than his usual Bob Dylan.

"Sal, are you feeling all right? I didn't realize you even had any music other than Dylan on your iPod," said David.

"Well, there are those moments, like now, when even Dylan seems out of sync. I think our group needs a little Mongolian soul," explained Sal.

"I agree," said Shugam. "I think a moment of thanksgiving and reflection is appropriate. Change and conflict is always stressful, and I think I make a much better philosopher and leader than a general. I would much prefer to negotiate with Viktor rather than fight against him and his men. I appreciate your work with our men, Jeffrey, but please understand that I only want them to retaliate if the Russians start an assault on us."

"Your men are superb fighters. They will respond well if called upon," said Jeffrey. "But I will follow your orders completely. I doubt that Viktor would want risk an assault in a foreign country, but if he does take that risk, it is unlikely with our weaponry we will be able to put up a fight for long. Our best bet may be to try to trick him in some way, which I will I need to discuss with David and Clint since they seem to be the craftiest people here. No offense, Chieftain Shugam. It's just a trait that comes from being lawyers."

Shugam nodded. "I agree. I was going to have to come up with some sort of intellectual challenge for David, but I think outsmarting Viktor would be much more helpful. Please see what you three can come up with."

David was amused by the chieftain's remarks. "It would be our privilege to try to figure some way out of this conundrum."

David, Clint, Jeffrey, and Bolormaa left the chieftain's tent and made their way to David and Clint's ger for a critical brainstorming session. Sal dropped off a few beers to help stimulate their thinking.

They knew the Russians would arrive by helicopter sometime in the next twenty-four hours, but they couldn't predict the exact time. They agreed that in order to avoid warfare they would need to give Viktor some information about the longevity formula. If he realized Bolormaa was the only one who could make it, he would definitely want her to leave with him.

At the mention of Bolormaa's possible danger, Jeffrey vehemently shouted, "No damn way! We can't just hand her over to Viktor! He cannot get his hands on her!" Jeffrey was nearly inconsolable.

David tried to settle him down. "Okay, Jeffrey, okay! We'll try another angle, but tell me this, in an all-out assault, do you really think you and your men could overcome Viktor's troops? You said yourself we'll likely be outnumbered and have less firepower."

Jeffrey tried to steady his breathing. "I think at best we could reach a stalemate, but there would be significant losses on both sides. It's all dependent on how many men Viktor brings with him and how well trained his army is. The nomad men are amazing, but there are limits to bows and arrows."

David paused and scratched his chin. "If only we had a way to take out Viktor…you know, like when you eliminate the queen ant and the rest of the colony dies," David said, thinking out loud. He then looked at Bolormaa. "Lady B., with your vast knowledge of chemistry and access to medicine, do you think you could come up with a way to knock out a man quickly and easily? I don't wish to suggest any illegal activities by you in the past, but…"

Jeffrey started to tense, but Bolormaa quieted him down. "I once had to concoct something like that when one of Dad's 'enhanced' men had a high fever and was delirious. He became violent and aggressive, so I had to give him an injection with something to knock him out. I kept some in case we needed it again. The tranquilizer is very quick acting, but it can only be administered via injection."

David smiled. "Bless you, my child. I think we have the basic makings of a plan. It may still take some luck and a bit of acting though. Jeffrey, were you able to get the explosives for the USB drive that Giselle sent with us?"

Jeffrey nodded. "The device is fairly small so the effective blast range will be limited, but it certainly could do some serious damage."

David got up and stretched. "Excellent! Clint and I have pulled off some plans more complicated than this, so it just may work. "

Clint let out a sigh. "Here we go again with one of David's famous plans. Somehow, I always wind up in some ridiculous costume cleaning the brass handrail of a five-floor staircase and feigning celibacy while he dresses like a king and sleeps with models. Be careful what you agree to, Bolormaa. David's roles aren't typically all fun and games," Clint teased.

"I do have to admit this venture has had an unexpected bonus for me. With your potion, Bolormaa, I can now outshoot your warriors and beat them at wrestling. If Victors men weren't armed I could inflict serious damage on the lot of them.

David pleaded his case. "Let me fill you in on the details of my plan, and you can decide for yourselves. It may not be the best plan, but on short notice, I think it will do. Besides, my plan has to beat having a war between Viktor and his men and Jeffrey and the nomad troops."

They rest of the group agreed it was worth trying David's plan, so they worked on the details of their plan for the next hour before deciding to retire to get some sleep before an eventful next day.

Jeffrey and Bolormaa had other plans though, and she had already farmed out her brothers and sister so they could have some well-deserved privacy in their own ger. The threats of the moment combined with their first intimate touches caused an explosion of passion. For a big man, Jeffrey was surprisingly gentle when he had to be, but both their athletic exertions eventually ended in a fury of entwined bliss. This was repeated twice more just for emphasis and ended only because they both felt they needed some sleep before the rigors of the next day.

28 THE BATTLE WITH
THE RUSSIANS

Dawn brought the sound of incoming helicopters. The nomad soldiers were already in position, and the rest had dressed and gathered in the chieftain's ger before the helicopters landed. Though the moment was tense, Shugam stood calmly sipping his tea.

Two older Russian helicopters came in to the landing site. The first came to a stop, and four soldiers with Kevlar vests and automatic rifles filed out. Then, without warning, the soldiers open fired on the nomad soldiers facing them. David and Clint could not believe their eyes.

"We haven't even begun negotiations! Idiots!" screamed Jeffrey. "Who would use automatic weapons on a nomad camp without any discussions whatsoever?" Jeffrey waved his hands to the soldiers, signaling them to stop their fire.

Fortunately, the nomads were mostly protected in their positions, and only one was wounded where a bullet had grazed his leg.

Within minutes, the nomads hidden in the trees around the landing strip peppered the four soldiers with barbed arrows. Soon, all four were on the ground with serious wounds, rendering them unable to keep firing at the nomads. The second helicopter landed, and Viktor, dressed in full Kevlar armor, jumped out, screaming in Russian and then Mongolian.

"Stop! All of you! Cease fire!" Viktor seemed frazzled by the sight of his injured men.

Ten more Russian soldiers piled out of the second helicopter and took up defensive positions, but this time, they did not fire. The nomads stopped their barrage of arrows, and the wounded soldiers were carried back into the first helicopter. Two of the wounded soldiers had serious injuries, one with an arrow to his chest and the other to his thigh, causing significant bleeding. They were attended to by a soldier with paramedical training.

Viktor shouted out in English this time, "Shugam, where the hell are you? We need to talk!"

The chieftain came out of his ger still carrying his cup of tea. "Viktor, you come to my home and bring chaos! Your men used automatic weapons on my village! Have you forgotten how civilized people interact? Has money addled your brain? Have your men retreat to the helicopters before we talk any further."

Viktor ordered most of the men to get back into the choppers, and despite his shameful introduction, he strolled confidently up to the ger to meet the chieftain accompanied by one of his men. Viktor and Shugam looked each other over. The rugged, wizened nomad tutored by the outdoor life and the cocky, self-absorbed billionaire could not have been more different. Shugam brought Viktor inside and gave him a cup of tea. Jeffrey, Bolormaa, Clint, David, and Sal posted themselves around the tent, ready to defend the chief and attack Viktor if necessary.

Upon seeing the smug look on Viktor's face, Jeffrey was unable to contain his fury. "That is the most irresponsible use of private military that I have ever seen! Are you unfamiliar with the concept of negotiation? Any good leader knows the threat of violence is generally more effective than the indiscriminate use of force."

Viktor was not one to be cowed by underlings, even if they were 6'5" and weighed close to three hundred pounds. He dismissed Jeffrey with a wave of his hand and then turned toward Shugam. "Shugam, you and I need to talk. Alone."

Shugam gave Viktor a sideway glance. "I have no wish for privacy here. You may speak freely in front of my family and friends. Please be aware your willingness to fire on my men does not help your position. The gift of our formula is not some commodity that can be sold to the highest bidder or whoever wields the greatest force, so I encourage you to tread lightly."

Viktor was not used to dealing with someone who could not be bought with money or cowered by force. He realized to get what he wanted he needed to rethink his approach. He softened his face and said, "My apologies, Chieftain Shugam. I really have no wish to harm your family or friends, but I must disagree with you. Your formula is a potential commodity. I understand it is untested on large groups of people and may turn out to be of little use, but if it has the benefits that have been reported, it could be very valuable. I am willing to share with you half the profits of this enterprise, which I believe is more than generous, under two conditions. You must turn over the details of the formula today, and since, as I've come to learn, your daughter Bolormaa is the sole chemical engineer in its production, she will need to accompany me back to St. Petersburg to supervise its development."

Jeffrey jumped up and pulled his Russian revolver from his waist. He grabbed Viktor and held the gun to his neck. "No one is taking my fiancée anywhere!"

Viktor looked more amused than frightened. Viktor's guard brought his gun up to Jeffrey's head. Viktor motioned to Shugam. "Is this the Mongolian hospitality one can expect while having a friendly discussion?"

The chieftain sighed. "No, it is not. Jeffrey, please put your gun away. This is my home, and if you are going to by my new son-in-law, you will act as such. However, Viktor, I might point out that a friendly discussion usually does not start with gunfire."

Jeffrey reluctantly put away his revolver, but he was still fuming.

"I guess I should be impressed that at least you had the courtesy to use a Russian weapon when trying to blow my head off." Viktor laughed. "Engaged or not, I insist your daughter accompany me. Perhaps her not-so-gentle giant can come as well, if he behaves himself."

"And if I decline your proposal?" asked the chieftain.

"Then, I'm afraid I would have to force the issue," said Viktor. "Keep in mind, I still have ten armed troops in my helicopters, who are chomping at the bit for some action. Your men in the trees wouldn't stand a chance. I'm sure they would even be able to persuade your daughter to come with us. I could try to stop them, but as you can tell from their actions on our landing, they don't always listen to me."

The chieftain looked at his daughter, the prize of his life. "What do you think, dear Bolormaa? I do not generally condone violence, but I hate to let you go with Viktor, even if Jeffrey is there to protect you."

Bolormaa put her arms around her father. "I see no alternative short of starting a major conflict. I couldn't bear matching poor little Mongolia against mighty Russia. Jeffrey and I will go with him, but, Viktor, you must guarantee our safety and to send us home once I have set up a center to develop our product in St. Petersburg."

Viktor was all smiles. "I knew we could come to an agreement," he said as he patted Shugam on the back. "That wasn't so hard, was it?" He winked at Jeffrey.

The rest of the group tried to hide their disgust. Bolormaa reached into a drawer and brought out a rather large USB drive. She handed it to Viktor.

"What in the world is this?" he asked

"That is the Mongolian version of a USB drive. It holds all the info on the production of the compound you want us to make," she replied.

Viktor shook his head. "I shouldn't have expected anything else from such uncivilized people," he said sharply.

As he plugged the USB into his computer, he did not notice Jeffrey setting a timer on his watch. Viktor was delighted to see chemical formulas and an explanation of how to combine certain elements.

"Well, as much as I have enjoyed our little discussion, it's time we head out. Some of my men need medical treatment, which I'll deduct the expenses for from your half of the profit we are about to generate."

Viktor then waltzed out of the ger followed by Jeffrey and Bolormaa. As they walked down to the helicopters, both Viktor and Shugam called out to their men to hold their fire. The Russian soldiers seemed very unhappy that they couldn't inflict more damage on the nomads. Viktor, Jeffrey, Bolormaa, and a few soldiers climbed into the older chopper.

Shugam shook his head. "With all your money, why would you fly around in this old rig? I'm not sure I trust my daughter flying in this thing!" he yelled over the sound of the blades to Viktor.

Viktor laughed. "I've flown in this beauty for the last five years across Russian and Siberia and back. It has never given me any trouble. I keep the parachutes aboard just for show. Now it's time to be leaving!"

The chopper with the injured soldiers took off, heading to Irkutsk to get medical treatment for the injured soldiers. Jeffrey and Bolormaa had one of the large Russian soldiers sitting between them. Their chopper took off with little fanfare.

Once off the ground, Viktor turned to the soldier and asked him to restrain Jeffrey's wrists with plastic cuffs. Jeffrey had expected this, but Bolormaa was horrified. She repeatedly objected, but was generally ignored.

Viktor glowered at Jeffrey. "Allow me to introduce you to Sergio Gremlin. Your employer's son managed to take advantage of my companion, and I am sure he would like return the favor."

With that, Sergio laughed and unleashed a series of blows to Jeffrey, ignoring Bolormaa's shouts and attempts to stop him. He truly enjoyed inflicting pain on his prisoners. If Jeffrey hadn't been bound, the two men would have fought evenly, but as it was, Jeffrey wound up bloodied and bruised. Sergio practiced his right cross and left uppercut blows to the restrained Jeffrey. He even threatened giving a couple of jabs to Bolormaa to shut her up.

With all the commotion, Bolormaa was able to sneak Jeffrey a small pair of wire cutters to cut his bonds.

The two soldiers sitting across from them cheered Sergio on, remembering Jeffrey from their beating in Paris. Unable to resist a shot at revenge, they jumped up to join in the fray. Their yelling and aggressive movements caused too much of a stir, so the pilot started screaming at them all to sit down or he was going to lose control of the chopper. With a laugh, the men wiped their bloodied knuckles on their shirts and returned to their seats. Sergio sat back between Jeffrey and Bolormaa while the other two decided to readjust the toppled over supplies in the back of the chopper. Viktor was too engrossed in analyzing the compound on his computer to even acknowledge the fight.

Bolormaa was enraged and could barely keep herself from trying to knock out Sergio. She eyed the revolver he kept pointed at Jeffrey and tried to steady her breathing.

When they started to get above the tree line, Bolormaa knew it was time to act. She saw Jeffrey had cut his plastic cuffs with the cutters she had slipped him. Then, in one swift moment, she plunged her little syringe into Sergio's thigh. He gave her a stunned look and started to point his gun at her, but was suddenly out cold. The two soldiers across from them were still readjusting the load and talking and did not react until Jeffrey had Sergio's gun trained on them. They silently dropped their weapons, which Bolormaa quickly recovered. She pointed the guns at the two men.

Viktor remained totally unaware of all of this and called out, "Sergio, I think it is time for our American passenger to lighten our load! Let's see if he can fly." He laughed at his own joke and kept his eyes glued to his computer screen.

Jeffrey backed up, keeping his eyes on the men, and moved behind Viktor. He clubbed him across the back of the head with his revolver. "I will be happy to lighten your load, but I won't be flying."

Viktor was startled and confused as to how Jeffrey got free. He frantically looked around for Sergio and saw he was knocked out. He screamed at the other two soldiers to attack Jeffrey, but they didn't move. They had no weapons and were still being held at gunpoint by both Jeffrey and Bolormaa. Realizing he was running out of options, he then screamed at the pilot to try to do something.

"Do not make any sudden movements, or you will be shot, and we will all die," Jeffrey said to the pilot.

The pilot remained in his seat, nodding his understanding.

Jeffrey and Bolormaa took turns strapping on parachutes while the other covered their captives.

As Jeffrey looked down, he realized this would not be an easy jump. They were at about five thousand feet above ground, just above the tree line. The air at this altitude would not support them too well, and the ground would be hard with some rocks. Unfortunately, there were no other options.

Jeffrey opened the door. Bolormaa kissed him, and then she jumped. He followed behind her shortly. The sudden cool air and free fall quickly brought back memories of the combat jumps he had made years ago. He hoped no one would be shooting at him from the ground, as he often had experienced in the combat jumps. For a moment, he felt completely at peace, as if he and Bolormaa were in their own world.

The sound of gunfire from the chopper quickly brought him back to the present. He looked up to see

Viktor had found a weapon on the chopper and was trying to shoot him as he fell. He felt a wave of relief as he remembered Sergio was still out cold. Otherwise, he would surely be dead by now.

He hoped Bolormaa remembered everything from last night that he had drilled into her head about parachuting. They were approaching their target, and he let out a breath when he saw her chute opening below him. *Thank goodness, she remembered,* he thought and then pulled his cord.

After the initial sudden deceleration when the chute opened, he felt an odd sensation as his three-hundred-pound frame drifted ever more slowly to earth. Unfortunately, he knew he would land fairly hard and the ground would not be kind.

He was right on both counts, though his muscles and rugged boots helped to brace him a bit. He felt a searing pain in his left lower leg and was briefly knocked out when he hit the ground.

For a moment, he was transported back to an EVAC unit with multiple shrapnel wounds, and then suddenly, he felt his fiancée rubbing his face and calling his name. When he opened his eyes and saw her, he felt as if he was being spoken to by an angel, though it may have just been the adrenaline and altitude. They embraced, and then he took an inventory on his basic body parts. He had multiple bruises and likely had a fractured left fibula, but he did not have any head, neck, or pelvis injuries. He might have also had a couple of bruised or cracked ribs, but he had been there before.

Bolormaa had faired even better, escaping with only a large bruise on her right thigh but otherwise generally intact.

Quickly, Jeffrey looked at his watch. He and Bolormaa counted down together. "Sixteen, fifteen, fourteen, thirteen, twelve, eleven, ten, nine, eight, seven, six, five, four, three, two, one, zero…"

They heard nothing and exchanged confused looks. They began to worry at the thought of that evil monster Viktor up in the chopper with all his resources aimed squarely at them. Jeffrey was starting to sit up when both of them heard a loud boom, like a muted clap of thunder coming over the mountain.

"I guess the timer was off a bit," said Jeffrey with a grin. "I'm going to thank Giselle for that explosive device USB drive when I see her next. That was good thinking on your part to put all that info on the drive to confuse Viktor. I can't believe we made it out of that alive!"

They embraced. Jeffrey had been in battle and knew taking another's life was not without consequence. This had not been an easy decision or one they had made on their own, but they knew the world was a better, safer place without Viktor Krashenko or Sergio Gremlin in it.

Bolormaa made a splint for Jeffrey's left leg with the parachute silk and some tree limbs. Jeffrey hobbled down the mountain with Bolormaa to get under cover of the larch forest. Clint and Sal were supposed to meet them on motorcycles with food and water, and Jeffrey hoped they would get there soon since he was famished and needed water more than anything else.

From her years exploring and camping growing up, Bolormaa had some memories of their current area. She was able to find a small stream with cold, clear water, and Jeffrey plunged his head into the pure frigid water. He quenched his thirst, and the icy water helped ease some of the bruising on his face. Bolormaa found a bush with bright red goji berries by the stream, and they both grabbed handfuls. They forced themselves to limit their intake because they knew the berries could cause an upset stomach if one ate too many. The snack helped to take the edge off their hunger.

Jeffrey's leg was sore, so they decided to wait by creek for Sal and Clint. Jeffrey had worn Timothy's AI gear and hoped the GPS would still work in the mountains. To help pass the time, he laid back onto the cool dirt and fantasized about a rare steak with all the fixings. Bolormaa joined him, laying her head on his chest.

They realized they had drifted off when they awoke to the sounds of motorcycles and Bob Dylan. Jeffrey and Bolormaa sat up and flagged down the riders. As Sal and Clint pulled up, they jumped up and hugged their friends.

"I can't believe you guys actually made it off the chopper and were able to parachute down! We were all scared shitless," said Sal. "Uncle Shugam had us leave immediately after you two took off. Thanks to the GPS we were able to find you, but I can't pretend I didn't worry we wouldn't. Man, Jeffrey, you really do look like you have been beaten and thrown out of a helicopter," Sal said, looking them up and down. "Bolormaa, you look as beautiful as ever. Are you sure you jumped out of the chopper too?"

Clint was unwrapping food they had brought, and Jeffrey was wolfing it down as fast as it appeared. Clint spoke quietly to Jeff. "Were you able to blow up the helicopter with Viktor on it?"

Jeffrey paused long enough to nod that Viktor was no longer a threat. He also told him Sergio Gremlin too had been on the chopper they blew up. Clint grinned and patted Jeffrey on the back.

"I still can't believe our plan actually worked! Though, Jeffrey seems to have taken the brunt of the injuries to accomplish that," said Bolormaa. "Without him, I would still be on my way to St. Petersburg with that evil man. It all seems like a dream—or nightmare, really." She threw her arms around Jeffrey. "And now this mangled mountain of a man is going to be my husband! I'm done wasting time. Jeffrey, I want to get married tomorrow at the Buddhist monastery before we have to leave our dear Mongolia for parts unknown."

Despite his facial injuries, Jeffrey kissed her and laughed. "Boy, things certainly aren't boring around here. Just a few hours ago, I was in a life and death struggle and jumping out of a helicopter, and now, I'm marrying the most beautiful girl on the planet."

They all laughed, and Bolormaa nuzzled Jeffrey's neck.

"I think getting married at the Buddhist monastery works for me. Just promise we won't take any wedding pictures of me until I look less like a head of cabbage and more like myself."

"Whatever you say, lover boy," Clint said as he refastened Jeffrey's splint.

Clint then helped Jeffrey onto one of the bikes. Sal's jaw dropped a bit at Clint's ability to lift the three-hundred-pound bodyguard. Bolormaa smiled and was amazed her "nomad potion" was already having a startling effect on Clint, making him much stronger.

Sal and Jeffrey sat on one bike, and Clint and Bolormaa sat on the other. Jeffrey had wanted to drive and ride with Bolormaa, but they all voted against that. With his broken leg, they felt it was going to be tough enough for him just to sit on the back. Thankfully, Shugam had thrown a few natural pain remedies into the medicine pack they had brought so Jeffrey's magic carpet motorcycle ride was more enjoyable than painful.

As they went down the mountain, Dylan wailed over the bike's speaker, "But I was so much older then, I'm younger than that now."

29 THE WEDDING
PREPARATIONS

Upon their return, they saw the women and children had rejoined the camp. The children's joy at seeing their dear Bolormaa and soon-to-be husband Jeffrey was explosive.

When they heard there was going to be a wedding tomorrow, the festivities really began in earnest.

Chieftain Shugam and David weaved through the eager children to meet with the returning motorcycle gang. They wanted to hear all the details of their helicopter adventure.

Shugam was quite upset about the beating Jeffrey had to take and was amazed that his loving Bolormaa had actually knocked out the evil goon with a concoction of her own. He could barely believe that they had survived a parachute jump into the mountains with only a broken leg to show for it. He was deeply saddened, however, to hear that the men on the helicopter had all likely died, even if they were evil and had tried to harm his family. He bowed his head and recited some Buddhist prayers for the recently deceased, especially for Viktor. He realized that Viktor had essentially kidnapped his daughter and would likely have killed Jeffrey, but he was remorseful that their actions had caused his death. As chieftain, he knew the group needed to move forward with their plans, so after his prayers, he swallowed his grief.

Shugam held his dear daughter in his arms and put his arm around Jeffrey as well. "I know you two just met, and I can't deny that the prospect of your getting married on such short notice is concerning. I am well aware that Bolormaa has been making her own decisions since she was a young girl, so I am sure nothing I could say would change her mind about marrying you, Jeffrey, not that I hope to do so. I would, however, like both of you to discuss this with the head Buddhist monk to get his blessing. Having the Great Spirit bless your union would bring me great peace. I gladly welcome you, Jeffrey, into our family, but I do need to remind you two that marriage is both a blessing and a responsibility. Do not let the exuberance of your recent battle influence your decisions that will forge the rest of your lives."

Both Bolormaa and Jeffrey embraced Shugam.

"Father, thank you for your words. We will gladly talk to the head monk before our nuptials. Though Jeffrey and I have only known each other a short time I feel both of us are absolutely certain that this is the right decision. Sharing this celebration with my family is very important to us and unfortunately time is of the essence," Bolormaa said.

The chieftain watched his daughter stare lovingly at Jeffrey. He knew she loved this man and felt at peace that the husband she had chosen was a strong and good man. Her life was going to be much different, but so might all of their lives. As he watched them, he realized he must let her go.

Teary-eyed, they all toasted with the obligatory vodka and set off for a mad evening of planning a wedding in one night. Sleep would have to wait until their long plane ride back to Europe. As the other dispersed, Shugam held David and Clint back for one last message.

"I will be flying to Brussels to meet with your boss, Mr. Marcum. We have been corresponding with one another via email and need to finalize our negotiations. I will have Jeffrey and Bolormaa fly with you to Paris so they can have a brief honeymoon there before they meet me, Mr. Marcum, and my cousin, the head monk at the monastery in Brussels. Thank you, David, for orchestrating your plan to save Jeffrey and Bolormaa, and thank you, Clint, for helping to retrieve them. I am surprised my daughter's formula has affected you so quickly, but I am happy to know it has served you well. Now, enough about business. We have a celebration to begin."

Bolormaa was already lining up her helpers to prepare for her wedding in seventeen hours. First in line was her mother who knew exactly what foods she wanted to prepare. In addition to their classic Mongolian fare, she would have to have one of their steers butchered in honor of her new son-in-law. Next in line was Bolormaa's aunt who would make her wedding dress and alter some clothes for Jeffrey as he certainly would not fit in any of the other men's clothes. Her aunt was an amazing seamstress, and she could be depended on to work miracles, even overnight. Bolormaa's uncle would coordinate with the Buddhist monks at the monastery for the ceremony and the proceedings for the wedding. Lastly, there was Sal who would coordinate the music and everything else that had to be done last minute, like finding some beer for their American guests.

Bolormaa held her cousin close to her. "Dear Sal, you really are the glue that holds our nomad camp together. Please help my father adjust to all the changes that may happen once we unleash our formula to the rest of the world. As far as the wedding tomorrow, try to stick with more traditional Mongolian music like throat singing. Try to go easy on the Dylan tunes please."

Sal cringed. "Throat singing is not my favorite. Please, before you make up your mind, listen to Bob Dylan's 'Wedding Song.' I really think it is one of his best and would work well for your wedding. It starts with the lyrics, 'I love you more than ever, more than time and more than love. I love you more than money and more than stars above. Love you more than madness, more than waves upon the sea. Love you more than life itself, you mean that much to me.'"

"Wow, that is very beautiful," said Bolormaa.

"Peter, Paul and Mary have a great wedding song as well. Although, theirs has a more religious tone. Kenny Loggins also has several great wedding songs."

Bolormaa grabbed Sal's hands. "Okay, I will leave it up to you. I should not have doubted your musical instincts. Now, please see what you can do about the beer for our thirsty guests."

Sal bowed before his cousin. "Your wish is my command!"

***

Things were humming through the evening at the nomad camp. Everyone worked busily at their own task and was happy to help another if needed. By eight the next morning, Jeffrey had bathed in the river; had herbs; was shaved by one uncle; had a type of make-up applied to his face by another; and had received a carefully molded posterior splint made by another uncle of leaves, algae, and grasses for his left leg. As the uncle was adjusting the mold to Jeffrey's leg, Sal dashed into their ger and announced the head Buddhist monk was there to interview Jeffrey before the wedding.

The monk could not be kept waiting, so they quickly bundled Jeffrey for his meeting. Jeffrey felt nervous about meeting the monk, which was a new feeling for him. Even though he had faced death many times over the years, including yesterday, he rarely felt anxious.

When he saw the monk, though, his fears evaporated. The monk exuded the serene qualities that the Dalai Lama displayed in his pictures and interviews. There was a peacefulness about him, and he seemed to have a harmonious nature.

The monk sat down in one of the chairs Sal had brought and motioned for Jeffrey to do the same. Sal translated for them.

"Jeffrey, I am Sha Wusshing, the head monk at the nearby Buddhist monastery. I am to preside over the ceremony of your betrothal to Bolormaa today. Some monks view marriage as a civil ceremony and do not officiate at weddings. I feel love and happiness as well as mutual respect and responsibility are key to our world and they are the foundation of all good spiritual unions. I know life can be challenging, so I believe it is wonderful to have a kindred soul to help one navigate life's perils and joys. I have known Bolormaa all her life, and she is one of the most determined, decisive people I have ever met. Despite your brief courtship, she is absolutely certain you are her soulmate. I must ask you, Jeffrey, is Bolormaa your love for all time?"

Jeffrey grinned. "I am absolutely sure that I will love Bolormaa for all my time. I'm not sure I would have believed in love at first sight before I met her, but we could spend another day, month, or a thousand years together, and I am certain my feelings for her will not change."

The monk pondered. "I know your feelings and words are genuine. I sense it may be time to for you to review your priorities now that you are taking a partner for life. Only you can know how to do that for yourself, so please spend some time today contemplating that. Then, meet me back at the monastery today at one this afternoon. I will bless you now and then you and your bride this afternoon."

Jeffrey bowed before the monk and received his blessing. His wounds immediately felt much better. He was not a religious man, but he had to admit the monk had powers he did not understand. After his meeting, he was rushed back into the ger and his aides finished their ministrations.

The morning flew by with frenetic activity. The nomads worked together like a beehive on steroids. Utterly against his will, Jeffrey was driven to the monastery on the back of one of the motorcycles by Clint. The nomad crowd was already gathering, supplemented by some of the curious fisherman from the fishing camp as well as tourists and monks from the area. The ceremony promised to be monumental and the food and music spectacular.

30 THE WEDDING & REVIEWS

The nuptials themselves were, of course, amazing, at least in nomad terms. The ceremony was simple, yet elegant and the bride ravishing and radiant. Part of the unique flavor of the wedding included the bride's brother, who rode by horseback through the dinner tent with a few goats and chickens trailing behind him. The groom, hungrier than he had ever been, astonished the guests by downing forty-eight ounces of steak, washing it down with six liters of Mongolian beer. After which, he arm-wrestled his new brother-in-law and soon-to-be wrestling great to an easy victory. There was just the right mix of spirituality and revelry to appease those who were present. The party lasted well into the night, and the amount of alcohol consumed was unfathomable.

* * *

Morning at the nomad camp was not like most mornings. The chieftain and his wife were up early, but the rest of the camp blissfully slept. Of course, once the children and animals were up, the rest of the tribe gradually opened their blurry eyes. The newlyweds met Bolormaa's parents and David, Clint, and Sal for a simple breakfast.

Shugam, as usual opened the discussions. "So, my dear daughter, did you enjoy your wedding? What was your favorite part?"

"Asking the bride for her favorite moments of her wedding is a bit like asking a child what their favorite part of Disneyland is. I savored every moment of the ceremony from the children riding out on their horses, to all my female relatives with flowers coming out to greet me, to my handsome husband wearing his cobalt blue deel with gold trim, to the magnificent deep purple and gold deel my aunt made for me with an embroidered eagle on the back. I will remember the words from the senior Buddhist monk as he blessed our union and future children. I will remember holding hands with my now dear husband while listening to my father and mother recite a prayer for happiness for Jeffrey and me. I confess the food, music, dancing, and singing seem more of a blur. I know I will not see you, my family, for some time so the memories of you all are all the more precious."

They all sighed, remembering the blissful night, and then Shugam turned to his new son-in-law and asked, "And you, Jeffrey? What will you remember?"

"Please don't expect any sophisticated memories from me. I was just happy to share this day with my beautiful wife, her family, and my friends. The ceremony and food were amazing—that was probably one of the best steaks I have ever eaten. I was surprised, though, to feel a real connection with the Buddhist priest here. I may have to give some more thought to this religion. I never expected to return from Mongolia with a new bride, but now I can't picture my life any other way. This has all been quite an experience!"

Shugam raised his cup of tea in the form of a toast. He beamed at his family. "Our simple wedding ceremony may be a footnote in history, forecasting changes that will soon be unleashed on our world. We have the potential to strengthen mankind and extend people's lives, and that may alter civilization's path for the next millennia. Yesterday's celebration will remain a stellar event in my life, and today, I am the proud father of my daughter Bolormaa and my new son-in-law!"

Bolormaa's mother raised her glass of tea as well. "Bolormaa, I have never seen you shine so brightly. I am sad you are leaving, but I have always known you would. Your destiny lies outside our nomad village with your new husband. I love that we were able to create a wonderful wedding for you both on such short notice. Jeffrey, I know you are a good man to be her partner, and I will always remember you two together, happily accepting the blessings from my husband and me."

Jeffrey and Bolormaa smiled at the chieftain and his wife and then kissed each other.

Sal took off his earphones. "Hey! Don't forget to thank Bobby D for providing us with endless tunes to dance to."

The chieftain sighed, and they all laughed.

Clint then raised his glass and said, "My deep congratulations to the bride and groom! I hope I can continue to develop a friendship with both of you through all the craziness that we and the world are likely to see in the coming years. Having some personal experience with Bolormaa's potion, I am not sure whether I or anyone is ready for the changes it can generate, so here's to proceeding with caution and utilizing some of the best minds on our planet to harness this power!"

"L'chaim!" said David as he clinked his glass against Clint's. "I have to admit, it was pretty amazing to watch the preparations in the nomad camp for this event. One could not have orchestrated such preparations in a well-oiled military operation. The event itself seemed like it had been planned for months, not twenty-four hours. My hat is off to you, Chieftain Shugam, and your wife for achieving this and my congratulations to the bride and groom."

"Thank you all for your kind words," Shugam said. "On a more somber note, the Russian news reported the unfortunate crash of a private helicopter in Southern Siberia yesterday with the apparent death of billionaire Viktor Krashenko and several of his employees. The news stated he was returning to St. Petersburg from scouting out a fishing trip in Northern Mongolia, though we know this is not true. The military is apparently sending out troops to investigate. I don't believe they will discover the real cause of his trip or his death, but I thought you all should know."

"Thank you for informing us and for your hospitality here. I hope we can proceed without any more deaths. Like Clint said, we are facing some potentially monumental changes in our society. Clint's own changes are a testament to that. I pray we do not face any more threats," David said.

Shugam silently agreed, nodding his head. They all quietly finished their breakfast and then spent the rest of the day relaxing and preparing for their departure the next day.

By evening, exhaustion entombed most of the inhabitants of the nomad village. The only three moving bodies were the newlyweds, who were deep in sexual embrace, and the "enhanced" Clint, who wandered the perimeter of the nomad village in search of wisdom and a release for his exploding muscles. Bolormaa was greatly amused that her sexual dance with Jeffrey was not only condoned by her tribe but welcomed now since they were legally as well as physically joined. Even at the height of passion, she knew that sleep was dangling its weary head and the morning awaited her like an oncoming train.

Clint was deep in thoughts about his return to Paris and Molly. He knew he had changed more than she could have suspected and wondered what this would do to their relationship. He could even see a change in his relationship with David and was not sure where that would lead. He knew that some answers to his questions would have to wait for their meeting back at the abbey in Brussels. He could not believe all that had transpired in their week in Mongolia. Eventually, he too decided that sleep was necessary, so he returned to his ger for a few hours of rest.

31 RETURN TO PARIS

Morning dawned on the idyllic nomad village. The usual emergence of its inhabitants began with the early rising women who heated up the water for the ubiquitous morning tea followed by the men and older children who fed and cared for the animals. They all knew that their guests, their chieftain, and even their beloved Bolormaa would be leaving at noon.

The group was scheduled to first fly by helicopter to Ulaanbaatar and then across Central Asia to Europe, landing in Paris. For most of the village who had never been out of Northern or Central Mongolia, they might as well have been flying to the moon.

During breakfast, Chieftain Shugam gave final instructions to his brother and Sal to carry out in his absence. Having satellite phones with rural connections and email certainly made communicating easier, even from a quarter of the way around the world. Shugam hoped he would only be gone a week, but as his new friends pointed out, a lot can happen in a week. His family would wait until his return to start the move to more southern territories for their fall residence. Though it was beautiful at their current site, the winters could be absolutely brutal, so a migration south was essential.

Shugam also discussed with his brother and Sal the latest Russian news briefing that confirmed Viktor had died in a helicopter crash along with his pilot and two crewmen in Southern Siberia. No specific cause of the crash was noted, but the media had noted the helicopter was surprisingly old, which was odd considering Viktor had been a billionaire and could easily afford more modern transportation.

David, Clint, Jeffrey, and Bolormaa enjoyed their last Mongolian breakfast, at least for a long time to come. Jeffrey downed his usual dozen eggs and two large beef fillets, courtesy of his mother-in-law. He was going to miss this sweet lady who worshiped the ground he walked on. Clint was doing his best to keep up with Jeffrey's appetite, but there was no contest between him and the big man when it came to eating.

Bolormaa eyed Clint. "I thought I heard you out roaming the grounds late last night. Were you having trouble sleeping?"

"Since I'm on this new potion of yours, I don't need as much sleep. My mind is readjusting to a different way of thinking. It's like my internal hard drive has had a sudden upgrade and the rest of my machinery is trying to adjust. Did the other men you have on this formula have similar reactions?"

Bolormaa shook her head. "The other subjects on this formula had much less education than you and are obviously of Mongolian ancestry. Your reaction may have something to do with your genetic makeup as it does seem to affect you more than the others who responded to it. We need to set up a clinical evaluation site ASAP and subject all those getting the formula to serial testing. We cannot release this as a medication without official medical and pharmaceutical testing, which is going to take time and money."

David patted his friend Clint on the back. "I think Clint needs a full medical evaluation and lab studies done as soon as we get to Paris. You might think about cutting the dose of his meds in the meantime. I don't know that this is harming him, but it certainly is affecting him in a major way. As you said, there may be some genetic differences. Most of your subjects have been Mongolian, not Caucasian, so we should be cautious. I am not suggesting that there is anything bad about this formula, but we need to know more about it."

Bolormaa switched to her scientist role. "Actually, six of the monks at the Belgian monastery are Caucasian and have been on both the brew from the monastery and my formula for the last year. They're all doing quite well. They are much older than Clint though, so that might have some effect. I do agree we will need to have a medical evaluation of Clint as soon as we get to Paris."

Clint laughed. "I'm glad you all are so concerned about poor Clint, but actually, I feel better than I have in my entire life. I will agree to medical tests, but I doubt the doctor will find anything wrong. I feel I am physically ten years younger than my age."

David and Bolormaa exchanged looks. David still felt worried for his friend. They all had certainly been through quite a bit on their journey.

They ended their breakfast so they all could finish packing. The helicopter was scheduled to pick them up soon.

Since he was done packing, Clint went down to the docks to watch the fly fishermen try to catch their elusive giant trout, the taimen. He heard loud shouts, and sure enough, a huge fish sparkling in the morning sun was brought on board one of the boats. It was quickly weighed, tagged, and then released back into the Üür River. The fishermen were as excited as if they had won an Olympic medal. It was a pleasant memory, a gift from Northern Mongolia and the River God's daughter.

Clint could hear the helicopter circle overhead and then drop into the area set up for its landing. He made his way back in time to participate in goodbyes. A few tears were shed, especially between Bolormaa and her mother. The villagers turned out to see them off. As they had been forewarned, they all used the facilities before takeoff since there were none to be had on the helicopter.

The forests, rivers, and Lake Khövsgöl in the distance were as beautiful from the air as on the ground. The flight was definitely no frills and took over four hours to go the roughly six hundred kilometers to UB.

They had little time to rest between flights as Mr. Marcum had again chartered the opulent Gulfstream G500 from Elite World Airways. The five were whisked along with their luggage to a gleaming aircraft outfitted with every possible extravagance one could possibly imagine. The contrast with the helicopter flight was like going from the Stone Age into a Mars mission. Jeffrey loved the food, Shugam the computerized newsfeed and books, Bolormaa the research composite, David the beer selection, and Clint all of the above.

The flight attendant, Elise, advised them that it would take fourteen hours to fly back to Paris, but they would gain seven hours flying west. They were scheduled to arrive in gay Paree at 7:30 p.m. local time.

"While you get some sleep, I should be able to book you a table at any of the top restaurants in Paris for after you land," Elise offered.

David gave Elise Giselle's number. "Please text her to get a reservation for seven at a restaurant of your choosing. She speaks French and English, so you can use either."

"As you wish, sir," Elise said with a smile.

The group settled into their flight, most of them managing to get four to six hours of sleep before arriving in Paris as scheduled.

When they landed, they hazily went through customs and then found a limousine waiting for them with their luggage and two very boisterous ladies who immediately jumped on David and Clint. David had not expected the impact of a flying Giselle, but Jeffrey helped him from being knocked flat. Clint easily caught Molly in midair and planted a well-timed kiss on her lips. He held her in his arms.

"Wow!" Clint said in awe. "How did you get more beautiful in the last week since I've been gone?"

Molly laughed. "Being stuck in Paris with Giselle has its perks. So many amazing spas and so little time.

Now, tell me how you changed into a beefcake model in one week?"

"It's the wonder of modern science gone mad. I'll tell you all about it as we discuss the current state of the world tonight," Clint responded, feeling relieved his relationship with Molly didn't seem to have been affected by the formula or their time apart.

"I'll bet your answer and the state of the world looks better from a horizontal position," said Giselle.

David introduced the chieftain, the newly married Jeffrey, and his wife Bolormaa to Giselle and Molly.

"Jeffrey, you old dog, you certainly didn't waste time landing this filly and importing her from Mongolia. Hell, if the others are half as good looking as these two, I might have to find my way to Mongolia myself," said Giselle, as she reached over and pinched Bolormaa's father on the bottom, which was much to his surprise.

The chieftain assumed this was an American custom and, in order not to offend, pinched her bottom as well.

"Well, well. You, Mr. Shugam, are one frisky Mongolian nomad! I'm starved as usual, and I'm sure you are too, so let's see how French cuisine matches up against Mongolian eats."

They all climbed into the limousine and headed off for their decadent meal in Paris, and when they arrived at their restaurant, David reminded them that both he and Clint would be one million dollars richer from their jaunt to Mongolia, so a significant celebration was in order. They wasted no time ordering Dom Perignon and Foie Gras, and the amount they consumed surprised even the maître d'. Jeffrey felt he was in heaven eating his fillet with true "French fries" while romancing his new wife under the cover of the table. In fact, there was a good deal of "romancing" going on at their table with Clint and Molly and David and Giselle.

Before the group exploded into an orgasm of gustatory delights, they exited back to their various hotel rooms to continue their reveries. Only Shugam was focused on getting some sleep since he had to catch an early train to Brussels to meet his cousin, Brother Antiochus. The rest of the hotel was alive with amorous activity on at least three floors.

* * *

The next morning, they were all up reasonably early and lounging in their comfy terrycloth hotel robes like a bunch of overgrown bunnies in Giselle's suite. Only Jeffrey and Bolormaa had any interest in exploring Paris since this was their chance for an abbreviated honeymoon. They had quickly dressed and escaped into the Paris sunshine to do as many touristy things as they could in the space of one day. The others enjoyed the luxury of doing nothing but soaking up the bliss of romance reunited. Even Giselle was less spunky than usual but not beyond certain innuendos.

"So, Molly, how would you rate our new Clint in comparison to the old Clint on an amorous index? Understand this is for pure scientific research that I am asking."

Molly gave this serious consideration. "Well, if it's for science...I would say a definite increase in endurance, precision, and strength with some loss of spontaneity, but overall, at least a nine out of ten on my pleasure index. This is from a pure scientific consideration of course."

Clint threw a pillow from across the room and hit her square in the chest. He then did an impressive leap over the settee she was sitting on, grabbed her, and then bit her on the ear.

David laughed. "Well, I would give him a ten out of ten for settee jumping. We should definitely be thinking of the next Olympics with Clint here. I think six gold medals in various events would be easy."

"Why do you have to come up with new challenges for me when we haven't even finished the last? Not to mention I don't think the Olympic committee would be pleased to have an 'enhanced' Clint competing in any events. They would have to come up with a different class of events for our formula contestants, which isn't a bad idea. It might make for a more interesting competition."

David thought for a moment. "You definitely have an idea there. Come out on the patio, and let's see if you can throw this orange through the basketball net across the street."

Clint walked out onto the patio, and with little effort, he threw the orange one hundred feet through the net across the street. Molly and Giselle clapped. David, now even more intrigued, had Giselle call down to two young boys playing baseball in the yard below to negotiate in French with the boys for their baseball. The boys were soon ten euros richer, and Clint had a new object and a new target.

"Okay, Clint, let's see if you can hit that stop sign down the block. It is at least three hundred feet away."

Clint looked at the sign and decided to take off his robe. He had worn his Bastille Day shorts, and his friends clapped and whistled in appreciation. He reared back and threw the ball like a bullet, hitting the sign so hard it was dented by the ball. His friends went even wilder, clapping and patting him on the back.

David shook his head. "There isn't a pitcher in the major leagues who could throw that hard and far. Who cares about the Olympics?"

"There you go again," said Clint. "It's just the potion that makes me stronger. It would never be fair for me to compete with others while I was affected by it. We really need to think about what this formula can do to our world. It scares the hell out of me."

Molly put her arms around Clint and ruffled his hair. "You're right. We do need to think about all this, and we have very little time to do so. We have to meet the group at the monastery tomorrow in Brussels, so we should come up with some plans for how to proceed. Cornwell Marcum is going to be there with Timothy, Shugam, Brother Antiochus, and the rest of the monks. It should be quite a gathering with all of us. I think a walk along the Seine is in order, at least for Clint and me."

Giselle was pensive for a change. "You long-legged ruffians take off for your walk. I need to check in with my client here in Paris and get ready to go to Brussels tomorrow with you to meet the group. We will see you two at dinner tonight. I never thought I'd say this, but perhaps a little less champagne tonight might be in order."

Clint and Molly nodded their heads as they left the suite. They quickly changed into street clothes before walking hand in hand along the Seine. The Seine was like magic that curved through some of the most interesting architecture on the planet. It exuded history and as much romance as any of its cousins across Europe.

Despite the overwhelming improbable odds, Jeffrey and his beautiful bride crossed paths with Clint and Molly. The newlyweds had been going warp speed, visiting Notre Dame Cathedral and the Louvre and taking a boat trip on the Seine. They had seen the Eiffel Tower from the boat and were now on their way to see it from the ground up.

Bolormaa had never seen anything like Paris and was more than a bit awestruck. Jeffrey was still overwhelmed at the thought that this amazing creature next to him was actually his wife. They both would need time and more than a few bedtime chats to get to know each other, but Paris was calling them.

As the couples continued on their separate ways, Clint and Molly realized that they too had a lot to discuss. Molly was getting more used to this construct walking next to her, but he certainly wasn't the Clint she had said goodbye to several days ago. Clint was well aware of the changes going on in his body, but he was unsure of how to adjust to them. They both agreed that hopefully with time they would be able to sort this out.

Clint held her hand. "You know I still am fond of you and want our relationship to move forward. It's just that my view of the whole world has changed."

Molly shrugged her shoulders. "I know you are trying, and I'm trying to understand what you've been through. I guess this is somewhat like couples who reunite after one goes off to war or after some major episode affects one of them. We will both have to see where things evolve."

Clint nodded and squeezed Molly's hand, reassuring her he agreed with her.

As the day melted away, Molly and Clint decided it was probably time to head back to their hotel for their last night in Paris.

The evening turned out to be very quiet. David and Giselle went down to the hotel restaurant and had a simple dinner—well, simple according to Giselle's meter; most couples would likely call this dinner rollicking or boisterous, but Giselle did have a certain image to maintain. After dinner, she and David went to the Crazy Horse so she could say goodbye to some of the girls she had seen while in Paris. David was certain he had never been kissed goodbye from so many half-naked, beautiful women in his life. "I could get used to this," he had told Giselle with a lipstick-covered face.

Clint and Molly and Jeffrey and Bolormaa stayed in their rooms and had dinner through room service.

Neither couple could resist the sight of Paris at night from their patios. It truly was the "City of Lights." This city had become a part of them, etching itself into their souls, and they were sad to leave it. Though they could have soaked up those lights all night, they couldn't resist the soft but persistent call of their down comforters and soon they were quietly tucked away in their beds.

* * *

Paris by night evolved into a crisp Paris morning soon enough, and the bunnies in their white robes were back in Giselle's suite sipping their morning coffees. They were booked on a 12:30 train back to Brussels where most of this adventure had started. They were all a bit subdued since the reality of some finality or new path to their travels was about to be imposed on them.

Giselle, never one for melancholy attitudes, barked, "Okay, you lackluster group of miscreants, I've ordered two dozen croissants from the kitchen and enough butter and strawberry jam to cover the walls if we want. No need to worry, Jeffrey, I specifically ordered a dozen just for you. Though, I could probably eat a dozen of these myself. I may have to have my own daily supply delivered by air freight to LA when we are back home."

With that, there was a knock at the door, and room service arrived with enough croissants to fill their dining table, the patio table, and the countertop. The aroma was palpable, and the group attacked as one. The only thing missing from this scrumptious breakfast was alcohol.

Jeffrey polished off his dozen as well as another two more that were somehow uncounted for. Bolormaa had never eaten anything like this before. The buttery, feather light layers of the croissants left one craving more. Giselle unabashedly lathered David's mouth in a thick layer of strawberry jam and carefully licked it off. It was a proper adieu to Paris, and the group couldn't have imagined it any other way. Once they finished stuffing their stomach with decadent croissants, they adjourned to their rooms to finish packing and to rinse off the butter and strawberry from various body parts.

Instead of the typical flock of cabs waiting to take them to the train station, there were only two. Giselle had decided to send most of her luggage back to LA directly instead of taking it to Brussels with her. She would have to make due with three large suitcases for her two-day stay in Brussels. Jeffrey and Bolormaa were staying behind to enjoy the rest of their brief Parisian honeymoon, so they hugged their friends tightly and made arrangements to stay in contact over the next few days.

32 BRUSSELS II

The main square in Brussels was a beehive of activity. After spending the last two days in Paris soaking up the city and each other, Bolormaa and Jeffrey felt a culture shock rejoining the rest of society again. Everything in Brussels was new to Bolormaa but little changed for the rest of the group. The little boy was still pissing in the fountain, and the glorious chocolates still awaited them.

They were staying at the Hotel Warwick, and when Bolormaa and Jeffrey checked in, she felt like she was entering the Pantheon in Rome with its majestic columns. The rooms did not disappoint either. Giselle's suite alone could have housed her entire nomad village.

Giselle, of course, had some Wittamer chocolates delivered to the room and had already booked a spa session for the ladies before the evening's meeting at the monastery.

David, Clint, and Jeffrey headed down to the hotel exercise room to try to work off the few extra pounds they had surely put on in Paris.

"Clint, try not to break any of the machines here. They haven't had to contend with anyone like you before," David said with a chuckle.

Clint laughed. "I promise not to break anything or frighten any of the Belgian guests. I am curious about my strength and endurance, though, since I've cut back on Bolormaa's formula over the last two days."

Jeffrey nodded. "I'm glad to hear that since we really don't know all the side effects of this formula. If this is anything like using steroids, it's probably better to err on the side of caution. I've known far too many athletes over the years with serious issues using anabolic steroids to gain muscle mass, and in those cases, less was always better."

Even though they worked the exercise equipment fairly hard, it did survive. Bolormaa and Molly managed to squeeze in a light work out after their massages as well. Giselle, on the other hand, opted for more spa treatments.

After their workouts, they all headed back to their rooms for some much-needed showers. David couldn't not stop thinking about their upcoming meeting with Mr. Marcum. He imagined Mr. Marcum to be like a bull and David the matador, both dancing around the arena. He didn't know what the evening would bring and, moreover, how it could affect his and Clint's heading home. He was surprised he felt a bit homesick. This had been quite the adventure, but a part of him missed the simplicity of his old life, his beer club, his California home. He also had to consider just where his relationship with this crazy woman Giselle was heading. Having a steady romantic relationship wasn't something generally high on his list, but he had to admit Giselle was an intriguing candidate. He took a long thoughtful look at her.

Giselle noticed the look and tried to decipher what was going on in David's mind. "What's with the perplexed look?"

"I'm just thinking about our meeting tonight," David said.

"I don't quite understand why you're concerned about our little soiree tonight. You already have the formula, a general agreement with the chief, and have beaten Viktor. I say it's time to sit back and enjoy the spoils of war."

"You of all people know that these negotiations aren't done until all the t's are crossed and i's dotted. There are far too many questions as to what happens next, and above all, I feel a responsibility to the nomads to ensure they can continue their existence as much as Mongolia will allow."

Giselle was surprised with David's somewhat morose tone. "You should be celebrating another successful venture—perhaps the biggest this world has ever seen. I think something else is bothering you. I know you like to weigh everything like the Jewish grocer from *Fiddler on the Roof*. Is it possible the famous David Collins is having some second thoughts about our flirtations and future interactions?"

David shrugged. "You are right, at least in one sense. I do like to plan for the future, and right now, the future is tossing an awful lot of balls in the air. I just hope some of those balls fall into place tonight. Then, maybe we can revisit this discussion about 'our future.'"

"Well, the only thing I like to weigh is caviar, so let's go meet the troops at the monastery and let the balls fall where they may."

David grabbed Giselle's hand, and the two headed out to meet the rest of their rat pack for their limousine ride to the monastery.

Inside the limo, Giselle and Molly popped a bottle of champagne and clinked their glasses. The rest were happy to enjoy various Belgian beers while on their way.

33 THE MONASTERY AND SO MUCH MORE

Twilight set a perfect scene for a summer's night at the monastery. They met in a large room the monks had set up as part of the brewery. The usual austere decorations had been embellished by the hand of Mr. Marcum and his minions. A speaker's platform with a microphone was set up, and some of Mr. Marcum's assistants were starting to circulate with appetizers and Lavro beer. The elderly monks stood at one end of the hall and were friendly but somewhat distant. Upon arrival, the chieftain had run over to the group, dragging his cousin Brother Antiochus along and had thrown his arms around Bolormaa and Jeffrey.

"My dear daughter and her newfound mate Jeffrey, allow me to introduce you to my cousin Antiochus, the head monk of this amazing monastery. So much has been happening in the last few days, but my greatest joy has been to see my cousin again."

The rest of the group was introduced, and Antiochus laughed as he was reintroduced to Clint.

"Brother Clint, I was wondering when our paths would cross again. I see you are looking very fit. Mongolia must agree with you, or maybe it's that beautiful young lady Molly on your arm. Perhaps it was just as well that monastic life was not for you."

Clint warmly embraced the monk. "Brother Antiochus, I am happy to see you again and must apologize for my rapid departure from the monastery and any deception David and I may have had while staying here. As you may know, a great deal has gone on since we last met."

"I am happy to see you are doing well and am anxious to hear what may be in store for all of us. Mr. Marcum has promised 'all will be revealed tonight'— whatever he means by that. Our only sadness is that Brother Adolphus was taken from us. We have hung his cloak and the dagger that caused his demise over the entrance to remind us of him."

They all turned to look at the cloak and dagger hanging from the wall, and Brother Antiochus recited a small prayer in remembrance. It seemed a bit odd that the monks hung the dagger as part of Brother Adolphus's memory, but life and death was as one to them.

There was a bustle at the door, and a stately silver-haired gentleman in stylish Brooks Brothers suit entered the room flanked by Timothy, his Parisian nurse, and his sister Marguerite. Mr. Marcum and his entourage had arrived, and everyone in the room took notice. They immediately came over to greet Brother Antiochus, the chieftain, and the rest of the expanding group. Timothy and Marguerite were excited to see their friends, and introductions to Mr. Marcum were made all around.

"He certainly carries the aura of a billionaire," Giselle whispered to David. "I think even his cologne is called *Essence of Money.*"

Jeffrey introduced his new bride Bolormaa to the stunned Marcums. Mr. Marcum made a quick recovery and offered his congratulations, adding that a substantial bonus would be on its way for his help and to celebrate their nuptials.

As if one surprise marriage hadn't been enough, Timothy added to the revelations by introducing his new fiancée Jolene—his Parisian angel of mercy. It seemed that romance was sprouting in every direction from this venture.

Mr. Marcum, true to form, brought the introductions to a close and indicated their meeting needed to get started. He climbed the podium, and everyone else took their seats around the table. Mr. Marcum took a long drink of his Lavro beer and studied the group.

"This whole endeavor started several years ago when I turned fifty," Mr. Marcum began. "I realized that, despite being fortunate enough to join the billionaire fraternity, my life was coming to an end, and at best, I only had about another thirty years left. Having certain resources available to me, I assembled a team to study potential means of extending my life. As you can imagine, most purported treatments were absolutely garbage and often turned out to be toxic. I even purchased a genetics firm in hopes they might come up with something on our own.

"Last year, I attended a gala, and some individuals at my table were discussing a trip they had recently taken to Belgium where they had visited an esteemed monastery filled with spry but older monks. This comment piqued my interest, so I had my staff look into this monastery to see if this was true. After a thorough investigation, I contacted Brother Antiochus and sent my son Timothy here to exchange some diamonds for information. Brother Antiochus needed funds for the monastery and felt it was time to release this gift to the world. Unfortunately, another wealthy Russian man, Viktor Krashenko, caught wind of the same information. He sent one of his thugs to Brussels who killed poor Brother Adolphus. My son Timothy barely escaped with his life.

"After talking further with Brother Antiochus, I was surprised to learn the monk's 'secret' to staying young was attributed to the private beer they made for themselves. He was uncertain of why it had this property since its ingredients are fairly standard, but our suspicions point to a specific combination of ingredients and the particular yeast they use. I was also shocked to hear that another component of their formula was made by Brother Antiochus's cousin in Mongolia. As some of you know, this Mongolian potion does not have the same effect on all people, only seeming to benefit a certain subgroup of men. These men seemed to become stronger and faster and may live longer. They have not been studying this long enough to know for sure.

"Unfortunately, when I pursued this avenue further, my son Timothy was beaten by Viktor's men and ended up in the hospital in Paris. I then hired David and Clint to go to Mongolia to get the last portion for this formula. They were successful, and since, the chieftain and I have been working with his daughter Bolormaa on how to perfect this formula so as not to inflict harm on the world."

"So, what do we know now about this formula? How do we determine if it will have a negative effect on anyone?" Molly asked.

"My geneticists have determined the men who respond to Bolormaa's formula have what is called the 'Khan gene' on their Y chromosome. Those with the Khan gene are all descendants of Genghis Khan. This finding is not terribly surprising since, supposedly, the formula was developed by Khan's mother to help him in his quests. Currently, .5 percent of the men in the world, or sixteen million, have this gene with up to 8 percent of men in Mongolia. As you probably have suspected by now, some of Chieftain Shugam's nomads have this gene, which is why their abilities are so remarkable when given Bolormaa's potion. Some of the monks here carry the gene as well, which has helped to increase their strength. It appears Clint also is a carrier of this gene.

"So, we now must decide where to go from here. We certainly cannot make any major decisions without more research, but it is time to put some things in motion. The monastery here does not want to ramp up supply of their private beer, so I have purchased the Anheuser Busch Budweiser plant in Los Angeles to help with production. My chemists feel that the beer itself is likely to increase the average life expectancy of the human race by ten years, which will have a staggering impact on the world's population. After our latest run-in with Viktor, we cannot afford any leaks of information. I need people on this who I can trust, which is why I'm proposing that you, David and Clint, supervise the production."

Clint nearly fell out of his chair. He had assumed that after his trip to Mongolia he was done with this episode in his life.

"At the request of the chieftain, I have also enlisted Roche Pharmaceuticals, based out of San Francisco, to recreate Bolormaa's formula. She will oversee the entire enterprise.

"We have many challenges proceeding from here. Producing and marketing the beer should be fairly straight forward. However, Bolormaa's potion will need to be studied and will eventually need FDA approval. The impact of our product will be global. Think about food supplies, healthcare costs, and the idea of possibly having sixteen million super humans running around. This is-"

All of a sudden, there was a huge crash, and the building literally shook. The group dashed into the adjacent brewing area and found a large Humvee had crashed through the side door and armed men were pouring out with handguns and rifles. Six men took up military positions around the exits and had killed the guard who had been standing at the door.

"What the hell is happening?" shrieked Giselle.

Jeffrey couldn't believe it when Sergio climbed out of the vehicle. His eyes oozed revenge. He then fired a few shots into the air just to get their attention.

"Did you miss me? I always did enjoy making a grand entrance at special occasions. Though, for some of you, it won't be so memorable since you won't be around much longer to remember it. Mr. Marcum and Bolormaa, you will be coming with us. And, Bolormaa, don't even dream of sticking me with anymore of your concoctions because I will not hesitate to shoot you. It would be shame to see you die because I need your help setting up our little chemical enterprise. My men would be sorry to lose such a pretty plaything as well," Sergio said.

Bolormaa didn't hold back her disgust.

"Jeffrey, you will be the first to die. I have always enjoyed killing big game, and I've fantasized about your death since our helicopter ride. Oh, this should be fun! Mr. Marcum, I think I'll have a beer now if you please. Crawl over here and bring me a cold one, or my second target will be your son Timothy. If I remember right, he is the one who had that massive dog nearly remove my right arm. Speaking of that night, I see my old dagger is hanging over the door. How kind of you to return it to me after all this time."

Mr. Marcum did as he was told and brought Sergio a beer on his knees. The guests were scared witless, and many were crying and holding each other. Jeffrey whispered to Bolormaa that he loved her and tried to think of a Buddhist prayer in the face of death. Clint surveyed the room, preparing for a display of chemical madness.

Sergio, tired of his banter, felt it time to play out his hand. He aimed his handgun at Jeffrey and fired off a volley of four automatic rounds, as Bolormaa screamed. Clint was a blur of motion before Sergio even pulled the trigger. He grabbed a heavy metal drink tray from a table and threw it across the room, landing it square in Jeffrey's chest only milliseconds before Sergio's rounds would have penetrated his heart. Jeffrey caught the tray and thanked the Buddha for Clint and the tray that saved his life.

Giselle realized some distraction was needed to prevent mass carnage. She channeled her days back at the Crazy Horse in Paris and started singing at the top of her lungs while stripping to distract the other armed Russians in the brewery. Her notes reverberated off the metal tanks, and her lingerie reverberated off the Russian's eyes, catching everyone by surprise for a moment. Molly decided to add to the distraction by doing back flips across the floor, remembering her days in gymnastics from school.

Before Sergio and his men could react, a huge furry object flew through the air toward him. Bernardus, the giant Saint Bernard of the monks, saw his old nemesis and had launched himself at Sergio. As Sergio tried to turn his gun on Bernardus, Clint vaulted over a table and grabbed the dagger off the wall, flipping it with deadly accuracy toward Sergio. His aim was true, and the dagger sunk deep into his neck, severing his right Carotid artery and piercing his trachea His final attempt to curse them all was lost to the world.

As he was dying, his last image was of Bernardus knocking him flat on the ground and again sinking his teeth into his right arm.

Sergio's demise caused some uncertainty among the rest of his accomplices. Their indecision was quickly used to the advantage of the elderly monks in the brew house who, thanks to the combination of the Khan gene and their brew, easily disarmed the thugs and had them tied up in a matter of moments.

Clint apologized to Brother Antiochus for killing Sergio in the monastery. Brother Antiochus, though he was always saddened to see a life taken, absolved him of this since he had acted in self-defense and to save others. The monk silently prayed to the Lord, thanking him for bringing Clint to them to help protect them all.

Both Molly and Bolormaa threw their arms around Clint and smothered him with kisses for his amazing actions in saving Jeffrey and ending what would have been true carnage.

The Belgian police and the medics arrived soon after and carted off the Russians and Sergio's body. The medics tended to the injured Russians, and things began to shift from utter chaos back to a more civilized manner. The whole group had exploded into joyful pandemonium. One moment they were facing certain death and the next, joyous celebration.

Mr. Marcum toasted Clint and the Belgian monks for their bravery. Clint was embarrassed by all the attention, but he didn't mind the attention he was getting from Molly.

Brother Antiochus thanked Giselle for her efforts in distracting the Russians and assured her the monks would likely need long hours of penance to repent for witnessing her performance.

Giselle laughed and petted a very happy Bernardus. "I wish we could take him home with us," she said to David. "I would buy up every seat on the plane to accommodate this giant fur ball."

David shook his head. "I know, but the monks have had him for years, and this is where he should stay. Maybe they could breed him and get you a puppy. You'd probably need to move into a barn though. I can't imagine any apartment would be big enough for his offspring."

"A barn? No one with my fashion sense belongs in a barn. I would keep him at the new brewery you are going to manage in LA. We could raise him together."

"Speaking of LA," said David, "I talked with Mr. Marcum, and we can fly back there tomorrow on his Gulfstream 500 along with Clint, Molly, his family, and him. And I can't say raising a giant Saint Bernard puppy with you is not altogether unappealing."

"Wow, I don't recall a less romantic invitation to the beginning a relationship, but I'll let this one slide. Let's seal the deal with a kiss."

"I'll have my attorney call your attorney to work out the details," David teased, and then, he leaned over and passionately kissed Giselle.

EPILOGUE

Three months had passed, and at lightning speed a lot had happened for Clint and David. By contrast, the group at Lucky Baldwin's was sitting in their usual seats, carrying on their usual conversations, and drinking their same Belgian beers. They were quite excited since David and Clint were back in town and able to meet with them for the first time since they went to Europe. They had heard all sorts of rumors of new ventures they were involved with and even semi- serious relationships that both had started during their adventures.

Bartley and Smithers anxiously awaited their long-lost world travelers. Instead of the usual throaty growl of Clint's motorcycle, a sleek black limousine pulled up to Lucky's, and David and Clint emerged. Not surprisingly, David was wearing a three-piece suit. Clint, however, was wearing a coordinated Patagonia outfit, which seemed strange to the old beer buddies. In addition, his slight limp was gone. Clint looked like he had been hijacked by a lumberjack. As David and Clint approached their old friends, they exchanged warm greetings, and one of the barmaids quickly took their drink orders.

"Clint, where is your Harley, and what's with the clothes and all the muscles? Did you buy a gym?" asked Bartley.

"I've been in the gym, but no, I don't own one," Clint said. "As chief of operations of our new company I have to dress the part, at times, and clients generally prefer to ride in the limousine instead of on the back of my Harley. What can I say? I had to make some accommodations. My girlfriend, Molly, and I still get to ride the Harley on weekends, and I even convinced her to get her own—though she has to take off her high heels to navigate it."

Bartley shook his head. "Chief of operations and girlfriend Molly—you guys certainly have been busy."

David laughed. "You can't imagine even half of what has been going on since we last met here three months ago. I am CEO of a new major entity, New Life Productions, and have a new female partner myself in both business and romance, Giselle Larson. She and I stick to four-wheeled vehicles, but have a 911 Porsche and a Humvee when we want to establish a 'presence' on the road or take our new Saint Bernard puppy with us."

Smithers choked a bit on his beer. "Giselle, as in Giselle from Chapman, Carter, and Godfrey? She has a reputation as a world class barracuda."

"Well," David smiled. "She can be a bit intense at times, but she does keep me on my toes. I think it's time to fill you in a bit about what Clint and I have been up to. We only have an hour since our ladies are meeting us at two. But before my long dialogue, I want to show you our first product from our new company. It just got off our production line." David pulled out two bottles from his backpack. "These are more for advertising and not for official release or consumption, but we are proud of the product."

Bartley laughed. "My French may be a bit rusty, but *Fontaine de Jouvence* I think means 'fountain of youth.' Pretty label and name, but is the beer any good? I see it's only 8 percent alcohol. That is a bit low for our standards."

"It is from a recipe from one of the Belgian monasteries, so don't dismiss it because of its alcohol content. Would you mind drinking it if I told you it could let you live ten years longer and still tastes great?"

"Okay, you have my attention," said Bartley. "Tell me about this mysterious beer."

David and Clint launched into their adventure and travelogue over the next hour. They were surprised how quickly time had passed when they saw Giselle's Humvee pull up slightly after two p.m. Bartley and Smithers's jaws dropped when a tall knockout blonde and a buxom hurricane and an teenage girl dragging a large Saint Bernard puppy got out of the car and headed their way.

The barmaid stopped the ladies, saying, "Ma'am, you can't bring your dog in here. It is against state health regulations."

"You might be able to see that this beautiful animal is a service dog by his collar, and I have the papers to prove it. You can save the 'ma'am' for your mother. Go make yourself useful and bring someone a beer!"

The barmaid sheepishly turned around and tried to make herself busy.

The women and their giant "service dog" squeezed between the tables, knocking a few items off, which were kindly wolfed down by the pup. He bounded into David's lap, seriously testing the integrity of Lucky's chairs. Clint provided the usual service of keeping David from any serious injury and then led introductions to the stunned beer club.

Clint and Molly exchanged kisses, and Clint patted her glorious behind. "This is my love, Molly Malloy, who helped start our jaunt across Europe and Mongolia. In addition to working at New Life Productions, she and I have started a new detective agency with a great detective, Enrico."

"Let me introduce the other joy in my life, my daughter Karen."

On que, she introduced herself and hugged her father and dodged a large wet tongue from Bernie. She began petting her new found charge in earnest.

"Did you manage to catch your friends up on at least half of what has happened since they last saw you?" asked Molly.

"They have had an abridged version and are up to our departure from Brussels with the Marcums," said David. "I was about to tell them about Giselle and I adopting a puppy from the Barry Foundation in Switzerland. I have to admit he has helped cement our relationship, as parenting sometimes does."

Giselle laughed. "The only cementing our relationship needs is to keep you grounded from all of your high-flying ideas. As CEO, you need to remember to keep things simple! However, yes, the dog has helped our relationship. The only negative is he has managed to shred half of my designer French lingerie in the last month. I will have to return to Paris soon to replace my vital outfits."

Smithers blushed.

"Getting back to the USA," David continued, "Mr. Marcum purchased the old Budweiser brewery in LA and refurbish it to start production of our Belgian beer. Giselle and I have a five thousand square foot apartment space there for us and our puppy Bernie. Molly and Clint use the space as well when we are working late, which happens quite often.

"Bolormaa and Jeffrey, the newlyweds we were telling you about, are up in San Francisco working with Mr. Marcum's genetic and biologic companies along with Roche chemicals. I am happy to report Bolormaa is now pregnant with triplets! She is extremely excited she will be expanding their Mongolian connection to California in a major way. Jeffrey, after some soul searching, decided a military focus no longer suited him and is now helping Bolormaa with her plant development. I'm fairly certain he is the largest Buddhist in Northern California.

"True to his word, Mr. Marcum is working with the Mongolian government to establish a large long-term area for the nomads to use in Northern Mongolia. Chieftain Shugam has been somewhat less involved with day-to-day operations at the nomad camp. I've heard his brother and son have taken over some of those responsibilities. Our dear friend Sal has found himself a girlfriend, one of Bolormaa's friends from college, and plans to come out to San Francisco to spend some time with his cousin. You guys would get a kick out of him! I hope he can make it down to the LA area sometime."

Smithers shook his head. "It sounds like you've made some interesting friends. I can't believe one of your schemes turned into this, David. Tell me something though. Do you seriously think this new brew of yours could extend the people's lives by ten years? That seems unbelievable."

David proudly lifted the sample of beer he had brought along. "Our chemists and biologists' findings and the studies on the monks in Belgium suggest that is true. We will simply have to continue to run studies. It certainly looks promising though."

"Wow," Smithers and Bartley said simultaneously.

Before Clint, Molly, David, Giselle, Karen and Bernie got up to leave, they all raised a toast to Lucky Baldwin for bringing them together and starting one crazy adventure.

When they got back to their vehicles, Giselle turned to David and said, "You didn't happen to get into the Khan gene and Bolormaa's formula when talking with your friends, did you?"

"No," said David. "I thought it best to save that little bit of information for another day."

ABOUT THE AUTHOR

I am a retired Family Physician/ Gerontologist, though
I prefer the term diversified to retired. I was brought up
in the great American beer city of Milwaukee, making it
no surprise that I would write a novel channeling beer.
History and storytelling have always fascinated me and
drew me to Mongolia for my first adventure. Who
knows where my next literary path leads.
I think China is beaconing me.

Made in the USA
Lexington, KY
19 July 2018